MW00636973

Eileen Yin-Fei Lo's

New Cantonese Cooking

新式廣州菜譜

OTHER BOOKS BY EILEEN YIN-FEI LO

The Dim Sum Book:
Classic Recipes from the Chinese Teahouse

The Chinese Banquet Cookbook:
Authentic Feasts from China's Regions

China's Food
(*co-author*)

Eileen Yin-Fei Lo's

New Cantonese

Illustrated by Lauren Jarrett

Calligraphy by San Yan Wong

Cooking

新式廣州菜譜

CLASSIC

AND

INNOVATIVE

RECIPES

FROM

CHINA'S

HAUTE CUISINE

VIKING

VIKING
Published by the Penguin Group
Viking Penguin Inc., 40 West 23rd Street,
New York, New York 10010, U.S.A.
Penguin Books Ltd, 27 Wrights Lane,
London W8 5TZ, England
Penguin Books Australia Ltd, Ringwood,
Victoria, Australia
Penguin Books Canada Ltd, 2801 John Street,
Markham, Ontario, Canada L3R 1B4
Penguin Books (N.Z.) Ltd, 182–190 Wairau Road,
Auckland 10, New Zealand

Penguin Books Ltd, Registered Offices:
Harmondsworth, Middlesex, England

First published in 1988 by Viking Penguin Inc.
Published simultaneously in Canada

10 9 8 7 6 5 4 3 2 1

Copyright © Eileen Yin-Fei Lo, 1988
Illustrations copyright © Viking Penguin Inc., 1988
All rights reserved

LIBRARY OF CONGRESS CATALOGING IN PUBLICATION DATA
Lo, Eileen Yin-Fei.
    New Cantonese cooking.
    Includes index.
    1. Cookery, Chinese—Cantonese style.   I. Title.
TX724.5.C5L5946 1988   641.5951'27   87-40602
ISBN 0-670-81519-5

Printed in the United States of America by
Arcata Graphics, Fairfield, Pennsylvania
Set in Trump Mediaeval
Designed by Fritz Metsch
Illustrations by Lauren Jarrett

Without limiting the rights under copyright reserved above, no part
of this publication may be reproduced, stored in or introduced
into a retrieval system, or transmitted, in any form or by any
means (electronic, mechanical, photocopying, recording or
otherwise), without the prior written permission
of both the copyright owner and the above
publisher of this book.

*This book, as always, is for
Stephen, Elena, Christopher and Fred.*

Acknowledgments

As ever, there are those who share this book: my children, Stephen, Elena, and Christopher, who tasted things they never thought they would and did so with grace and forbearance; my husband, Fred, who ate, critiqued, often angered me, but always cared; the many chefs of Hong Kong and Canton who shared their knowledge and their skills with me; my sister and brother, Rosanna and San Wong, who helped shape the book; my agent, Joseph Spieler, who had faith in it. I thank them all.

Contents

The
Cooking
of Canton

廣州食譜

The occasion I remember was the day of the wedding of my grandmother's grandson, who was my mother's nephew, and so my cousin. I was ten years old and in Sun Tak, the suburb of Canton in which I lived, the wedding was to be an exciting event. My grandmother, who loved to have big parties for her family, had decided the wedding meal would be in her home. And I was to help prepare it. True, her servants would be there, and my aunts and my mother, but Grandmother, mindful that my mother had always urged me to learn to cook, said that I was to be in the kitchen that day.

I felt ambivalent about the honor. My young cousins would be playing catch or hide-and-seek or jumping rope; the older cousins would be chattering away in the garden around tables set up under the trees for the games of Mah-Jongg that would go on before and after our dinner. But I would be inside. I thought about it and decided that I preferred the honor of cooking with my elders.

And so that day I helped pluck the chickens, some of which would later be steamed with fresh ginger, black mushrooms, and the sausages we knew as *lop cheung*, and some of which would be boiled in soup, then later cut up to make white cut chicken. I cut tender pieces of *choi sum*, so that later the servants could cook the young stalks with oyster sauce; and I soaked dried mushrooms so they could later be cooked with the expensive delicacy of cooked webbed duck feet that we all liked so much.

I helped prepare the fish we call the yellow croaker, a favorite in my town, salting it so that when it was cooked with pork the resulting sauce would be so good that my cousins and I would compete to see which of us could pour it first over our cooked rice. I helped boil the dried abalone until it was tender enough to braise, and I washed the oranges, persimmons, tangerines, and the grapefruit-like pomelos so that they would glisten as they sat in bowls in the centers of the tables set up in the big central room of my grandmother's house, a room filled with heavy carved blackwood chairs and tables and paper images of the various deities she prayed to as a practicing Buddhist.

There would be roast suckling pig and fresh carp. The grown-ups would eat raw, tissue-thin slices of this sweet and oily fish, dipping them in a sauce of ginger, soy sauce, boiled peanut oil, scallions, and white pepper. Those under sixteen—which meant me and two handfuls of cousins— would not be permitted to eat the raw fish because the adults said it was too strong for our constitutions, but we could have thick rice porridge called congee, into which pieces of the carp, cooked, would be mixed. But I helped prepare the fish, the sauce, and the congee, which at least put me one leg up on my cousins.

I had so much enjoyment that day, not the least of which was occasioned when my grandmother, whom we called *paw paw*, came over to me and told me I had worked well and rewarded me with a handful of candied lotus seeds. It was something she did not do often. After that I really didn't care that I had missed jumping rope.

And later, after I had changed into the new clothes which my mother had bought for the party, and which I had carried to my grandmother's and stowed away until I finished my kitchen work, I sat with my cousins at the table reserved for all of us children and felt wonderful, a little superior, for I had been, temporarily, an adult.

That is the sort of memory I have of my first days in the kitchen, the Cantonese kitchen of my Sun Tak girl-hood. It was the food, the importance of the food, the joy in the food, that my grandmother wanted to impart to me, even though I was so young. It is memories such as this that I take with me to my kitchen.

Though I cook the foods of all of China, the table I truly love is that of Canton, and I cannot say how happy I am that finally these days the Cantonese kitchen has come to be recognized for what it is: China's finest classic cuisine. True Cantonese food, subtle, sophisticated, creative, adaptive, is now appreciated not only in the world of the West but in the rapidly changing People's Republic of China, where in every city, it seems, fine Cantonese restaurants are being opened.

What, then, is Cantonese food? What is its essence?

Canton, Guangzhou, the surrounding province of Guangdong, and the Hong Kong New Territories are China's food basket, and the Cantonese will say that with pride, pointing out that when the women of Shanghai gather together over tea the talk is always of fashion, but when the women of Canton meet, the talk is always of food.

Cantonese food is fresh, but more than that, there is the belief among the Cantonese that in preparing it for consumption its essential character should not be altered. The tastes of vegetables, meats, and fish should not be changed; therefore cooking should be simple, straightforward, and brief. Lightly blanched and stir-fried vegetables and fish steamed in the Cantonese manner retain appearance and taste. Although some dishes are cooked for extended periods, they are the exceptions in the Cantonese kitchen.

Cantonese cuisine is a light cuisine, with no heavy sauces, and though occasionally the Cantonese will employ peppery spices and oils, this is done for contrast, for the "ting," as it might be recognized in New Orleans, not in the overpowering manner of Sichuan and Hunan, where

such heat is often applied to mask the tastes of food that
has been preserved.

Just a touch of oil is used to stir-fry. Food is whisked
through this oil in a manner described as *wok hei,* a Cantonese phrase that translates as "flame and air" and simply means food cooked precisely and quickly over an
extraordinarily high flame that curls around the bowl of
the wok, food cooked so that it retains its character and
taste.

A Cantonese will mix fruit and meat, nuts and poultry, roots and seafood. For spiciness the cook will use
fermented black beans, fermented soybeans, touches of
chilis, but more often dishes will be subtly scented by
wrapping them in lotus leaves, perhaps bamboo leaves,
touching them with sesame oil, or dropping flower buds
into them.

Should it be thought that only the Japanese eat raw
fish, let it be known that the Cantonese have always had
a delicacy called *yueh song,* that dish from my cousin's
wedding, in which a fresh carp is pulled from the water,
knocked on the head and stunned, split, gutted, scaled,
and filleted; then the fillets are dipped into that sauce of
ginger, soy, boiled peanut oil, scallion, and white pepper,
and eaten immediately. Which came first—Cantonese
yueh song or sashimi?

A Cantonese cook will make two visits to the market
each day: first in the morning for the vegetables, meats,
and fish that will be the basis for lunch, and again in the
afternoon to purchase food for the dinner table.

A fish will be selected as it swims about in a huge
square vat; shrimp will be darting about in a freshwater-
filled glass tank, unfed, so that their veins will become
clean and they can be cooked in their shells, which the
Cantonese say is the only way. Chickens, ducks, and
pigeons will be strutting around in their bamboo cages;
pigs and steers, killed that dawn, will be hung in the
market waiting to be butchered to order. Buying in advance and refrigerating or freezing is unheard of. The peo-

ple of Hong Kong, for example, will tell you that the reason Colonel Sanders failed in his attempt to sell Kentucky Fried Chicken there was because his chickens were frozen and the Cantonese would not eat frozen meat.

A Cantonese kitchen is a laboratory in which a creative cook adapts. Give him a fish and he will quickly devise thirty ways to prepare it. A Cantonese cook's head is a computer that never stops processing: it never rests; it always creates.

If chicken, duck, shrimp, and lobster can be cut up and steamed so that their inherent tastes are not lost, why cannot a shrimp be cut in half, dotted with minced ginger and a fermented black bean or two, and then steamed so that three pure tastes are presented, not in competition as so much of today's "new" cookeries seem to be, but as complements to each other?

Why cannot that wonderful Cantonese basketlike *dim sum*, *siu mai*, a mixture of minced pork, shrimp, and mushrooms, be made with pork, shrimp, pungent chives, and crisp bamboo shoots? Why not indeed, so that the *dim sum* becomes new and fresh? Why cannot that other mainstay of the Cantonese kitchen, the *won tun*, be packed with veal to create a new tradition? Why not stir-fry chicken with sweet honeydew and cantaloupe melons? Why not substitute roast duck for chicken and create a new dish out of that traditional chicken *ding*, a dish further enlivened with fresh pistachios? For centuries in Canton, chicken has been marinated in rice liquor, then steamed and subsequently deep-fried. Why not alter the process so that the marinade is Cognac? All of these I have done, and they have become "new" Cantonese dishes while remaining faithful to the essential character of the cuisine from which they came, the cuisine into which I was born.

It is the Cantonese who created the great banqueting delicacies of Chinese cooking: the celebrated shark fin, either braised or in broth; the equally celebrated bird's nest, the nest of the swallow, cooked to resemble pieces of transparent noodles; those wonderful *dim sum*, of which there are about two thousand varieties and which are unknown in most other parts of China.

And their cousins and brothers have contributed to the greater variety of the Cantonese table. The people of Chiu Chow, south of Canton, have made the widest possible use of foods from the sea, utilizing fish sauce akin to, but so different from, those of southeast Asia; an intense master sauce, *lo soi*, that never dies, and tangerine jams as new heightening flavors. The Hakka people, wanderers from Mongolia who settled in Canton, have contributed to the Cantonese table the fine tastes of chicken baked in coarse salt and pungent preserved vegetables.

The cuisines of other parts of China are limited by geographical circumstance, tradition, and history. The food of Peking is the food of the royal court, wheat-oriented and often given to excessive decoration and oil. The food of the west, of Sichuan and Hunan, is quite often too searingly hot to allow discernment by the palate. The food of Shanghai is cosmopolitan, an amalgam of all of the foods of China, beautifully cooked but often overly sweet and oily. Only the food of Canton has no limitations, no restrictions. It is a cookery open to experimentation and creativeness, China's ever-growing cuisine.

A traditional Chinese adage suggests that the perfect life on earth is attainable, and that to achieve it one should be born in Suzhou, the city of beautiful women; clothed in Hangzhou, where the most beautiful silks are said to come from; and buried in Luzhou, which makes the finest coffins. But if one is to taste the best, one must eat in Guangzhou—in Canton.

A Chinese will think of Cantonese cooking in a classical way, with such a proverb. A non-Chinese, anywhere, will also think of Cantonese cooking when he considers Chinese food.

Why?

Because it is Cantonese cuisine, though altered—and generally for the worse, I might add—with which they

are most familiar. Things cloyingly sweet and sour, ge-
latinous stir-fried mixtures of vegetables thick with cornstarch, overdone omelets such as the ubiquitous egg *fu
yung,* are all regarded as true Cantonese cooking. And the
concepts that gave rise to them were indeed Cantonese
in origin, but as produced in the West, they are these days
inadequate, short-cut imitations unworthy of their history.

Why Cantonese in the West?

The first immigrants to leave China for the West, for
Hawaii, for the North American West and East coasts,
for London, and all stops in between, were from Canton,
from the districts of Toi San and Sun Tak and neighboring
areas. They came from a fertile land, a tropical place where
fruits and vegetables were in year-round abundance, where
there were more fresh fish than could ever be caught,
where grains were plentiful and crops of rice followed
hard on one another, where ducks and chickens and their
eggs were dietary staples. These Cantonese had been raised
with a devotion to what was fresh, what had just been
dug from the ground, tugged from a branch, pulled from
the sea or lake or river; and though they left Canton they
retained that devotion.

But when they reached the West, as a womanless so-
ciety, some of these immigrant men were forced to become the cooks, first for those of their fellows who were
building the roadbeds and laying the rails of the trans-
continental railroad, and then for others who were pros-
pecting for gold. They cooked what was at hand and they
cooked it quickly, at the end of a day's work. And the
food they cooked was plain and, though fresh, was without subtlety.

Later they were to be the proprietors of the first Chinese
restaurants of the West, chefs of a cuisine that, although
Cantonese, was greatly altered by circumstances, cli-
mates, available produce, and distance from tradition. The
further corruption of what is a classic cuisine is the one
that is familiar to most of us.

But that is changing. I have sensed an increasing interest in true Cantonese cookery. People are interested to learn that *chau mein* is an elegant noodle preparation with mixed vegetables and meats, rather than the coarsely chopped cabbage and celery mired in cornstarch. There is surprise, and again interest, when I tell people that tomatoes and their catsup have long been known to the Cantonese. There is interest in knowing that a spring roll is delicate, the size of a finger, not the loglike egg roll found in most restaurants. There is interest in knowing that egg *fu yung* is a mixture of lightly cooked eggs and tiny shrimp—that the very words *fu yung* mean "beautiful and delicate"—rather than the hard-scrambled omelets with which most of the West is familiar.

I mean to fuel that interest, to further it.

The Cantonese Kitchen

廣卅廚房

The Foods | 食物

Though a few of the ingredients needed for the recipes in this book are not universally available, most are, and you will find them in Chinese and Asian markets and in better supermarkets simply because of the demand for them as a result of the continuing interest in the cooking of China and other Asian countries. Most foods of Chinese origin are imported from the People's Republic of China, from Hong Kong, and from Taiwan. More recently they have been coming from Southeast Asia, from the Philippines, Korea, and Japan. Most are available by mail order as well, particularly ingredients that are prepared, preserved, or dried, and advertisements for them can be found in the better cookery magazines.

Brands have also proliferated. I have refrained from specifying brands except in cases where I believe a particular brand is far superior to its counterparts and thus essential to the recipe.

腊肉 **Bacon, Chinese**
Chinese bacon is cured with sugar and a thick soy sauce. It does not have the smoked flavor of American bacon, is not as salty, and is drier. Sold in butcher shops and Chinese groceries, it will keep, refrigerated, for about one month.

13

竹
筍

Bamboo Shoots

The spear-shaped beginnings of bamboo trees, they are rarely available fresh. Use those that have been cooked and canned in water. There are bamboo shoots and winter bamboo shoots, the latter more tender and of better quality. Cans will be labeled "Winter Bamboo Shoots" or "Bamboo Shoots, Tips." The latter are often as good as those labeled "Winter" and are less expensive. Once the can is opened, shoots can be kept in water in a covered container, refrigerated. They will keep for two or three weeks if the water is changed daily.

Bean Curd

Called *dau fu* by the Chinese, tofu by the Japanese, bean curd comes in square cakes, 2½ to 3 inches on a side. Made from soybean liquid, or milk, the cakes have a custardlike consistency. Fresh, individual cakes are preferred to those that come several to the package. Bean curd has little taste of its own, and its versatility lies in its ability to absorb the tastes of the foods it is combined with. It can be kept refrigerated in a container of water, tightly covered, with the water changed daily. It will keep for two to three weeks.

Bean Curd, "Wet"

This fermented or preserved bean curd comes in cans, jars, and crocks and is labeled "Wet Bean Curd." It consists of small cakes of bean curd, cured with salt, wine, and either chilis or "red rice." Red rice is just that, a rice reddish in color, used basically as a vegetable dye. The "Wet Bean Curd" I refer to is the one with the red rice added and gives a fine flavor to barbecued pork.

Bean Thread Noodles

These are often called bean threads, or vermicelli bean threads, or cellophane noodles. They are made when mung beans are moistened, mashed, and strained, and are formed from the substance that is left. They come in ½-pound packages, or in 2-ounce packs, eight to a 1-pound package.

豆豉 **Black Beans, Fermented**
These black and fragrant beans are cooked and preserved in salt and come in plastic sacks and in cans. I prefer those in packages, lightly flavored with orange peel and ginger. Before they are used, the salt should be rinsed off. They can be kept for as long as a year, without refrigeration, so long as they are in a container that is tightly sealed.

白菜 **Bok Choy**
Perhaps the most famous vegetable in Canton, it is called the "white vegetable" there. The white-stalked, green-leafed vegetable, so versatile in Chinese cookery, is sweet and juicy and sold by weight. It is often called Chinese cabbage, but that is a misnomer because it bears no resemblance to cabbage. It will keep for about a week in the vegetable drawer of a refrigerator, but it tends to lose its sweetness quickly, so I recommend using it when fresh.

 Catsup, or Ketchup
The catsup from China comes in bottles, like its Western counterpart. The best brand is Koon Yick Wan Kee, manufactured in Hong Kong, and is made from tomatoes, vinegar, and spices. The difference between it and Western catsup, with which we are familiar, is its use. In China, catsup is used more as a food-coloring agent than as a flavoring. It is often difficult to obtain, however, so the use of Western catsup will suffice.

Chili Oil. See Hot Oil.

Chinese Mushrooms. See Mushrooms, Black Dried.

Chinese Sausage. See *Lop Cheung.*

Chinkiang Vinegar

This very strong, aromatic red vinegar is used primarily in the Hakka and Chiu Chow kitchens and is quite distinctive. Red wine vinegar may be used in its place but is not a true substitute.

Chives, Chinese

Also known as garlic chives, they are more pungent than the American chive and are wider and flatter, though of the same deep green color.

Coriander

Similar in appearance to parsley, fresh coriander is also called cilantro and Chinese parsley. It has a strong aroma and taste and is used either as a flavoring agent or as a garnish. It should be used fresh so that its bouquet will be appreciated, but it can be kept refrigerated in a plastic bag for a week to ten days.

Curry Powder

Although there are many brands of curry powder on the market, I prefer the stronger, more pungent and intense brands from India.

Eight-Star Anise, or Star Anise

A tiny eight-pointed hard star, this spice has a flavor more pronounced than that of anise seed. It should be kept in a tightly sealed jar in a cool dry place. It will keep for a year, though it will gradually lose its fragrance.

Fen Chiew

This is a spirit distilled from sorghum. Quite strong, at 130 proof, it is used often in the Cantonese kitchen. Usually available in shops in Asian neighborhoods.

Fish Sauce

This sauce is a thin, amber-colored extract of fish diluted with water and with salt added. There are many kinds of fish sauces, from China, Hong Kong, Thailand, Vietnam, and the Philippines. Fish sauce is used widely throughout Southeast Asia. The Chiu Chow people use it as a dip with many of their preparations. Fish sauce from China or Hong Kong most closely resembles that of the Chiu Chow kitchen.

五香粉 Five-Spice Powder

A distinctive powder, this spice imparts the taste of anise to food. It can be made from a combination of spices, including star anise, fennel seeds, cinnamon, cloves, ginger root, licorice, nutmeg, and Sichuan peppercorns. There are, to be sure, more than five spices listed, but different makers use different combinations, although anise and cinnamon dominate. It should be stored similarly to eight-star anise. It, too, tends to lose its fragrance after six months.

生薑 Ginger

A constant of Chinese cookery, this root is a necessity in the Cantonese kitchen. Look for roots with smooth outer skins, because ginger begins to wrinkle and roughen with age. It flavors, it is used to overcome strong fish and shellfish odors, and it is said to greatly reduce stomach acidity. Use it sparingly. When placed in a heavy brown paper bag and refrigerated, it will keep four to six weeks. I do not recommend trying to preserve it in wine, or freezing it, because it loses strength. I do not recommend ground ginger as a substitute because for fresh ginger root there is no substitute.

薑汁 Ginger Juice

Although this is available in small bottles, you can make a better quality yourself simply by grating fresh ginger root into a bowl, then pressing it through a garlic press. Do not store it; make as needed.

Ginger Pickle (see recipe, page 114)
Young ginger is pickled with salt, sugar, and white vine-gar. The ginger used must be pinkish white and smooth, and quite crisp. In Canton, young ginger grows in two crops, one in late summer, another in January and Feb-ruary. In the United States, it is available from mid-spring to mid-fall, and is often referred to, mistakenly, as spring ginger.

 Glutinous Rice
This is often called sweet rice and is shorter-grained than other rices. When cooked, it becomes somewhat sticky. Its kernels stick together in a mass instead of separating the way long-grain rice does.

 Hoisin Sauce
This thick, chocolate-brown sauce is best known as a complement to Peking duck and roast suckling pig. It is made from soy beans, garlic, sugar, and chilis. Some brands add a little vinegar; others thicken the sauce with flour. Hoisin comes in large cans or jars. If in a can, it should be transferred to jars and kept refrigerated. It will keep for many months.

 Hot Oil
This is available in bottles, but you will be more satisfied with your own. Here is how to make it: Add ½ cup of dried hot pepper flakes to ¾ cup sesame oil and ¾ cup peanut oil. Put all in a large jar, mix, close the jar tightly, and put in a cool, dry place for four weeks. It will then be ready for use. It will keep for one year, without re-frigeration.

 **Lop Cheung**
These Chinese sausages are traditionally made of pork, pork fat, and duck liver. In North America the most com-mon are of pork, threaded through with pork fat. They usually come in pairs, held together by string. They are

cured but not cooked; thus they must first be cooked before eating. They can be kept refrigerated for about a month, and frozen, from three to four months.

Lotus Leaves
Dried leaves used as wrappings for various steamed preparations, lotus leaves impart a distinctive, somewhat sweet taste and aroma to the food around which they are wrapped. If you are able to get fresh lotus leaves, by all means use them fresh; or sun-dry them yourself for future use.

Lotus Root
The gourd-shaped root of the lotus. Often four to five grow together, connected like a string of sausages. Each is about 2½ inches in diameter, 4 to 6 inches long. When the root is cut through, there is a pattern of holes, not unlike those in Swiss cheese. The texture is light and crunchy. Lotus root should be kept refrigerated in a brown paper bag and used within a few days of purchase, since it tends to lose both flavor and texture.

Lotus Seeds
The olive-shaped seeds from the lotus pod are regarded as a delicacy and are priced accordingly, by weight. They can be kept for as long as a month in a tightly sealed jar at room temperature, though I do not recommend keeping them that long, because their texture roughens and their flavor weakens.

Mushrooms, Black Dried (Chinese)
A staple of Chinese cooking, these black, dark gray, brownish-black, or speckled dried mushrooms are not only flavorful but versatile. They come in boxes or in cellophane packs and range in size from those with caps about the size of a nickel to those with 3-inch diameters. Those in boxes are choice in size and color and are more expensive. These mushrooms must always be soaked in hot water for at least thirty minutes before use, the stems

removed and discarded; and then they should be thoroughly cleaned on the undersides of the caps, and squeezed dry. Dry, they will keep indefinitely in a tightly closed container, in a cool, dry place. If you live in an especially damp or humid climate, they should be stored in the freezer.

Mustard, Hot
This is made by mixing equal amounts of mustard powder and cold tap water. There are many hot mustards on the market, but I prefer the English-made Colman's Mustard, Double Superfine Compound. It must be the dried mustard powder, not the Colman's prepared mustard that comes in jars. For normal use, combine 2 to 3 teaspoons of mustard with a similar amount of water.

Mustard Greens
This leafy, cabbagelike vegetable is called *kai choi*, or "leaf-mustard cabbage." Its taste is strong and it is used fresh in soups or stir-fried with meats, but it is more commonly used in its preserved forms. Water-blanched and cured with salt and vinegar, it is used in stir fries or soups. It comes loose (sold by weight) or in cans labeled "Sour Mustard Pickle" or "Sour Mustard Greens" or "Mustard Greens." If you buy them loose, place them in a tight plastic container and keep, refrigerated, for not more than two weeks. Once cans are opened, greens should be stored in the same manner and have the same storage life.

Mustard Pickle, or Sichuan Mustard Pickle
This pickle is made from Chinese radishes cooked with chili powder and salt. It can be added to soups and stir-fried with vegetables. It is never used fresh, only in its preserved form. It can be bought loose by weight, but more often can be found in cans, labeled "Szechuan Preserved Vegetables" or "Szechuan Mustard Pickle."

There can be instances of loose or confusing labeling, so be careful when you buy, so that you obtain the correct vegetable. Once a can is opened, place pickle in a glass jar. It will keep for one year, refrigerated.

蠔
油
Oyster Sauce
A thick sauce of oyster extract and salt, it imparts a rich taste. There are many brands, but I prefer bottles labeled Hop Sing Lung, manufactured and bottled in Hong Kong.

米
粉
Rice Noodles
Very fine noodles made from rice flour, they are also called rice sticks and rice vermicelli. They are sold in 1-pound packages and come from Thailand, Hong Kong, and the People's Republic of China. I prefer the superior quality of a Chinese brand called Double Swallow, except that for Chiu Chow soups my preference is for a Thai brand labeled Banh Pho. The noodles, packed in plastic bags and stored in a cool dry place, will keep for a year.

冰
糖
Rock Candy, or Rock Sugar
A compound of white sugar, raw brown sugar, and honey, it comes in 1-pound packs and looks like a collection of light amber rocks.

沙
薑
Sand Ginger
A dark brown root, smaller and more gnarled than regular ginger root, it is available sliced and dried or powdered, both in plastic envelopes. The envelope for the dried pieces is labeled *"Kapurkachi"*; the label for the powder is *"Kaempferia Galanga."* It is wonderfully aromatic. Both the dried root and the powder should be kept in tightly sealed containers in a cool, dry place. They will keep for a year. However, as the root ages, it tends to lose some of its fragrance. Used particularly in the Chiu Chow kitchen.

Scallion Oil

This is an ingredient that cannot be bought in markets. It was devised by an elderly Hong Kong chef who told me the ingredients, from which I created the recipe. It is delicious when added to many dishes. Here is how it is made:

Ingredients:

1 cup of the stringy whisker ends of scallions, washed and dried thoroughly
2 cups green portions of scallions, cut into 3 sections, washed and dried thoroughly
2 cups peanut oil

Directions:

Heat a wok over medium heat. Add the peanut oil, then add all the scallions. When the scallions brown, the oil is done. With a strainer, remove and discard the scallions. Strain the oil through a fine strainer into a mixing bowl and allow to cool to room temperature. Pour the scallion oil into a glass jar and refrigerate until needed. It will keep for about 2 months. The recipe may be cut by half, or into thirds.

 Sesame Oil

An aromatic oil with a strong, almost nutlike aroma, made from sesame seeds, it is used mainly in sauces and marinades and as a finish to many dishes. Adding a little to an already prepared dish imparts fine flavor, particularly in the case of some soups. It is thick and brown in versions from China and Japan, thinner and lighter from the Middle East. I recommend the former. Stored in a tightly capped bottle at room temperature, it will keep for at least four months.

 Shao-Hsing Wine

A sherrylike wine made and bottled in the People's Republic of China and in Taiwan. There are several grades.

I use the basic wine, but also the best grade of Shao-Hsing, which is labeled Hua Tiao Chiew (pronounced Far Jiu by the Cantonese) for particular dishes, as noted.

Shark Fin
This is the dried dorsal fin of a shark. Usually sold in packages, it must be cooked repeatedly until it comes to the noodlelike consistency favored for soups. It is a great delicacy, and expensive. It also comes frozen, ready for use. I prefer preparing it myself, but this is most time-consuming. The packages of dried fins, stored at room temperature in a cool, dry place, will keep for many months.

Shrimp, Dried
These are precooked, shelled, and dried shrimp, which usually come in packages of ½ and 1 pound. To be used for the recipes in this book, they should be soaked, as instructed.

Sichuan Mustard Pickle. See Mustard Pickle.

Sichuan Peppercorns
Quite different from the usual peppercorn, this is reddish in color, not solid, but open. The Cantonese call it "flower peppercorn" because of its shape. It is not peppery, but rather mild. Store in a tightly capped jar as you would ordinary peppercorns.

Sichuan Preserved Vegetables. See Mustard Pickle.

Smithfield Ham
Cloth-wrapped hams cured in Virginia, they are used to replace the traditional Yunnan ham of the Chinese kitchen. It is not necessary to buy an entire ham. Slices of up to 1 pound are available in butchers' shops. To prepare for use in the recipes in this book, soak in water to remove salt for 4 hours, then place in a steamproof dish, add ⅓ cup of brown sugar, and steam for 2 hours. The ham is then ready for use.

It can be kept in a closed container for four to six weeks.

 Soy Sauces

There are both light and dark soys. The light soys are usually taken from the top of the batches being prepared; darker soys, from the bottom. Both are made from soybeans, flour, salt, and water. There are many brands, but I believe the best quality is a Hong Kong brand called Yuet Heung Yuen.

The light soy sauce from this manufacturer is labeled "Pure Bean Soy Sauce"; the dark soy (it is often called Double-Dark) is marked "C Soy Sauce." Dark soys are best with meats—for roasting, for sauces, and for rich, dark coloring. Light soys are best for seafood, chicken, and pork. There is even a soy with mushroom flavoring, and bottles of this dark soy are so labeled. The Chinese believe, rightly, that soys give a sweetness of taste to other foods. I often combine the various soys for different tastes and colorings.

Some soys come in cans, though most come bottled. If in a can, transfer the sauce to a bottle. It can be kept in a tightly capped bottle at room temperature indefinitely.

 Tangerine Skin, Dried

The dried, wrinkled, brown skin of the tangerine, this is sold in packages and can be stored indefinitely. The darker the dried skins, the older they are; the older the better—and also the more expensive.

 Tapioca Flour

Also called tapioca starch, it is made from the starch of the cassava root. Much of it comes packaged from Thailand. It is used as a basic ingredient in some *dim sum* doughs, as a thickener for sauces, or as a coating. Store as you would any flour.

Tianjin Preserved Vegetable

This is a mixture of Tianjin cabbage, garlic, and salt. It comes either in crocks from the People's Republic of China or in plastic bags from Hong Kong. The crocks are labeled "Tianjin Preserved Vegetable"; the bags, "Preserved Vegetable." Do not confuse this with the "Sichuan Preserved Vegetables" (mustard pickle) listed earlier. The Tianjin Preserved Vegetable contains garlic; the other does not.

Water Chestnut

Though it is called a nut, it is not. It is a bulb, deep purplish brown in color, that grows in muddy water. To peel fresh water chestnuts is time-consuming, but once this is accomplished, the meat of the water chestnut is sweet, juicy, crunchy, and utterly delicious. Canned water chestnuts are a barely adequate though serviceable substitute. Quite versatile, they can be eaten raw or lightly stir-fried with meats, poultry, and vegetables.

They should be eaten while very fresh for the most enjoyment. As they age they become less firm, more starchy, dried out. If you keep the skins on, with mud residues on them, and refrigerate them in a large brown paper bag, they will keep for four to five weeks. Peeled and placed in a container with cold water, and refrigerated, they will keep four to five days, provided the water is changed daily. Canned water chestnuts can be stored similarly, once the can is opened.

Water Chestnut Powder

White, lighter than cornstarch, it will make a sauce of a thinner consistency than will cornstarch. Packages of ½ pound are labeled either "Water Chestnut Powder" or "Water Chestnut Flour."

Wheat Starch

The remains of wheat flour when the wheat's protein is removed to make gluten, this starch is a basic ingredient for doughs. These powders will keep for at least a year if stored in a tightly sealed container and kept in a cool dry place.

White Wine

In China a white wine called Bok Jau is used in various seafood preparations. For years this was unavailable. These days, Bok Jau can be bought in Chinatown markets, or in other Asian markets, where it is often labeled "Chinese Cooking Wine." I use Chablis in its place, because I find the two wines quite alike for cooking purposes—and of course Chablis is more easily obtainable.

Winter Melon

This melon looks somewhat like watermelon and grows in the same oval shape. Its skin is dark green and occasionally mottled, while the interior is greenish white with white seeds.

Winter melon has the characteristic of absorbing the flavors of whatever it is cooked with. When it is cooked, usually in soup or steamed, the melon becomes beautifully translucent. Often the whole melon is used as a tureen, with other ingredients steamed inside it after it has been seeded and hollowed out a bit. It should be used immediately, for it tends to dry quickly, particularly when pieces are cut from a larger melon. It is usually sold by weight.

Won Tun Skins

Made of flour, eggs, water, and baking soda, they come in packages of 1 pound—about 75 to 100 in a package—and can be found in the refrigerator sections of markets.

Yellow Chives

This chive variety is bright yellow in color, rather than the customary green. These chives are grown in the dark, deprived of the sun and thus of their color, and they have a decided onion taste. They are often chopped and put into soups or stir-fried. They are most tender but should be eaten immediately, for their storage life, even refrigerated, is no more than two days.

The Tools | 厨俱

The tools of the Cantonese kitchen are not many. The most important is that all-purpose cooker the wok. It and the other specialized tools you will need are easily obtainable and not expensive. Whatever else you require will most likely be in the drawers and on the shelves of your kitchen cabinets.

鑊 Wok
The range of woks these days is immense, although unfortunately most of them are inadequate. The best to buy is one of carbon steel, with a diameter of about 14 inches. It is the all-purpose Chinese cooking utensil and can be used for stir frying and deep frying, dry roasting and sauce making; with the addition of bamboo steamers, it is a perfect steamer as well. Its seasoning and care are discussed in the section on cooking techniques.

鑊刷 Wok Brush
This is a slightly oversized oar-shaped wooden brush with long and very stiff bristles. It can be used, with exceedingly hot water, to clean all of the cooking residue from the wok, without any detergents.

Wok Ring

This is a hollow steel base that nestles over a single stove burner. The round base of the wok settles into it firmly, thus ensuring that the wok is steady on the stove, and that the flames of the burner will surround it.

Bamboo Steamer

Circular frames of bamboo with woven bamboo mesh bases and covers, these come in various sizes, but those 12 to 13 inches in diameter are preferred, for they sit quite nicely in a wok. Foods rest on the woven bamboo and steam passes up through the spaces. They can be stacked two or three high so that different foods can be steamed simultaneously. Steamers are also made of aluminum, and of wood with bamboo mesh bases. There are also small steamers, usually of bamboo or stainless steel, that are often used for individual *dim sum* brunch servings. For use with the recipes in this book, two bamboo steamers and a cover should be sufficient.

Chinese Spatula

This is a shovel-shaped tool available in either carbon steel or stainless steel, and in different sizes. I prefer a medium-size carbon-steel spatula.

Chinese Cleaver

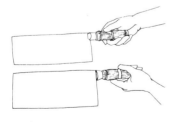

Still another all-purpose tool, it cuts and dices; its flat blade and its handle can mash; it can be used as a pastry scraper; it will cut dough. Usually of carbon steel with a wood handle, it is also available in stainless steel, either with a wood handle or as a one-piece tool with blade and handle of one piece of steel. The carbon steel is preferred because of its keener edge and because it is capable of such heavy-duty jobs as cleaving through bone. The preferred size is one with a blade 8 inches long and between 3½ and 3¾ inches wide. You may prefer to have a second cleaver, of stainless steel and of much lighter weight, with a blade 8 inches long by 3¼ inches wide. Chinese chefs call such a cleaver a chef's knife and reserve it only for slicing and cutting.

 Bamboo Chopsticks
In addition to being what the Chinese eat with, these are marvelous tools. They make fine stirrers, mixers, and serving pieces and are available usually in packages of ten. Avoid plastic chopsticks. They cannot be used for cooking and they are more difficult to manipulate than bamboo ones.

Chinese Strainer
This is a circular steel-mesh strainer attached to a long split-bamboo handle. Strainers come in many sizes, from as small as the average human palm to as large as 14 inches in diameter. For all-purpose use, I prefer one 10 inches in diameter.

The following will complete your Cantonese kitchen:

Oval Dutch oven
Large roasting pan
Frying pan, cast-iron, 10 inches in diameter
Round cake pan
A selection of heatproof, steamproof dishes
Strainer, fine, all-purpose
Rolling pin, heavy hardwood
Cutting board, wood preferred
Wooden spoon
Paring and boning knives
Small utility knife
Dough scraper
Small hand grater
Garlic press
Kitchen shears
Rubber spatula

Cooking thermometer, especially for deep frying
Kitchen scale
Ruler
Cheesecloth

These days most kitchens have electric mixers and food processors. Some fillings in this book can be mixed in either and some slicing and chopping can be done with a food processor, if desired, but I prefer the control I can exert with the hand and the cleaver. It is the traditional way, the way the finest Cantonese chefs follow, and I recommend it. Once you become a convert to the cleaver, I think you will agree.

The Techniques | 厨藝

Learning to cook in the Chinese way is not difficult. I have taught many people who have had no previous experience to cook everything from perfectly boiled rice to the exotic dish of the Hakka, salt-baked chicken. Although food from all of China's regions is served in restaurants these days, that is no reason for not learning what is surely one of the most creative and varied cuisines in the world.

Of particular interest should be the cooking of Canton, at once the most enjoyed and least understood cuisines of China. People who have eaten food in their neighborhood Chinese restaurant and take it for granted are always amazed when they go to Hong Kong and find "real" Chinese food. What they eat, of course, is the finest Cantonese cooking in the world, and perhaps without realizing it, they are set down square in the middle of a living cuisine, one in constant flux, as opposed to cuisines such as those of western China, where repertoires, while exquisite and delicious, are limited. Cantonese cooking is limited only by the creativity of its practitioners.

Nor is it mysterious. Its bases are easily learned, and mastering the techniques of Chinese cookery is anything but tedious. Nor should you be awed by any preparation. There is joy in preparation. To me the preparation of Cantonese food, fine Cantonese food, is as enjoyable as eating it. And this enjoyment is enhanced by doing things correctly, of course, and with economy.

Prepare your utensils and your ingredients. Any cookery can become overpowering and frustrating if you are ill prepared, and Chinese cuisine, particularly Cantonese cooking with its ubiquitous stir frying, which demands a certain discipline, is no exception. But if you prepare well and take care of your basics, you will be able to cook without worry and with pleasure. This preparation means not only familiarizing yourself with the different vegetables, sauces, and spices of the Cantonese kitchen, but also learning their properties. It means as well becoming familiar with the tools necessary to work with these foods, and learning *their* capacities.

COOKING WITH THE WOK

The wok is a thousand-year-old Chinese creation, and there is nothing more traditional in Chinese cookery. Woks were first made of iron, later of carbon steel, and even later of aluminum, but whatever its material it was always, is always, shaped like an oversized soup plate. Due to its concave shape, its base fits right into the burner flame or heat source of a stove and makes it the ideal cooker for stir frying, pan frying, deep frying, steaming, blanching, and sauce making. It is the perfect cooking utensil. Though it is not a pot or a pan, it functions as both. Its shape permits foods to be stir-fried—tossed quickly through tiny amounts of oil so that the foods cook but do not become oily. Its shape permits the wok to be converted into an efficient steamer simply by placing bamboo steamers in its well. Wok cooking is natural cooking.

If you buy only one wok, it should be of carbon steel. Avoid those with nonstick finishes because they will not take an oil coating. Avoid plug-in electric woks because their heat cannot be controlled as precisely as is needed. Stainless-steel and aluminum woks are fine for steaming, but cannot compare in versatility with the carbon-steel wok.

A wok of carbon steel is not pretty when it is new, because of its coating of heavy, sticky oil, but once cleaned and seasoned properly, it is ideal and will last for years. As I said earlier, woks come in many sizes, but one 14 inches in diameter is the perfect all-purpose size.

A new carbon-steel wok should be washed in extremely hot water with a little liquid detergent. The interior should be cleansed with a sponge, the exterior with steel wool and scouring-type cleanser. Then it should be rinsed and, while wet, placed over a flame and dried with a paper towel to prevent instant rust. With the wok still over a flame, tip a tablespoon of peanut oil into its bowl and rub it around with a paper towel. This oiling procedure should be repeated until the paper towel is free of any traces of black residue. Your wok is now ready to cook with.

To break in a new wok, I usually cook a batch of julienned potatoes in it. That is a perfect way to season it, although a bit unorthodox. I pour in 4 cups of peanut oil, heat the wok until I see wisps of white smoke rising from it, then put in the potatoes. What a delicious way to break in a piece of cookware!

After that initial washing, detergents should *never* be used in the bowl of the wok. It should be washed with extremely hot water, perhaps with a stiff-bristled brush made especially for woks (such brushes are inexpensive and available where you buy your wok) or a sponge. After rinsing, it should be dried quickly with a paper towel, then placed over a flame for a thorough drying. If you have finished cooking in it, then reseason it by rubbing the bowl with a little peanut oil. Do this for the first fifteen to twenty uses, until the wok becomes shiny and dark-colored, which indicates that it is completely seasoned.

If the wok is to be used several times in the course of one cooking session, then it should be washed, wiped with a towel, and dried over heat after each use.

The carbon-steel spatula you use with your wok requires the same care.

STIR FRYING

The Cantonese have a word for it: *wok hei*, or "wok air"; and what it means is simply the high heat created by flame and oxygen surrounding the wok. And it is *wok hei* that is illustrated by stir frying, certainly the most dramatic of all Chinese cooking techniques. Finely sliced and chopped foods are whisked through a touch of oil in a wok and tossed with a spatula. There is constant motion. Hands and arms move; the wok is often tipped back and forth. Stir frying is all movement, all rhythm. What leads to a perfect stir fry is preparation.

The object of stir frying is to cook vegetables precisely to the point at which they retain their flavor, color, crispness, and nutritive values. Meat is generally shredded or thinly sliced and seared to retain its juices. To do this you must prepare all of the ingredients of the recipe before stir frying.

All vegetables, thinly and evenly cut, must be next to the wok, ready to be tipped into the heated oil, and so must the meat and shellfish that will accompany them. This is simply organization, so that as you cook you will have everything within reach and the rhythm of stir frying will not be interrupted.

To Stir-fry

Heat the wok, usually over high heat, pour oil into the wok, and coat the sides by spreading the oil with a spatula. You will note in this book that varying times are designated for heating the wok. These times have been carefully tested, and there is indeed a difference in heating a wok for 30 seconds, 45 seconds, or 60 seconds. What I do is match the degree of heat with the foods to be cooked.

I suggest that if you are to cook on an electric range, you heat the burner for 10 minutes before placing the wok on it. This will heat the wok faster and more efficiently. Another burner should be heated to medium. If heat is too high on the first burner, transfer to the second to control heat.

Slide a slice of ginger into the oil; when it becomes light brown, the oil is usually ready. Place the food in the wok and begin tossing it through the oil: 1 or 2 minutes for such soft vegetables as *bok choy* or sweet red peppers; about a minute longer for harder vegetables such as cabbage, carrots, or broccoli. Scoop out the vegetables with a spatula and they are ready to be served.

If vegetables are too wet they will not stir-fry well, so they should be patted dry with paper towels. If they are too dry, however, you may have to sprinkle a few drops of water with your fingertips into the wok while cooking. When water is sprinkled in this manner, steam is created, which aids the cooking process.

油 DEEP FRYING
炸

The object of deep frying is to cook food thoroughly inside while outside it becomes golden and lightly crisp. Most foods that are to be deep-fried are first seasoned, marinated, and dipped in batter. Here is how to convert the wok into a deep fryer: heat it briefly, then pour in 4 to 6 cups of peanut oil and heat the oil to 325°F. to 375°F. depending on what you are to cook.

Oil should be heated to a temperature a bit higher than that required for frying the food because, when food is placed in it, the oil temperature will drop. It then rises again. I use a frying thermometer, which I leave in the oil, to help me regulate the oil's temperature.

When the oil reaches the proper temperature, slide the food down the sides, from the rim of the wok, into

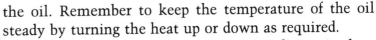

the oil. Remember to keep the temperature of the oil steady by turning the heat up or down as required.

The utensil to use for moving ingredients in deep frying is the Chinese mesh strainer. Its large surface and stout bamboo handle are ideal for removing foods from oil and straining them as well. In my view, this strainer is far more useful and efficient than a slotted spoon.

If you don't have a wok, you can deep-fry in a very large pot, using a Chinese mesh strainer (or a mesh spaghetti strainer), as described above.

OIL BLANCHING

A relatively simple cooking technique that is basically a sealing process. Its aim is to seal in the flavor of vegetables, meats, and shellfish, and to retain the bright color of vegetables.

Vegetables
Heat the wok, pour 3 cups of peanut oil into it, and heat to exactly 300°F. Vegetables should be added to the oil for no longer than 30 to 45 seconds, then should be removed with a Chinese strainer.

Meats and Shellfish
Heat the oil to 400°F. to 425°F. Place the food on the mesh of the strainer and lower it into the oil for 1 to 1½ minutes.

When you remove foods from the oil, drain off the excess oil and set aside the oil-blanched foods to use as required.

WATER BLANCHING

Water blanching removes water from vegetables, meats, and shellfish. For both vegetables and meats, pour 3 to 4 cups of water into the wok, add ¼ teaspoon baking soda to the water, and bring to a boil.

Vegetables

Place in the boiling water until their colors brighten, then immediately drain the vegetables in a strainer placed over a bowl, run cold water over them, and drain again.

Meats and Shellfish

Bring the water to a boil. Add in the foods and bring back to a boil. Remove immediately and drain the foods, then place them in a bowl, run cold water over them, and let stand for the times indicated in the recipes. Drain and set aside.

蒸 STEAMING

To the Cantonese, steaming is perhaps the most important cooking process. It helps foods retain natural flavors and nutrition. When steamed, doughs become soft, light, and firm dumplings. When subjected to steam's wet, penetrating heat, food that is dry becomes moist, and food that is shrunken expands. Steaming bestows a glistening coat of moisture on foods. It is an art as well, because foods can be arranged in decorative ways within bamboo steamers and, once cooked, can be served without being disturbed.

Steaming requires no oil, except a little used to coat the bamboo reeds at the bottoms of the steamers, to prevent sticking. If lettuce leaves of any variety are used as liners the need for oil is eliminated.

To Steam

Pour 4 to 5 cups of water into a wok and bring it to a boil. Place steamers in the wok so that they sit evenly above, but not touching, the water. This can be done by using a cake rack. (You may not even need a cake rack;

your bamboo steamers may just rest comfortably against the sides of the wok, above the water.) You will be able to stack two steamers, even more. Cover the top one, and the contents of all will cook beautifully. Keep boiling water on hand at all times during the steaming process, to replace any water lost because of evaporation.

Clam steamers and pots with holed steamer inserts may also be used for steaming.

TEMPERING PORCELAIN AND PYREX FOR STEAMING

Occasionally foods are placed within steamers in porcelain or Pyrex dishes to cook and to serve from. These dishes must first be seasoned, or tempered.

Fill the wok with 5 to 6 cups of cold water. Place a cake rack inside and stack the dishes to be tempered on the rack, making certain they are completely covered by the cold water. Cover with a wok cover and bring the water to a boil. Let the water boil for 10 minutes, turn off the heat, and allow the wok to cool to room temperature. The dishes are then seasoned and can be placed in steamers without fear that they will crack. They may be used in place of steamers themselves. Foods are placed in the seasoned, tempered dishes, which are in turn placed on cake racks in the wok. Cover and steam as described in the previous section.

Once tempered, the dishes will remain so for their lifetime. They need not be tempered again.

 ## DRY ROASTING

In this process there is no need for oil, salt, or anything else in the wok.

To dry-roast cashews or peanuts, heat the wok over high heat for 30 to 45 seconds. Add the nuts and lower the heat to very low. Spread the nuts in a single layer and use the spatula to move them about and turn them over to avoid burning on one side and leaving the other side uncooked. This process takes about 12 to 15 minutes, or until the nuts turn brown. Turn off the heat, remove the nuts from the wok, and allow to cool.

Nuts can be dry-roasted 2 to 3 days in advance. After they cool, place them in a sealed jar.

Use the same process to dry-roast sesame seeds, except that the roasting time is only 2 to 3 minutes.

PREPARING BROTHS

In this book I use chicken broths a good deal in sauces, marinades, and soups. I also use fish and vegetable broths as recipe ingredients. These are basically stocks, which I make myself. They are intense and delicious and add to any recipe. Here is how I make them.

CHICKEN
BROTH

10 cups water
 8 pounds chicken bones and skin
 3 quarts cold water
 1 piece fresh ginger, 1 inch thick, smashed lightly
 2 peeled garlic cloves, whole
 1 bunch scallions (usually 4 or 5), ends trimmed and discarded, washed, dried, and cut into halves crosswise
 2 medium onions, peeled and quartered
   Salt to taste

1. In a large pot, bring the 10 cups of water to a boil. Add the chicken bones and skin and allow to boil for 1 minute. This will bring the blood and meat juices to the top. Turn off the heat, pour off the water, and run cold water over the skin and bones to clean them.

2. Place the skin and bones in a stockpot; add the 3 quarts of cold water, the ginger, garlic, scallions, onions, and salt. Cover and bring to a boil, partially uncover, and allow the broth to simmer for 3½ to 4 hours.

3. Strain the contents, discard the solid ingredients, and reserve the liquid. Refrigerate until used. This recipe makes 6 cups.

⟶ This stock will keep 2 to 3 days refrigerated, or it can be frozen for about 1 month.

FISH
BROTH

10 pounds fish heads and bones, washed well in cold running water
4 quarts cold water
2 pounds onions, peeled and quartered
2 stalks celery, cut in halves
6 scallions, washed, dried, with both ends trimmed, and cut into halves crosswise
1 piece fresh ginger, 2 inches long, smashed lightly with a cleaver
6 whole, peeled garlic cloves
1 teaspoon white pepper

1. In a large stockpot, place all the ingredients. Set over high heat and bring to a boil. Lower the heat, partially cover the pot, but keep at a boil at all times. Cook for 6 hours.

2. Turn off the heat. Using a large strainer over a mixing bowl, ladle the broth through the strainer. Refrigerate until ready to use. Discard the solids.

⟶ This broth can be kept, refrigerated, for 2 to 3 days. It can be frozen for about 1 month. This recipe makes 8 cups.

VEGETABLE | 蔬   10 cups water
BROTH | 菜   1½ pounds large yellow onions, cut into quarters
_____ | 湯   8 stalks celery, cut into thirds
                  3 large carrots, cut into thirds
                  1 pound fresh mushrooms, trimmed and cut into halves
                  1 large piece fresh ginger, about 1 by 2 inches
                  2 teaspoons salt
                 ⅛ teaspoon white pepper
                  3 tablespoons Scallion Oil (page 22) or peanut oil

1.   In a large pot, bring the water to a boil. Meantime, scrub and cut up the vegetables as described, but leave the skins on. Add all the ingredients to the boiling water, reduce the heat, and simmer, partially covered, for 3½ hours.

2.   When the broth is cooked, remove from the heat and strain the liquid through a metal strainer. Discard the solids. Store the broth in a covered plastic container in the refrigerator until needed.

ﯦ   This broth can be kept in the refrigerator for 4 to 5 days, or can be frozen for 3 to 4 weeks. This recipe makes 6 cups.

WORKING WITH THE CLEAVER

Just as the wok is an all-purpose cooker, so the cleaver is the all-purpose cutting instrument of the Chinese kitchen. Nobody who cooks Chinese food should be without the broad-bladed, wood-handled cleaver. It is a rather formidable-looking knife, and many beginners think they will cut off their fingers when they begin slicing vegetables. Not true. The cleaver, when held correctly, so that its weight and balance will be well utilized, can do virtually anything a handful of lesser knives can. It can slice, shred, thread, dice, cube, chop, mince, and hack, all with great ease. It mashes, it is a scoop, it can scrape dough.

Cleavers come in various sizes and weights, some about ³/₄ pound, which are ideal for slicing and cutting; those heavier, about 1 pound, which are better for mincing; and still heavier cleavers of about 2 pounds, which will chop through any meat and all but the heaviest of bones. If you are to have, however, only one cleaver, I recommend one that weighs about 1 pound, is about 8 inches long, and has a blade 3¹/₂ to 3³/₄ inches long. It must be kept very sharp, always.

The cleaver can be held in different ways for different tasks, but it should be held comfortably. I use three basic grips:

For chopping and mincing:

Grip the handle in a fistlike grasp and swing it straight down. The stroke will be long and forceful if bone or a thick substance is being cut. If you are mincing, the strokes will be short, rapid, and controlled. The wrist dictates the force.

chopping   mincing

For slicing, shredding, and dicing:

Grip the handle as before, but permit the index finger to stretch out along the side of the flat blade to give it guidance. The wrist, which barely moves with this grip, is virtually rigid and almost becomes an extension of the cleaver, as the blade is drawn across the food to be cut. When you use this grip, your other hand becomes a guide. Your fingertips should anchor the food to be cut and your knuckle joints should guide the cleaver blade, which will brush them very lightly as it moves across the food.

slicing

Vegetables and meats are sliced, shredded, and diced. Garlic, occasionally ginger, and shrimp are generally minced.

slicing meat

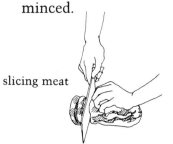

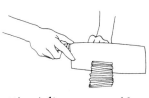

cutting julienne vegetables

For trimming meat and peeling vegetables:

Grip the handle tightly, with thumb and index finger holding the sides of the flat of the blade. The cleaver is almost horizontal. Then, as the free hand lifts pieces of gristle away from meats and fowl, the cleaver blade is gently inserted and follows the hand, cutting the gristle as the hand lifts it. When peeling, as with water chestnuts, the cleaver is steady; the free hand manipulates what is to be peeled. The blade edge is always away from you as you peel.

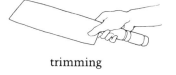

trimming

peeling

knicking out sprouts

trimming meat

A cleaver, because it is made of carbon steel, should be washed and dried quickly to prevent rust. Under no circumstances should you place it in a dishwasher. If your cleaver should show a spot of rust, it should be rubbed with steel wool, dried, and touched with a bit of vegetable oil.

CUTTING UP FOWL

Most people buy their fowl and poultry already cut up. You need not do this, for cutting up your fresh-killed bird is simple. Here is the procedure for cutting up a chicken.

Sit the bird up on its neck, its back to you, its tail and legs up. Using the cleaver, cut downward from the spinal joint. As you cut through, use your hands to pull the chicken apart. With the cleaver, cut the center joint of the breast bone. The bird is now cut into halves. Cut off the thighs and wings at their joints. Cut each half of the body into halves lengthwise, then cut these lengths into bite-sized pieces.

The procedure is identical for cutting up a duck.

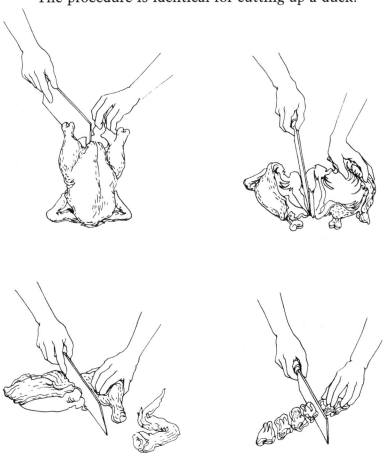

MASHING

mashing

The handle of the cleaver is used in this process. Hold the handle firmly, with the index finger and thumb at the base of the blade where it meets the handle. The other fingers are clenched. The blade faces outward. The handle becomes, in effect, a hammer that is used to make a paste, including fermented black beans and garlic, for example.

CLEANING AND PREPARING FRESH FISH

Your cleaver is fine for the preparation of fresh fish for cooking. To scale a fish, hold the cleaver with the blade at about a 45-degree angle to the side of the fish, against the grain of the scales. Move the blade from the tail toward the head and the scales will come off readily.

Use the cleaver to cut the body of the fish along the stomach line. Remove intestines and discard. This interior cleaning can also be done with the cleaver blade.

With kitchen shears, cut the tendons connecting the gills to the head and remove them.

Wash the fish inside and out thoroughly under cold running water, taking care to remove any membranes that may remain in the stomach cavity. Dry the fish with paper towels. The fish is ready to cook.

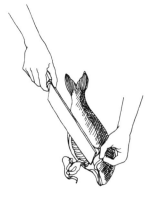

EATING WITH CHOPSTICKS THE CHINESE WAY

There is really only one proper way in which to hold chopsticks, despite what you may be told and despite what you may see. Since you are learning to master all of the other Chinese cooking techniques, you should master eating with chopsticks as well.

There is also a proper way to hold a rice bowl, a soup bowl, and one of those small, oval porcelain soup spoons. Observe:

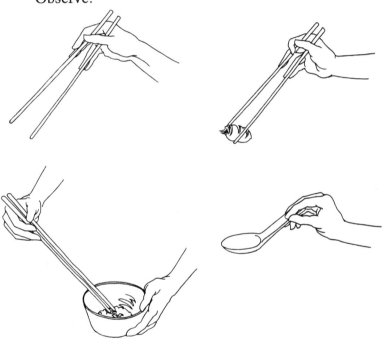

A BASIC SHOPPING GUIDE

Poultry

Chicken
Fresh-killed chickens are preferred, though I know that these are becoming more difficult to find. They are worth

the effort, however, for their taste, so try to buy fresh-killed chickens if possible, and if possible buy those that have been hand-plucked. Otherwise they are dipped into boiling water in order to facilitate removal of the feathers by machine, which diminishes the taste.

If you are buying chicken that is not freshly killed, first look for the date on the wrapping label. If the date is past, do not buy it. Check to see if the chicken has been frozen. Frozen chickens are usually permitted to defrost in meat cases. Often they will be hard to the touch and there will be traces of crystallization. If a chicken has been in a display case too long, its packaging will contain too much reddish, blood-colored liquid. If you buy chicken cutlets, ask your butcher to remove them from a whole chicken breast, rather than buying them packaged.

Duck
Ducks should be fresh-killed as well. All of the shopping criteria for chickens apply to ducks. If fresh-killed ducks are not available, you may use frozen ducks. Again, look for dates and signs that will indicate relative freshness, or its lack, before making your purchase. Frozen ducks can be used in all recipes.

Meat

Pork
Fresh pork will be quite pink. When you have access to fine-quality fresh pork, as I have in my home state of New Jersey, you can buy with confidence. Buying from a butcher is recommended, however. When pork is mentioned in the recipes in this book, I suggest the use of double-cut pork chops, fresh pork butt, or fresh ham, all of which can be supplied by a butcher. In a supermarket

those cuts are available packaged. A sign that packaged pork has been lying about in a meat case too long is an excessive amount of liquid in the package and a dull color to the meat.

Beef
Buy fresh beef, preferably from a butcher, and age it yourself before using. Allow beef to rest in the meat-keeping compartment of a refrigerator for several days until liquid drains off and the meat turns from bright red to a darker brownish red.

Specific cuts include London broil and flank steak. With London broil, look for the "oyster cut," which is a bit smaller than regular London broil. It is shaped like an elongated oval, a bit pinched in the center, like two oysters side by side. A kosher butcher will know this cut readily. Others may not, so be specific. With flank steak, choose a thick cut because it will cook well on the outside but retain pinkness and moistness inside.

Veal
Select meat from the leg. Have the butcher cut off a piece of about ½ pound, then slice it yourself. The best veal is milk-fed, pale in color, more tender, less inclined to toughness. The pinker the color of veal, usually, the older it is.

Fish and Seafood

When you are buying fish, any fish, buy freshness. Look for eyes that are clear, not cloudy, and gills that are red. If the fish has been frozen, its eyes will seem to have sunk into its head. Obviously the best fish to buy should be swimming, but that is not always possible. Perhaps what you should do is befriend a fisherman!

Sea Bass

This fish has a fine flavor and a firm texture. If you have access to fresh, pure striped bass, then it is preferred. But sea bass is cheaper and easier to obtain.

Red Snapper

Quite like sea bass in most respects, red snapper can be substituted wherever sea bass is called for.

Flounder

This is a flat fish, easily obtainable, used in steamed and pan-fried recipes. Flounder has a pleasant, mildly sweet flavor, softer flesh than bass or snapper, and therefore cooks in less time than those fish.

Carp

This is a fish with many bones, but with a fine, sweet taste. When it is small, from 2 to 3 pounds, it is exceptionally bony and is not recommended. Buy it by the piece. Have your fishmonger cut a thick slice from the center of the body of a carp that weighs at least 8 to 10 pounds. The bones will be bigger and easier to remove. Carp is oily but extremely tasty.

Shrimp

Fresh shrimp are virtually unobtainable in most parts of the United States. Notable exceptions are areas around the Gulf of Mexico, and occasionally in Maine. But in all likelihood you will buy frozen shrimp that have been defrosted. Look for those of gray color. A pink color indicates that the shrimp have probably been dropped into boiling water briefly, then frozen. These are not recommended.

Lobster

Lobster should be fresh, and freshly killed in front of you before buying. Frozen lobster, including lobster tails, usually has a dull and uninteresting taste, while fresh lobster is sweet and juicy and has a fine, crunchy texture. The size I recommend for tenderness is 1½ to 2 pounds.

Scallops

These days it is quite difficult to tell fresh sea scallops from imitations, which have been stamped by machine out of shark meat or from the meaty wings of the manta ray. If the market price seems inordinately expensive, the scallops are usually genuine. Unfortunately, it is easy to tell real scallops from fakes only after cooking. Those not real will often have offensive, excessively fishy aromas. The best advice I might give is to buy your scallops from a reliable fishmonger. Or if you are lucky enough to live near that font of fine seafood Seattle, buy all of your scallops fresh in their shells. They are delicious.

The advice is ended. The introduction to the foods of the Cantonese kitchen has been made, the ways to prepare them have been outlined. It is now time to cook.

⤵ All of the recipes in this book will yield four to six servings. Of course, if you cook a large, many-course meal then they might serve as many as eight or ten, because of smaller portions. In addition, Cantonese family-style eating dictates that rice be served with each dish so that even small recipes will feed four to six people. When Cantonese eat out or have banquets, usually no plain white rice is served. The meal will then contain a special rice preparation, perhaps an imaginative Fried Rice (page 58), Almond Rice (page 62), or Sun Tak Fried Rice (page 60).

Eating in Canton

菜譜

Rice | 白米

Rice is the Cantonese universal. No day passes without a Cantonese man, woman, or child having rice at least twice, for it is said that unless a Cantonese eats rice at least two times daily, he or she will have no energy. Rice eaten in Canton is white rice, usually eaten after it has been cooked plainly, with water, and properly, so that each grain of white rice is fluffy, is separate from other grains, and though not moist, has absorbed all of the water in which it has been cooked.

South China, along with India and other parts of East Asia, is perhaps the world's most abundant rice-growing region. Two crops are harvested each year in southern China, in and around Canton and throughout Guangdong Province, and the mark of a man without material care is said to be that "his rice bowl is full." A person who has fallen upon lean times has a "broken rice bowl." Rice in Canton is food, respect, tradition.

In the morning a family might eat plain cooked rice, perhaps with an egg broken into it, perhaps with a stir-fried vegetable, perhaps as part of a congee, a rice porridge that is a cooked combination of long- and short-grain rices, often with bits of meat or fish added to it. At noon a Cantonese will eat not lunch but *n'fon,* or "afternoon rice," and in the evening he will eat *mon fon,* or "evening rice." And the words signifying that a meal is to be eaten are *sik fon*, which are translated to mean "eat rice and other foods."

At a family celebration it is customary for the younger ones to wish each older person at the table *sik fon*, and no one may eat until all of the *sik fon*s have been said. I can recall an occasion when I was a young girl in Sun Tak, sitting at the table with my grandmother, my mother and father, my brother who was older, two aunts and two uncles, and five older cousins and having to wish each of them *sik fon*. This turned out to be thirteen wishes, and I felt sorry for myself until my two younger cousins, who were also there, had to wish *sik fon* to everybody, *including* me.

The rice eaten most widely in Canton today is extra-long-grain rice, which is said to have been first cultivated in the area around Laos. There are also short-grain rices and glutinous rice, both somewhat shorter in length than the extra-long-grain rice and somewhat sticky when cooked. Brown rice, which is simply rice in which only the outer husk has been milled off, is not widely eaten because it is regarded as inferior.

To a Cantonese the finest rice is completely milled white rice that is then washed, cleaned, and polished. And the whiter the better, for it is the whiteness that is prized. In all the years of my growing up in China, I can recall eating brown rice only once, and that was in the late days of World War II when our family, and others, were forced to eat it. We did not like it at all.

In North America the best rice to accompany Cantonese food—or for that matter, any Chinese food—is extra-long-grain rice. I prefer the sort grown in Texas, which can be bought in sacks labeled, naturally enough, Texas Extra-Long Grain. It is virtually identical to the best rice of the Canton region. And when cooked properly, it is a joy to eat. In Canton this fine rice is called *see miu mai*, which merely describes its extra-long grain. I suppose we can call the Texas kind Texas See Miu Mai. It has a nice ring to it.

RICE | 白飯

Fon

For many beginners, the most mystifying of cooking preparations is cooking rice properly. It is not difficult. Here is a virtually foolproof recipe for creating fine cooked rice, which can accompany many, if not most, of the dishes in this book.

Use extra-long-grain rice, preferably Texas-grown. Place it in a pot with cold water and wash it 3 times. As you wash it, rub it between your hands. Drain well after washing. Then add water and allow the rice to sit 2 hours before cooking. A good ratio is 1 cup of rice to 1 cup less 1 tablespoon of water, for two people.

So-called old rice, which has been lying about in sacks for extended periods, will absorb more water and be easier to cook.

Begin cooking, uncovered, over high heat and bring the water to a boil. Stir with chopsticks and cook for about 4 minutes, or until the water evaporates. Even after the water is gone the rice will be quite hard. Cover the pot and cook over low heat for about 8 minutes more, stirring the rice from time to time.

After turning off the heat, loosen the rice with chopsticks. This will help retain fluffiness. Cover tightly until ready to serve. Just before serving, stir the rice with chopsticks once again. Well-cooked rice will have absorbed the water but will not be lumpy, nor will the kernels stick together. They will be firm and fluffy.

Sik fon.

FRIED RICE
WITH
CHINESE
SAUSAGES
AND
SHRIMP

*Lop Cheung Sin
Har Chau Fon*

This is the classic Cantonese fried rice, the *chau fon*. I remember it as a special treat for the Lunar New Year and during the winter months, when *lop cheung*, the Chinese sausage, was available to us. It was, and is, wonderfully tasty, and you needn't wait for winter, for *lop cheung* is available the year round.

    4 Chinese sausages
1½ cups extra-long-grain rice
1½ cups cold water
  ¼ pound fresh shrimp, shelled, deveined, washed, dried, cut in half lengthwise, then half again, making 4 pieces each

Make a sauce—combine in a bowl:

1½ tablespoons oyster sauce
  2 tablespoons Chicken Broth (page 40)
  1 teaspoon light soy sauce
 ¼ teaspoon salt
 ½ teaspoon sesame oil

Make a marinade—combine in a bowl:

½ teaspoon grated ginger mixed with 1 teaspoon white wine
½ teaspoon sugar
½ teaspoon sesame oil
 1 teaspoon oyster sauce
½ teaspoon light soy sauce
  Pinch of white pepper

  2 tablespoons peanut oil
  3 large eggs, beaten
  1 teaspoon minced ginger
  1 teaspoon minced garlic
  1 teaspoon coriander, chopped
  2 scallions, washed, dried, with both ends trimmed, and finely sliced

1. Wash the Chinese sausage, place in pot with the rice and water and cook the rice (page 57). After cooking, remove the sausage and allow to cool. Cut into quarters lengthwise, then into ¼-inch pieces.

2. While the rice is cooking, make the sauce and reserve. Add the shrimp to the marinade and allow to marinate for ½ hour. Reserve.

3. Heat wok over high heat for 45 seconds to 1 minute. Add 1 tablespoon of the peanut oil, coat wok with spatula. When a wisp of white smoke appears, add the beaten eggs. Scramble the eggs. Turn off heat and use spatula to break the cooked eggs into small pieces. Remove and set aside.

4. Wash wok and spatula; dry. Heat wok over high heat for 45 seconds to 1 minute. Add the remaining peanut oil; coat wok. When white smoke appears, add the ginger and garlic. When the garlic turns light brown, add the sausage and stir-fry together for 1 minute. Make a well in the center of the mixture and add the shrimp and marinade. Stir together for another minute. Add cooked rice and mix all together well for 5 to 7 minutes. The rice should become very hot.

5. Stir the sauce, pour it into the rice, and mix it well, making certain the rice is completely coated. Add the coriander and scallions and mix well into the fried rice. Turn off heat, transfer rice to a preheated serving bowl, and serve immediately.

FRIED RICE
SUN TAK
STYLE

———

*Hom Yu Chau
Fan*

The Chinese call all preserved fish *hom yu*. This particular fish, a toothed croaker, is widely eaten in Canton. It is usually dried and preserved in salt after it has been caught. The Cantonese use small pieces of it, very sparingly, because of its strong taste. This Sun Tak Style rice is a very special dish from my childhood in the Cantonese suburban town of Sun Tak.

   1 ounce of preserved fish (see note at end)
   2 cups peanut oil
1½ cups extra-long-grain rice
1½ cups cold water
   2 Chinese sausages
   2 tablespoons peanut oil
   2 eggs, beaten
1½ teaspoons minced ginger
1½ teaspoons minced garlic
   1 scallion, washed, dried, with both ends trimmed, and finely sliced

Make a sauce—combine in a bowl:

   1 tablespoon oyster sauce
1½ teaspoons light soy sauce
  ¼ teaspoon salt
  ½ teaspoon sugar
  ½ teaspoon sesame oil
    Pinch of white pepper
   2 tablespoons Chicken Broth (page 40)

1. Deep-fry the fish in the 2 cups of peanut oil until very crisp, about 4 to 5 minutes. Remove from oil, allow to cool, remove bone, and mince to make 1 tablespoon. (The remainder may be reserved for another use.)

2. Make the sauce; reserve.

3. In a bowl, wash the rice 3 times in cold water, rubbing it between your palms. Drain off water and place the rice in a cake pan. Add the 1½ cups cold water. Wash the

Chinese sausages and place atop rice. Steam the rice for about 40 minutes (see steaming instructions, page 38).

4. Remove the rice from steamer and allow to cool. Cut the sausages into quarters, then cut these into ¼-inch pieces. Reserve the sausages. Loosen the rice and reserve it separately.

5. Heat wok over high heat for 1 minute. Add 1 tablespoon of the peanut oil. Pour the beaten eggs into wok. Soft-scramble the eggs, then remove from wok and cut coarsely with a knife. Reserve.

6. Heat wok over high heat. Add the remaining 1 tablespoon of peanut oil. When a wisp of white smoke appears, add the minced ginger, stir for 20 to 30 seconds, then add the minced garlic. When the garlic turns light brown, add the fish and stir together for 30 seconds. Add the diced Chinese sausage and stir for 1 minute. Add the rice and mix all ingredients thoroughly until the rice is hot. If heat is too high, lower it to avoid burning the rice.

7. Add the sauce to the rice and continue to mix, raising the heat once again. When the rice has become an even light brown and is well coated, add the reserved egg. Stir well. Turn off the heat and add the sliced scallion; stir until well mixed. Serve immediately.

❧ The preserved fish, the *hom yu,* is usually available in Chinese groceries, on shelves, not in refrigerated compartments. It is labeled either "Toothed Croaker" or "Preserved Han Yee." Be certain the fish used is this because other preserved fish will yield very different results. If the fish is unavailable, the closest approximation is dried codfish, the sort found in Italian food stores.

If your preference is not to use fish, then the recipe can be made beautifully without it, in which case a touch of salt might be needed in the sauce. The sweet taste of the Chinese sausage will be dominant.

ALMOND
RICE
IN LOTUS
LEAVES

蓮
包
杏
仁
飯

*Lin Bau Hung
Yun Fan*

Almonds are eaten widely in China and are thought to add to one's good health. What I have created with them is a variation on a classic dish of the Hakka people, in which rice and vegetables, meats, or shellfish are steamed in closed fresh lotus leaves. Fresh lotus leaves impart an utterly marvelous fragrance to the rice. Unfortunately, only dried lotus leaves are available in Asian food stores. The dried leaves, when soaked and wrapped around the rice, do, however, give some of that aroma. In my recipe the dominant flavors are those of the leaves and the almonds.

2 cups rice, preferably short-grain, though long-grained rice may be used
2 cups cold water
6 Chinese sausages, washed
½ cup whole blanched almonds (skinless)
2 cups water
1 tablespoon peanut oil
2 cloves garlic, minced
¼ cup dried shrimp, soaked ½ hour in hot water, then cut into ¼-inch pieces
6 Chinese mushrooms, soaked ½ hour in hot water, stems removed, cut into ¼-inch pieces
4 fresh water chestnuts, peeled, washed, dried, and cut into ¼-inch cubes
2 scallions, washed, dried, with both ends trimmed, and cut into ¼-inch pieces
1½ tablespoons oyster sauce
1 tablespoon sesame oil
1½ teaspoons dark soy sauce
1½ teaspoons light soy sauce
1½ teaspoons sugar
½ teaspoon salt
   Pinch of white pepper
2 whole lotus leaves, soaked in hot water for ½ hour

1.   Wash the rice 3 times in cold water, rubbing it between your hands. Drain well. Place in a cake pan 9 inches
in diameter and add 2 cups cold water. Place the Chinese
sausages on top of the rice. Place the cake pan with the
rice and sausages in a bamboo steamer and steam for 30
to 40 minutes. (See "To steam," page 38.) When the rice
and sausages are cooked, turn off heat and allow them to
remain in the steamer.

2.   Place the almonds in a small saucepan with 2 cups
of water. Bring to a boil, lower the heat, and cook, partially covered, for 30 minutes. Drain and reserve.

3.   Remove the sausages from the rice, quarter them
lengthwise, then cut them into ½-inch pieces. Reserve.

4.   Heat wok over high heat, add the peanut oil, and coat
the wok with a spatula. Add the minced garlic, and when
it turns light brown add the shrimp and mushrooms and
stir together for 1 to 1½ minutes. Reserve.

5.   When the rice is at room temperature, place in a large
mixing bowl. Add the sausages, shrimp and mushroom
mixture, almonds, water chestnuts, scallions, oyster sauce,
sesame oil, soy sauces, sugar, salt, and pepper. Mix thoroughly and set aside.

6.   Remove the lotus leaves from the water, drain, and
wipe dry. Spread the first leaf out on a large work surface,
smooth side up. Place the second leaf on top of the first,
positioning them so that no holes can be seen. Mound
the rice mixture in the center. Form a bundle by folding
the leaves over to cover the rice on all 4 sides.

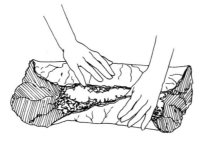
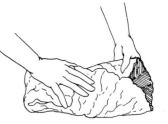

7. Place the bundle, folded side down, in a steamer and steam for 30 minutes. Transfer to a serving dish. Cut a round hole out of the top of the bundle with a pair of kitchen shears, and scoop out the rice to serve.

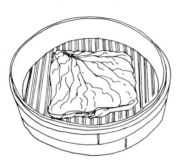

↘ If lotus leaves are unavailable, you may use aluminum foil. Or you may follow the recipe through step 5, keeping rice warm instead of allowing it to cool. Serve immediately after the ingredients are combined.

↘ The recipe may be made 1 day in advance. Keep refrigerated, then allow to come to room temperature before steaming.

LOTUS LEAF
RICE
WITH
DUCK

———

*Siu Op Hor
Yip Fon*

Lotus Leaf Rice exists in many versions in Canton. The quiet taste of the lotus leaf when steamed with rice is quite pleasing, and the combination of the two is beloved by chefs, who become very creative with them. The most traditional version has glutinous rice surrounding Chinese sausages, fresh pork, chicken, shrimp, and mushrooms. There is a Hakka version that combines chicken and shrimp and utilizes extra-long-grain rice. I have created a different version, using almonds and short-grain rice. And here is my conception of yet another, using glutinous rice. It is almost traditional, but with the tastes of roast duck and a bit of honey roast pork at its center, I might even call it a new tradition.

1½ cups glutinous rice
1½ cups cold water
1½ tablespoons peanut oil
 ½ teaspoon salt
1½ teaspoons minced ginger
1½ teaspoons minced garlic
  2 cups Roast Duck meat (page 174) cut into ¼-inch dice
 ½ cup Honey Roast Pork (page 181) cut into ¼-inch dice
  4 Chinese mushrooms, soaked in hot water for 30 minutes, squeezed dry of excess water, stems discarded, and cut into ¼-inch pieces
  1 tablespoon Shao-Hsing wine or sherry
  4 fresh water chestnuts, peeled, washed, dried, and cut into ¼-inch dice
 ½ cup scallions, washed, dried, with both ends trimmed, and finely sliced
  2 tablespoons oyster sauce
1½ tablespoons Scallion Oil (page 22)
1½ teaspoons sesame oil
  1 teaspoon sugar
  2 teaspoons light soy sauce
    Pinch of white pepper
  2 large lotus leaves, soaked in hot water for 30 minutes

1.   Wash rice 3 times. Drain off water. Put rice in a round cake pan of 8-inch diameter, add the cold water, place the cake pan in a steamer, and steam for 30 to 40 minutes, or until rice becomes creamy white in color (page 38).

2.   Heat wok over high heat for 45 seconds. Add the peanut oil and coat wok with spatula. When a wisp of white smoke appears add the salt, ginger, and garlic. Stir together. When the garlic turns light brown add the duck meat, roast pork, and mushrooms. Mix well and cook for 1 minute. Add the Shao-Hsing wine by drizzling it down into the wok along the sides. Stir together for 30 seconds. Remove from wok and place in a large mixing bowl.

3. Add the steamed rice, water chestnuts, scallions, and all the other ingredients except the lotus leaves. Mix well.

4. Wipe the water from the lotus leaves. Place flat on a work surface, one on top of the other, smooth sides up, making certain that the top leaf seals all the holes in the bottom one. Mound the rice mixture in the center of the leaves and fold inward, one side, then the opposite, then repeat with other 2 sides, to create a package.

5. Place the package in a steamer, folded side down, and steam for 30 to 40 minutes, or until the rice package is heated through. Turn off heat, transfer the package to a serving dish using two spatulas, and serve immediately. To serve, cut a round hole in the middle of the package and spoon the rice mixture out.

➴   Instead of one large package, this recipe can be made into 4 to 6 packages. Use smaller leaves, or cut large ones in half; portion out the filling, wrap, and steam for 30 minutes.

➴   The dish can be prepared up to 2 days in advance and refrigerated. Before steaming, allow to come to room temperature.

Doughs and Noodles 麵糰和麵

One of the pleasures of cooking is making doughs. The transformation of flour, water, and eggs into a kneadable mass and then into plump *dim sum*, or into noodles, dumplings, and pastries, is a joy. I never tire of working with dough. Perhaps my fondness for it is a childhood remembrance I have. Often when I see packages of freshly made noodles in the Asian markets in which I shop, I think of the "bamboo stick noodles" of my youth in Canton. I recall that my mother first urged me to watch the noodle makers, saying I would learn something useful. But after seeing them for the first time I needed no further prodding, for not only did I learn, I had fun.

The noodles were made in this manner. One end of a long bamboo pole would be attached to the top of the noodle maker's floured worktable, near an edge. He would pound and knead his dough, and when it was a substantial ball he would bring the bamboo stick over it, and bend the other end until it was between his legs. Then he would jump and dance back and forth, as if he were riding a rocking horse, from side to side, smacking the dough until it became very flat and thin. Then he would cut the dough into thin, flat noodles, which were later separated into fine strands. Unfortunately, I never got to dance around and make noodles that way because that was highly skilled work, but I did get to eat those noodles, often, to my great delight.

And that is what Chinese doughs and noodles are all about. They are a continual delight, certainly one of the more versatile aspects of the Chinese kitchen, particularly in Canton. The Cantonese use doughs to make an infinite variety of *dim sum*, dumplings, steamed and baked breads, and noodles. They boil noodles, cook them in soup, or add them to soups. They steam them, toss them with an endless variety of sauces, fry them softly or crisply, eat them hot or cold. In Canton there are restaurants devoted exclusively to noodles and doughs.

Noodles, by their length, signify long life and are always served on birthdays. In Taiwanese villages, noodles are presented as grave offerings so that those who have passed away will have some added enjoyment in heaven.

Chinese doughs can be divided into two general categories, dried and fresh; and within these there exist doughs of wheat flour, flour and egg, rice, and beans. These doughs can be factory-made or rolled, kneaded, flattened, and cut by hand. In Peking a mass of dough is braided, pulled, twisted, and thrown in the air repeatedly until it emerges, somehow, into a pile of noodles as fine as hair. These noodles, called the "dragon's beard," are deep-fried and folded into wheat flour pancakes, a treat that had its origins in the imperial court. In Canton there is a character in an opera, Mo Dai Long, who does nothing but eat noodles. When we were children, anyone who loved noodles was called by his name.

Marco Polo notwithstanding, doughs and noodles have existed in China since the Han Dynasty, which began in 206 B.C., more than 1,400 years before Marco Polo made his way to Peking. It was the Han who milled flour and boiled the noodle. Doughs of various kinds and noodles, boiled, fried, steamed, and sauced, were a constant in China by the time of the Yüan Dynasty, the period when Marco Polo arrived. The Ming are reported to have included noodles flavored with sesame in an elaborate court banquet.

In Canton there are fresh noodles of wheat flour and water, and of simple flour and water to which eggs have been added. There are fresh rice flour noodles as well. There are dried wheat flour and water noodles, dried egg noodles, and dried rice noodles. And there are also dried noodles made from the processed starch of the mung beans, often called bean thread noodles. All Chinese noodles, fresh or dried, should be boiled first before eating, and in the case of many *dim sum*, they should be carefully steamed.

Soft noodles of fresh wheat flour, of eggs, of rice, are usually freshly made and can be found in the refrigerated compartments of markets. They are best when cooked fresh, but may be kept refrigerated for 2 to 3 days. They may also be frozen for 4 to 6 weeks without losing their textures. Both *won tun* skins and spring roll wrappers are soft doughs as well. They may be kept refrigerated for 2 days and may be frozen from 4 to 6 weeks.

The many kinds of dried noodles available can make for some confusion. There are as many as twenty different kinds, from so-called rice sticks to Japanese-style noodles made with sweet potato starch dough. All come packaged in cellophane in bundles ranging in size from 2 ounces to as much as a pound. Dried noodles can be kept, in tightly sealed packages, unrefrigerated, for as long as 6 months. The most common dried noodles are of eggs, of rice, of mung bean starch. Often shrimp roe is added to noodles in the preparation process, and when they dry they will appear flecked with the tiny eggs. These are more expensive than other noodles, but they have a distinctive taste.

For most *dim sum*, doughs should be fresh and soft, so that they can be molded and folded into the many distinctive shapes of *dim sum*. The dough used in most *dim sum*, particularly *har gau*, those famed Shrimp

Dumplings, is of wheat starch and tapioca flour. The wheat starch, very white, makes for a translucent dumpling after it has been steamed, and the tapioca flour, ground from the roots of the cassava, adds tensile strength to the Har Gau Dough.

Another dough, quite easily made, is the dough for those wonderful dumplings known as the *won tun*. It is made of flour, eggs, water, and baking soda, and while the Cantonese do not strictly regard it as a dumpling, as they do many *dim sum*, it is indeed a wrapping enclosing a filling. *Won tun* skins, packages of dusted squares of dough, are widely available these days in supermarkets and Asian food markets.

However, if they are unavailable—and because I am aware that virtually everyone in America, like every Cantonese, likes *won tun*—I have included a recipe for that dough, too, and for some unusual *won tun* creations of my own.

SHRIMP
DUMPLINGS

———

Har Gau

This tiny, pleated dumpling might well be the most familiar food of Canton. There is no other *dim sum* which is as popular. There is no teahouse which does not serve it. In fact, when I think of *dim sum* as a genre, what jumps into my mind is a picture of a woman pushing a cart full of steaming containers through a teahouse in Canton, intoning in a singsong voice, *"Har gau, har gau."*

The dough for it and its filling are made in virtually the same way by every chef who fashions *har gau*, yet one finds differences. Sometimes the cooked dough covering is thicker than usual, sometimes like tissue. Sometimes the filling is thick and meaty, sometimes spongy, sometimes light and crunchy. I expect these differences lie with the hands that make the *har gau*.

I, too, make it the traditional way—the only way, for a Cantonese cook—but at times with a minor variation. Occasionally I add extra egg white to the filling, as below, and the result is a lighter-textured filling.

   2 tablespoons pork fat, either bought packaged or trimmed from a fresh ham or from pork chops
1½ cups boiling water
  ½ pound shrimp, shelled, deveined, washed, dried, and cut into ½-inch dice
  ¾ teaspoon salt
   1 teaspoon sugar
   1 medium egg white, beaten
1½ tablespoons tapioca flour
1½ teaspoons oyster sauce
  ¾ teaspoon sesame oil
    Pinch of white pepper
  ¼ cup fresh water chestnuts, peeled, washed, dried, and diced into ⅛-inch pieces
  ¼ cup white portions of scallions, finely sliced
   2 tablespoons bamboo shoots, cut into ⅛-inch dice
   1 recipe Har Gau Dough (page 73)

1.   Place the pork fat in the 1½ cups boiling water and allow to boil until it cooks fully, about 30 minutes, or until translucent. Remove from water and place in a bowl, run cold water over it, let stand for several minutes, then remove from water, dry with paper towels, and cut into ⅛-inch dice. Reserve.

2.   Place the shrimp in bowl of an electric mixer. Start mixer and add, mixing thoroughly after each addition, the salt, sugar, egg white, tapioca flour, oyster sauce, sesame oil, and white pepper.

3.   Add the reserved pork fat, water chestnuts, scallions, and bamboo shoots. Combine evenly and thoroughly.

4.   Remove the mixture from mixing bowl and place in a shallow bowl or dish, cover, and refrigerate for 4 hours, or put it in the freezer for 25 minutes.

5.   Using Har Gau Dough skins, form the dumplings: place 1½ teaspoons shrimp filling in the center of each skin, then fold the skin in half, forming a crescent, or half-moon.

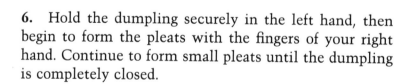

6.   Hold the dumpling securely in the left hand, then begin to form the pleats with the fingers of your right hand. Continue to form small pleats until the dumpling is completely closed.

7. Press the top edge of the dumpling between your thumb and index finger to seal it tightly. Tap the sealed edge lightly with your knuckle to give the dumpling its final shape.

8. Steam for 5 to 7 minutes (page 38) and serve immediately.

⊁ This recipe will make about 45 to 50 *har gau*. As you gain experience, you may put more filling into each *har gau. Har gau* can be frozen for future use. They keep for 4 to 6 weeks when piled neatly and wrapped in a double layer of plastic wrap and then in aluminum foil. To reheat, defrost, then steam for 3 to 5 minutes.

HAR
GAU
DOUGH

─────

Har Gau Pei

蝦
餃
皮

The small, individual pieces of dough made from this recipe, when formed into thin wrappings, are called *pei*, which means "skin."

1⅓ cups wheat starch
⅔ cup tapioca flour
¼ teaspoon salt
1 cup plus 3 tablespoons boiling water
2 tablespoons liquefied lard

1. In the bowl of an electric mixer, place the wheat starch, tapioca flour, and salt. Start the mixer, and as the bowl and dough hook rotate, add the boiling water. (If electric mixer is unavailable, mix by hand in the same order, pouring water with one hand while mixing with a wooden spoon with the other.)

2.   Add the liquefied lard and mix thoroughly. (You may have to assist the process with a rubber spatula.) If dough is too dry, add 1 teaspoon boiling water.

3.   Continue to mix until a ball of dough is formed. Remove from bowl, knead a few times, divide into 4 equal pieces, and place each ball in a plastic bag to retain moisture until ready for use.

4.   Before working with dough, oil the work surface. Soak a paper towel in peanut oil and repeatedly run cleaver across the towel so that the blade is oiled.

5.   Roll each ball of dough into sausage-shaped lengths about 8 inches long, 1 inch in diameter. Cut a ¹/₂-inch piece from the length. Roll into a small ball, then press down with palm of your hand to flatten it.

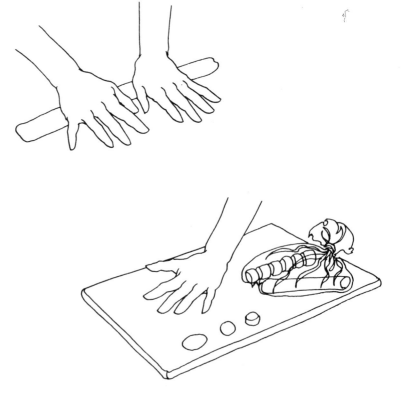

6. Press flatter with the broad side of the cleaver to create the round skin, 2¼ inches in diameter.

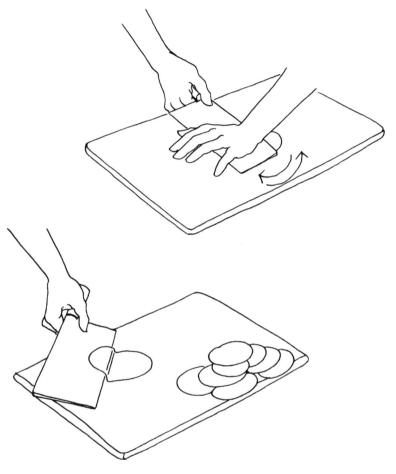

↘ The recipe will make 64 skins. The filling is sufficient for 50. I specify the extra so that failures can be discarded.

Dough can be set aside for a few hours, or overnight in cold weather. It must remain at room temperature; it cannot be refrigerated or frozen.

If your electric mixer does not have a dough hook, you must mix and knead the dough by hand. You cannot use a hand mixer with beaters.

LOBSTER DUMPLINGS

龍蝦餃

Lung Har Gau

The Cantonese for these lobster dumplings translates into "Dragon Shrimp Dumplings." "Dragon shrimp" is what lobster is called in Canton. This *dim sum* utilizes a traditional shape, called "Phoenix Eyes," because it is shaped somewhat like the eye of a woman. Usually it is filled with diced shrimp. I have chosen to make a lobster filling and to create a *new* tradition, that of the dragon shrimp.

1 pound lobster meat from the tails of 2 lobsters, each about 9 to 10 ounces, shelled, deveined, washed, dried, and cut in 1/4-inch dice
3/4 teaspoon salt
1 medium egg white, beaten
2 tablespoons tapioca flour
1 3/4 teaspoons sugar
1 1/2 tablespoons diced pork fat (see Shrimp Dumplings, page 71, Step 1)
1 teaspoon sesame oil
1 tablespoon oyster sauce
Pinch of white pepper
1 teaspoon white wine
2 tablespoons fresh water chestnuts, peeled, washed, dried, and cut into 1/8-inch dice
2 tablespoons scallions, white portions only, finely sliced
2 tablespoons carrots cut into 1/8-inch dice
3 Chinese black mushrooms, soaked in hot water for 30 minutes, washed, squeezed dry, with stems removed, and cut into 1/8-inch dice
1 recipe Har Gau Dough (page 73)

1. Place the lobster meat in bowl of electric mixer. Add the salt and blend for 1 minute. Add the egg white and blend for 1 minute.

2. Add all other ingredients except the dough and blend thoroughly for 1 1/2 minutes. The consistency should be slightly coarse; pieces of lobster meat should be visible.

3. Transfer the mixture to a shallow dish and place in refrigerator for 4 hours, or 25 minutes in freezer.

4. Using Har Gau Dough recipe, form dumpling wrappings.

5. Place 1 tablespoon of filling in center of each wrapping. Fold the skin in half to create a crescent shape. With your index fingers, create a pleat on each side of the dumpling. Press and seal the edges of the dumpling to form the Phoenix Eye shape.

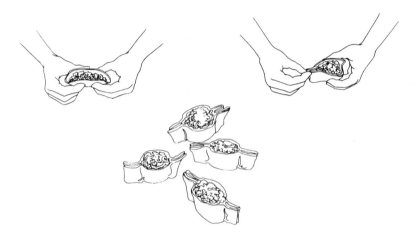

6. Steam for 5 to 7 minutes (page 38) and serve immediately.

⌖ Lobster Dumplings may be frozen and will keep 4 to 6 weeks. To freeze, wrap in a double layer of plastic wrap and cover with foil. To reheat, defrost thoroughly and steam for 3 to 5 minutes.

WON
TUN

These are most often called *won ton*, but the Cantonese pronunciation is *won tun*. The words literally mean "swallowing a cloud" and denote lightness. In the city of Canton, around midnight, young men sent by restaurants walk the streets hitting pieces of bamboo together, and the "tok tik" sounds indicate that midnight *won tun* snack time is at hand. I remember we used to lean out of our windows and give our orders, which were later delivered.

The *won tun* comes in a wonderful variety. Once made, it can be boiled, put into soup, pan-fried, deep-fat-fried, or steamed. It can be eaten at any point in a larger meal. Perhaps best of all, if it is left over, it can be frozen to be enjoyed on a future day. Following is my version of the traditional *won tun*.

25–30 *won tun* skins (these come in 1-pound packages of 75 to 80 skins; freeze and reserve those not used—see instructions at the end of the next recipe for Won Tun Dough)

In large mixing bowl, combine and stir clockwise:

½ pound fresh ground pork
¼ pound shrimp, shelled, deveined, washed in salt water, drained, dried with paper towels, and finely diced
3 scallions, washed, dried thoroughly, with both ends trimmed, and finely sliced
1½ teaspoons minced garlic
3 fresh water chestnuts, peeled, washed, dried, and finely diced
1½ teaspoons white wine mixed with ½ teaspoon ginger juice (page 17)
½ teaspoon salt
1 teaspoon sugar
1 teaspoon light soy sauce
1 teaspoon sesame oil

1 tablespoon oyster sauce
   Pinch of white pepper
2 tablespoons cornstarch
1 medium egg

1. Skins should be kept in plastic wrap at room temperature. Twenty minutes before preparation, peel off the plastic wrap and cover the skins with a wet towel.

2. Keeping a bowl of water at hand so that the 4 edges of the *won tun* can be wetted, place about 1 tablespoon of the mixture on the nonfloured side of the skin. Then the skin should be folded and squeezed along the wet edges so it seals like an envelope.

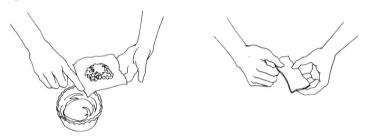

3. Once it is folded and sealed, the 2 corners of the folded sides are wetted and then drawn together and squeezed with the fingers to create a bowlike dumpling. As each *won tun* is made, place it on a floured cookie sheet so that it will not stick.

4. Cook the *won tun* in 3 quarts of water to which have been added 2 tablespoons of salt and 1 tablespoon of peanut oil. The water should be boiling before the *won tun*

are placed in it. The usual cooking time is 5 to 7 minutes, or until the *won tun* become translucent and the filling can be seen through the skin. Use a wooden spoon to stir 3 or 4 times during cooking to avoid sticking. Cook in 2 batches.

5.   Remove pot of *won tun* from heat and run cold water into it. Drain. Run more cold water through the *won tun*. Drain again. Place them on waxed paper and allow them to dry. Consult page 83 for various ways in which to cook and present *won tun*.

WON
TUN
DOUGH

This recipe will make about 100 squares of these wrappings. As I have said before, *won tun* skins are widely available, but if they are not, this recipe will make them quite nicely. The skins, which come in 1-pound packages, are of varying thicknesses. I prefer the thinner ones, and it is because of this that I recommend you buy them commercially. These will, of course, be thinner than those you will make. Nevertheless, here is a fine recipe for a traditional Cantonese staple.

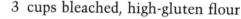

>   3 cups bleached, high-gluten flour
> 1¼ teaspoons baking soda
>   1 teaspoon salt (optional)
>   4 extra-large eggs
>   ¼ cup water
>   ⅔ cup of cornstarch, for dusting

1.   Place the flour on a work surface and mix with the baking soda and salt. Make a well in the center and add the eggs, unbeaten. Work the dough with your fingers until the eggs are absorbed. Slowly drizzle the water into the dough, mixing with your hands as you do, until it is thoroughly blended. Use a dough scraper to collect the excess pieces. Then begin to knead the dough.

2. Knead for about 10 minutes, or until the dough becomes elastic, then set aside, covered with a damp cloth, for 3 hours.

3. When the dough is ready, dust the work surface with cornstarch. Divide the dough into 2 equal pieces. Roll each piece with a rolling pin until you have a sheet $1/4$-inch thick. Pick up sheet, dust the surface again, and roll again, continually, until the dough's thickness is reduced to $1/8$ inch, or less.

4. Roll up the dough around a length of broom handle or a dowel. Dust the work surface again. Roll the dough off the broom handle, then roll with the rolling pin again, as thin as possible, then again roll up around broom handle to lift it from the work surface. You must use the broom handle, or dowel, because otherwise the dough will tear.

5. Dust the work surface again, unroll the sheet onto it, and with rolling pin roll out a sheet about 18 by 21 inches. Repeat with the second piece of dough.

6. Cut the *won tun*. Before cutting, make certain the surface is dusted again. Using the edge of the dough scraper, cut squares 3 inches by 3 inches. Reserve the skins for use.

When freshly made, the skins cannot be used because they are brittle. Store overnight, refrigerated and wrapped in plastic to renew elasticity. Be certain that there is a dusting of cornstarch between all skins. The skins can be frozen for 4 to 6 weeks. Defrost and allow to come to room temperature before using.

WON
TUN
WITH
VEAL

牛
仔
肉
雪
吞

*Won Tun Ngau
Jai Yuk*

My variation of the traditional *won tun* is one made with fresh ground veal. The Chinese name for these means "*won tun* made with meat from the baby cow." In it I replace the scallions and water chestnuts with fresh chives and bamboo shoots. While the texture of the *won tun* are similar, their taste is very different and very delicious.

30 *won tun* skins

In a large mixing bowl combine and stir clockwise:

- ³/₄ pound ground veal
- 1¹/₂ cups Chinese chives, or regular chives, washed, dried, with ¹/₈ inch trimmed off the white end, and cut into ¹/₄-inch dice
- ¹/₄ pound shrimp, shelled, deveined, washed in salt water, dried, and cut into ¹/₄-inch dice
- ¹/₄ cup bamboo shoots, cut into ¹/₄-inch dice
- 1 teaspoon grated ginger mixed with 1¹/₂ teaspoons Shao-Hsing wine or sherry
- 1¹/₂ teaspoons minced garlic
- ³/₄ teaspoon salt
- 1¹/₄ teaspoons sugar
- 1¹/₂ teaspoons dark soy sauce
- 2 teaspoons sesame oil
- 1 tablespoon peanut oil
- 1 tablespoon oyster sauce
- 2¹/₂ tablespoons cornstarch
  Pinch of white pepper
- 1 medium egg

To prepare, follow directions for traditional *won tun* (page 78).

This basic recipe can be used to create Chicken Won Tun, or as we call them, *Gai Yuk Won Tun*. To make them, use ¹/₂ pound ground fresh chicken meat, white and dark mixed, and all of the ingredients in the traditional pork *won tun.* However, you should add an additional ½ tea-spoon of sesame oil and 1 tablespoon of peanut oil to keep the chicken mixture moist.

All of the different *won tun* can be eaten as they are after cooking, or they can be:

Pan-fried:

Place 3 tablespoons of peanut oil in a frypan, nonstick preferred, heat oil until a wisp of smoke appears. Place the *won tun* in pan and fry on both sides, until brown.

Deep-fat-fried:

Place 4 to 5 cups peanut oil in a wok. Boil the oil (it is boiling when white smoke rises from it), and a ½-inch slice of ginger and a clove of garlic, and fry the *won tun* to a golden brown. Drain on paper towels and serve.

Steamed:

Line a steamer with any kind of lettuce leaves. Place *won tun* in a layer on the leaves and steam (page 38), covered, for 4 to 5 minutes until quite hot. These are best served in the steamer. Set it on a large dish so that any excess water will drip down into it.

Put into Soup:

To 4 cups of chicken broth brought to a boil, add the *won tun*, 3 per person. Let the soup come to a boil again, then add 4 cups of shredded lettuce and serve.

I also serve *won tun* as a first course with a spicy sauce.

To make the sauce, mix together:

1½ teaspoons white vinegar
1 teaspoon sugar
   Pinch of white pepper
4 teaspoons Shao-Hsing wine or sherry
4 teaspoons dark soy sauce
1 tablespoon sesame oil
1 tablespoon chili oil
½ teaspoon chopped fresh coriander
½ teaspoon white portions of scallions, chopped
1 teaspoon minced garlic

Simply pour this over the boiled *won tun* and serve.

➘ Leftover *won tun* skins can be frozen for future use. Double-wrap them in plastic wrap and aluminum foil. *Won tun* can be frozen as well. Be certain they are thoroughly dry, then double-wrap in plastic and aluminum foil. Completely defrost before using.

SHRIMP
SIU
MAI
———
*Har Yuk Siu
Mai*

These *dim sum* are called "Cook and Sell" dumplings in Canton, because they are shaped like tiny cookpots filled with food. The Cantonese say they are so good they are never left unsold; thus their name. The traditional *siu mai* filling is pork and shrimp, dominated by the pungency of Chinese black mushrooms. I have made my *siu mai* more delicate, with minced shrimp, water chestnuts, ginger, and scallions.

35 *won tun* skins
  1 pound white shrimp, shelled, deveined, washed, well dried, and minced into a paste with Chinese cleaver
  1/3 cup fresh water chestnuts, peeled, washed, dried, cut into 1/8-inch slices, and diced
  1/3 cup scallions, white portion only, washed, dried, and cut into 1/8-inch slices
1½ teaspoons minced ginger
  1 teaspoon salt
  2 teaspoons sugar
  1 teaspoon sesame oil
  1 teaspoon white wine
  2 tablespoons cornstarch
  2 large egg whites, beaten
    Pinch of white pepper

1. Cut the *won tun* skins into rounds, 2½ inches in diameter. All the skins should be cut before preparing *siu mai.* Keep the *won tun* skins covered with plastic wrap at all times, including as much as possible during use, because they will dry out otherwise.

2. Combine all the other ingredients in a bowl. Mix thoroughly with chopsticks or a wooden spoon in one direction. When mixed, place in a shallow dish and refrigerate for 4 hours.

3. Make the *siu mai.* In the middle of each round, place 1 tablespoon of filling. Holding the filling in place with the blade of a small rounded knife in one hand, and holding the dumpling in the other hand, gradually turn knife and dumpling slowly in the same direction, so the dumpling naturally forms a basket shape.

4. Remove the knife, and pack down and smooth the filling on top of the dumpling. Squeeze the dumpling lightly to create a waist so that the dumpling and filling will remain intact during the steaming process. Tap the bottom of the dumpling on work surface to flatten it so that it will stand upright in the steamer.

5. Steam for 5 to 7 minutes (page 38). Serve immediately.

↘ *Siu mai* can be frozen either before or after steaming. They will keep 4 to 6 weeks. To reheat, defrost, allow to return to room temperature, then steam for 3 to 5 minutes.

BEEF
SIU
MAI

Ngau Yuk Siu Mai

Here is another of my versions of *siu mai*. When I was a child, the only *siu mai* that existed were the traditional ones of pork and shrimp. Most of the people my family knew were Buddhists, who did not eat beef, and beef dishes were not served in our teahouse. But this is another time.

45 to 50 *won tun* skins
1 pound ground sirloin
1/3 cup fresh water chestnuts, peeled, washed, dried, and cut into 1/8-inch dice
1/3 cup bamboo shoots, cut into 1/8-inch dice
1/4 cup scallions, white portions only, washed, dried, and cut into 1/8-inch slices
2 1/2 tablespoons minced ginger
1 tablespoon blended whiskey
1 teaspoon salt
2 teaspoons sugar
1 1/2 teaspoons dark soy sauce
1 1/2 tablespoons oyster sauce
3 tablespoons peanut oil
2 1/2 tablespoons cornstarch
1 teaspoon sesame oil
Pinch of white pepper
2 large egg whites

Preparation and cooking instructions for Beef Siu Mai are identical to those for Shrimp Siu Mai (page 84).

WATER
DUMPLINGS
WITH
CHIVES

韭
菜
水
餃

——————

*Gau Choi Soi
Gau*

This is another variant on a Cantonese tradition. The water dumplings that I remember, so called because they are boiled in water, were basic mixtures of pork and shrimp. I have added the very special taste of fresh Chinese chives. I prefer these flat chives, also known as garlic chives, but if these are not available, then regular chives will suffice.

45 *won tun* skins
2 teaspoons peanut oil
2 cups chives, washed, dried, with the tip of the root end discarded, and cut into ¼-inch lengths
½ pound shrimp, shelled, deveined, washed, dried thoroughly, and cut into ⅛-inch dice
¼ cup fresh water chestnuts, cut into ⅛-inch dice
¼ cup bamboo shoots, cut into ⅛-inch dice
1 pound ground pork
1 teaspoon ginger juice mixed with 1 teaspoon white wine
1½ teaspoons sugar
2 teaspoons sesame oil
2 teaspoons light soy sauce
1 tablespoon oyster sauce
2 tablespoons cornstarch
1 teaspoon salt
Pinch of white pepper

1. Cut the *won tun* skins into circles 2½ inches in diameter. All the skins should be cut before preparing the dumplings. Keep the skins covered with plastic wrap at all times, including during use, to prevent drying out.

2. Heat wok over high heat. Add the peanut oil; coat sides of wok with spatula. When wisp of white smoke appears, add the chives. Stir until the chives become bright green, about 30 to 45 seconds. Remove from wok and reserve.

3. Combine all the other ingredients (except the *won tun* skins) in a bowl and mix thoroughly with chopsticks or wooden spoon, stirring in one direction. When mixed, place in a shallow dish, cover, and refrigerate for 4 hours.

4. Make the dumplings. Place 1 tablespoon of filling in center of each skin. Keep a bowl of water at hand. Seal by wetting the edges of the *won tun* skin. Fold the skins in a half-moon shape, and press edges together to seal.

5. Cook the dumplings in 3 quarts of boiling water for 4 to 5 minutes, stirring 3 or 4 times with a wooden spoon to avoid sticking. Run cold water over them and drain. Serve immediately as a snack or as the first course in a meal. Cook in 2 batches.

 ﹆ These dumplings can be kept refrigerated for 3 or 4 days, or frozen 4 to 6 weeks. If you plan to freeze them, cook them only 2 to 3 minutes, drain, and dry thoroughly. To freeze, wrap in double plastic, then in foil. To recook, defrost, allow to come to room temperature, then either boil for 3 to 4 minutes, or steam (page 38) for the same period.

SCALLION
PANCAKES

———

*Sahng Chung
Bok Bang*

This is a very special preparation that in Canton is cooked for the pleasure of guests. It is customarily served with afternoon tea. My grandmother used to serve these Scallion Pancakes with slightly bitter *bo lei* tea. This recipe is a preparation for the home and virtually unknown in restaurants.

1¼ cups flour
1½ teaspoons baking powder
 1 medium egg, beaten
1½ cups plus 2–4 tablespoons cold water
 ¾ teaspoon salt
   Pinch of white pepper
 2 tablespoons dried shrimp, soaked in hot water for
   ½ to ¾ hour, then finely diced
 ⅓ cup Chinese bacon, finely diced
 7 scallions, washed, dried, with both ends trimmed,
   and sliced into ⅛-inch pieces
1½ tablespoons peanut oil, plus more oil for pan

1.   Mix the flour and baking powder. Add the egg and 1½ cups cold water, then mix in one direction until smooth. Add the salt and pepper and mix well.

2.   Add the shrimp, bacon, scallions, and peanut oil and blend thoroughly. The batter should be thin. If not, add the additional 2 to 4 tablespoons water.

3.   Heat a crepe pan or a nonstick frypan of the same size, then add enough peanut oil to coat bottom. Pour about 3 tablespoons of batter into pan and cook about 1 minute, until the pancake sets. Turn over with a spatula and cook until browned. Remove from pan and place in a preheated dish in an oven set at "warm."

4.   Repeat process until all the pancakes are cooked (about 12 pancakes). You will need to add more oil to the pan between pancakes, about 1 teaspoon or less. Keep regulating heat to avoid either overcooking or undercooking.

5. Serve pancakes with tea as a snack, or as the first course in a larger meal.

NOODLES
WITH
GINGER
AND
SCALLIONS

———

*Geung Chung
Bon Mein*

This is truly a Cantonese classic. It presents the fine tastes of fresh ginger, particularly the young ginger of spring, summer, and fall, a taste that is subtle and less hot than that of older ginger root. When fresh ginger is available, the Cantonese always demand that this noodle dish be made with *ji geung,* which translates into "baby boy ginger."

8 cups cold water
2 teaspoons salt
½ pound fresh egg noodles, flat, like linguine
2 tablespoons peanut oil
4 tablespoons fresh young ginger, shredded (if unavailable, use 3 tablespoons regular ginger, shredded)
1 cup scallions, washed, dried, with both ends trimmed, cut into 1½-inch pieces, and white portions quartered lengthwise

Make a sauce—combine in a bowl:

1½ tablespoons oyster sauce
1½ teaspoons light soy sauce
¾ teaspoon sugar
3 tablespoons Chicken Broth (page 40)
1 teaspoon sesame oil
Pinch of white pepper

1. Place the water and salt in a large pot and bring to a boil. Add the noodles and cook for 30 seconds, or *al dente,* stirring and loosening them with chopsticks or a fork as they cook. Turn off heat, run cold water into pot, and drain noodles immediately through a strainer. Place noodles back in pot and fill with cold water. Mix with your hands and drain noodles again through strainer. Repeat once more until noodles are cool. Allow to drain for 10 to 15 minutes, loosening with chopsticks to assist draining. Reserve.

2. Heat wok over high heat for 45 seconds. Add the peanut oil and coat wok with spatula. When a wisp of white smoke appears, add ginger and stir-fry for 30 seconds. Add the noodles and mix well with the ginger until noodles become very hot.

3. Add the scallions and mix well and cook for 1 minute. Make a well in the center of the wok, stir the sauce, and pour it into the well. Cook for 1 minute, mixing well, making certain the noodles are well coated. Turn off heat, transfer to a preheated serving dish, and serve immediately.

SESAME
NOODLES
——————
Chi Ma Mein

This recipe is a simple combination of two ingredients, fresh noodles and roasted sesame seeds, but its taste is far from simple. Like the other noodle preparations, its antecedents are Cantonese, but the tastes are mine.

     1 tablespoon white sesame seeds
    10 cups water
     2 teaspoons salt
     1 pound fresh egg noodles, quite fine, like a capellini, #11
  2½ tablespoons Scallion Oil (page 22)

Make a sauce—combine in a large mixing bowl:

  ½ tablespoon dark soy sauce
  ½ tablespoon light soy sauce
  1½ tablespoons oyster sauce
   1 teaspoon white vinegar
  1½ teaspoons sesame oil
  ½ teaspoon minced garlic
   1 teaspoon sugar
  ½ teaspoon salt
     Pinch of white pepper

1. Mix the sauce ingredients well and reserve.

2. Dry-roast the sesame seeds over low heat for 1 minute (page 39); reserve.

3. Add the water and salt to a large pot and bring to a boil. Add the noodles and cook for 30 seconds, stirring and loosening as they cook with chopsticks or a fork. Turn off heat, run cold water from tap into pot, and drain noodles immediately through a strainer. Place the noodles back in pot and fill with cold water. Mix with your hands and drain the noodles again through strainer. Repeat once more until the noodles are cool. Allow to drain for 3 minutes, loosening with chopsticks to assist draining.

4.   Place the noodles in a bowl, add the Scallion Oil, and mix thoroughly. Add the mixed noodles to the large mixing bowl holding the sauce and mix well again. Add the roasted sesame seeds and toss well. Serve immediately.

PAN-FRIED
NOODLES
WITH
SHREDDED
BEEF

———

*Ngau Yuk See
Chau Mein*

Pan-fried noodles are a favorite in Canton. The combination of the thin noodles, crisply fried, with different toppings is irresistible. This basic preparation, covered with pork, chicken, beef, and various seafoods, is, of course, best when made with fresh egg noodles. These are available in Asian markets and will keep 2 to 3 days refrigerated. But the noodles are available dry as well and can be kept for longer periods of time, like any boxed pasta, and therefore are more convenient that way. The following dish may be made with fresh or dry egg noodles.

2 teaspoons salt
8 cups cold water
¹/₂ pound dried egg noodles, thin, like a capellini, #11
¹/₄ pound London broil, cut across the grain, julienned

Make a marinade—combine in a bowl:

1¹/₂ teaspoons oyster sauce
¹/₂ teaspoon dark soy sauce
¹/₄ teaspoon salt
¹/₂ teaspoon sugar
 1 teaspoon sesame oil
¹/₂ teaspoon Shao-Hsing wine or sherry
¹/₂ teaspoon cornstarch
    Pinch of white pepper

Make a sauce—combine in a bowl:

$1/2$ teaspoon dark soy sauce
$1/4$ teaspoon salt
1 teaspoon sugar
1 teaspoon sesame oil
1 tablespoon oyster sauce
$1^1/2$ tablespoons cornstarch
Pinch of white pepper
1 cup Chicken Broth (page 40)

4–5 tablespoons peanut oil
2 teaspoons minced ginger
$1/2$ cup broccoli stems, peeled, with strings discarded, washed, dried, and julienned
$1/4$ cup red sweet pepper, seeded, washed, dried, and julienned
2 scallions, washed, dried, with both ends trimmed, and cut in $1^1/2$-inch sections, the white portions quartered
2 teaspoons minced garlic

1. Add salt to the water and bring to a boil. Add the noodles and cook for 1 minute, or until *al dente*, stirring with chopsticks or a fork to prevent sticking. Run cold water into the pot and drain through a strainer. Place noodles back in pot, add cold water, drain again. Repeat once again. Allow noodles to drain thoroughly for 2 hours, turning them occasionally so they dry completely.

2. Marinate the beef in the marinade for 20 minutes; reserve. Make the sauce; reserve.

3. Pour 2 tablespoons of the peanut oil into a cast-iron frypan over high heat. Heat for 40 seconds. When a wisp of white smoke appears, place the noodles in an even layer in the pan, covering the entire pan. Cook for 1 minute, moving pan about on the burner to ensure that the noodles brown evenly. Turn the noodles over, using dish placed over frypan. Cook the other side for 1 minute, moving pan about as before. If a little more oil is needed at this point, pour 1 additional tablespoon into pan, but only if necessary.

4. As the noodles are cooking, heat wok over high heat for 40 seconds. Add 1 tablespoon peanut oil and coat wok. Add the ginger and stir; when the ginger browns, add the vegetables. Stir and cook for 1 minute, or until the green portions of the scallions turn bright green. Turn off heat. Remove from wok, set aside.

5. Using paper towels, wipe wok and spatula clean. Heat wok over high heat for 30 seconds. Add the remaining 1 tablespoon of peanut oil and coat wok. When white smoke appears, add the garlic and stir. When the garlic turns light brown, add the beef and its marinade, and spread in a thin layer. Cook for 30 seconds, stir and mix, then add the vegetables and mix well for 1 minute. Make a well in the center, stir the sauce, and pour into the well. Stir-fry all the ingredients together until well mixed. When the sauce bubbles and thickens turn off heat.

6. Transfer the noodles to a preheated serving dish, pour the contents of wok over the noodles, and serve immediately.

LEMON
NOODLES

———

Ling Mung Mein

This is Cantonese in spirit, though the execution is mine. I have combined the noodles and the fresh citrus of Canton with the strong taste of cured ham, and the result, I think, is fresh and exciting.

2 quarts water
2 teaspoons salt
1/2 pound dry rice noodles
3 tablespoons Scallion Oil (page 22)
1 1/2 teaspoons minced garlic
1/2 teaspoon salt
1 teaspoon grated lemon rind
1/4 cup finely shredded Smithfield ham (page 23)
1 tablespoon fresh lemon juice
4 teaspoons Tabasco sauce
1 teaspoon sesame oil
2 tablespoons finely sliced scallions

1. Place the water and salt in a large pot and bring to a boil. Add the noodles and cook for 1 minute, loosening them with chopsticks as they cook. Cook until *al dente,* then remove from heat, run cold water into pot, and drain noodles through strainer. Place noodles back in pot, run cold water in, and strain again. Repeat once more, then reserve.

2. Place large pot over high heat. Add the Scallion Oil, garlic, and salt; stir. When the garlic turns light brown, add the lemon rind. Stir. Add the ham; stir for 30 seconds. Add the noodles, lower heat, and mix all ingredients thoroughly.

3. Add the lemon juice and toss. Add the Tabasco and toss. When the noodles are well coated, add the sesame oil and toss again. When the noodles are well mixed, turn off heat, add the sliced scallions, mix well, and serve immediately on a preheated platter.

SINGAPORE
NOODLES

————

*Sing Jau Chau
Mai Fun*

This has come to be a Cantonese tradition, though it is not Cantonese. Its use of curry derives from the Malay Peninsula, Singapore, and Indonesia, but over the years the chefs of Canton have made it their own. My guess is that there exists no Cantonese restaurant that does not offer this noodle dish. Master this recipe and you will make it as well as anyone.

6 ounces dry rice noodles
3 quarts cold water
1 tablespoon salt

Make a curry mixture:

  1 tablespoon peanut oil
  1 garlic clove, minced
  1½ tablespoons curry powder mixed with 1½ table-
      spoons cold water
  2½ tablespoons cold water
  2 beef bouillon cubes

  4 tablespoons peanut oil
  1 slice fresh ginger, ¼-inch thick
½ cup julienned celery
⅓ cup julienned carrots
  2 fresh water chestnuts, peeled, washed, and julienned
½ cup green peppers, seeded, washed, and julienned
¼ cup julienned bamboo shoots
  3 scallions, washed, dried, with both ends trimmed,
      and cut into 1½-inch pieces
  1 garlic clove, minced
  6 large shrimp, shelled, deveined, washed, dried, and
      cut lengthwise into quarters
¾ cup Honey Roast Pork (page 181), julienned
  1 tablespoon oyster sauce

1. Cook the noodles at least 2½ hours before assembling this dish. Place the water and salt in a large pot and bring to a boil. Add the noodles and boil for 1 to 2 minutes, or until *al dente.* Stir with chopsticks while cooking to loosen the noodles. Remove and rinse twice by filling pot with cold water. Drain. Loosen noodles with chopsticks to assist drying. Reserve.

2. Make a curry sauce: in a saucepan, heat the 1 tablespoon of peanut oil over high heat. Add 1 minced garlic clove and stir. When the garlic browns, add the curry powder mixed with the 1½ tablespoons water. Stir and let cook for 1 minute. Add the 2½ tablespoons cold water; mix well. Add the bouillon cubes. Lower heat, cover, and cook for 10 to 15 minutes, stirring 3 or 4 times, until smoothly blended. Set aside.

3. Heat wok over high heat, add 1 tablespoon of the peanut oil, and coat wok with spatula. When a wisp of white smoke appears, add the ginger. Cook for 30 seconds. Add the vegetables and stir-fry for 2 to 3 minutes, until the colors turn bright. Remove from wok and reserve. Remove wok from stove and clean. Replace on stove. Also clean spatula.

4. Heat wok over high heat, add 1 tablespoon of peanut oil, and coat wok. When wisp of white smoke appears, add the minced garlic clove. When the garlic turns light brown, add the shrimp. Stir and cook for 20 seconds, or until the shrimp begins to turn pink. Add the pork. Stir-fry for about 30 seconds, add oyster sauce and mix, then add curry sauce and stir together. Turn off heat, remove from wok, and reserve. Clean wok and spatula, replace wok on stove and dry with paper towel.

5. Heat wok over high heat for 45 seconds and add the remaining 2 tablespoons peanut oil; coat the wok with the spatula. When white smoke appears, add the noodles, allowing them to slide over spatula into wok, thereby

avoiding having them splatter in the hot oil. Use chop-sticks to toss noodles and loosen them. If noodles start to burn, lower heat. Cook for 5 minutes, or until noodles are very hot, then add the shrimp-pork-curry mixture and combine well with noodles. Add the reserved vegetables and stir well, making certain to mix thoroughly. When everything is combined, turn off heat, remove from wok, place in a preheated platter, and serve immediately.

Vegetables and Fruit

The Cantonese are fortunate indeed to be surrounded, year round, by the abundance of the earth, the growing things they call *choi*. The tropical climate of southern China lends itself to two crops of vegetables each year—often three—and accommodates an astonishing variety of vegetables and fruit.

In spring, I remember, we used to await with eagerness the first papaya, which would then be with us until late fall. We would have mangoes and hairy squash, watercress and the sweet and tender *choi sum*, lotus root and *bok choy*. But then *bok choy* would be harvested continuously throughout the year and water spinach would be grown three times in its watery fields.

Summer was the season for lettuce, cabbage, peppers, carrots, squash, turnips, and cucumbers, for sweet lichees and longans, guava and pomelos. We enjoyed Hami melons, watermelons, and pineapple and picked peaches, pears, plums, and apricots, using the last to make preserves.

In the fall the tangerines would come, small and sweet; they would be with us through the New Year, constant reminders of the sweetness of life that is to be wished at the beginning of each year. And there would be oranges, lemons, and grapefruit, big taro roots and another crop of *choi sum*.

And in winter we ate pomegranates, always counting

the seeds, because we knew then how many children would be born into the family that year. We cooked winter melon and lotus root and picked arrowhead roots and water chestnuts to give our dishes texture.

The fruits of the earth are dear to the Cantonese, and more so to those who are Buddhists. Buddhists will eat no meat, no poultry, no fish, and living amid such plenty, sense no lack of variety or sensual satisfaction. I recall how my grandmother, not a strict vegetarian though a Buddhist, observed her faith with a ritual of vegetable eating. On the first and fifteenth of every month she would eat only vegetables, and on those days she would sit in her salon and pray as she slid her beads through her fingers. But at the beginning of the Lunar New Year, she would eat only vegetables for the first fifteen days of the new year.

The Cantonese also enjoy creating imitation meats and fish from their vegetables, in a kind of culinary prank to fool their palates. "Oysters" would be made from eggplants, the skimmed skin of processed mung beans would become "chicken" or "duck," taro root would become "fish," with almonds as its "scales."

It is not widely known in the West that the Chinese, particularly the Cantonese, enjoy salads and pickles. In Canton, where, as I have described, fresh fruits and vegetables are plentiful throughout the year, the processes of pickling and of making salads are highly regarded.

The Cantonese cure and pickle many fresh products, including mustard pickles, dried *bok choy*, ginger, and various kinds of turnips and bamboo shoots, and make salads from cabbage, cauliflower, sweet potatoes, cucumbers, turnips, and broccoli. Most of these are eaten as refreshing, piquant snacks, but they are also ingredients in other dishes. For example, I use pickled peaches, pears, and ginger with fresh roast duck meat to make an unusual salad.

On the Cantonese table there will be small dishes of

different salads and pickles to be enjoyed alone or as accompaniments to other dishes. Cantonese salads are also versatile: I take two of my salads, broccoli and cauliflower, and mix them together for a dish that is not only tasty but beautiful to look at as well. I call it "green and white jade."

The range and extensive use of vegetables and fruits in this book reflect how they are regarded in Canton, but I have chosen as well to highlight some of the more unusual *choi* dishes and pickles and salads, because these will be new discoveries to many people.

BEAN
SPROUTS
STIR-FRIED
WITH
CHIVES

清炒拾菜

*Ching Chau
Sub Choi*

The name of this dish illustrates a typical Cantonese play on words and a touch of humor. The Cantonese name translates literally into "Lightly Stir-fried Ten Vegetables." But the word for chives is *gau choi*, which means "nine vegetables." So that nine vegetables plus bean sprouts equals ten. Is that clear?

    4 cups cold water
 1/2 pound bean sprouts, washed and drained
    1 tablespoon peanut oil
 1/4 teaspoon salt
    2 teaspoons minced ginger
    1 cup chives, washed, dried, with 1/8 inch of the hard
        end discarded and cut into 1-inch pieces

1.   In a large pot, bring the water to a boil. Place the bean sprouts in the water, stir for no more than 20 seconds. Turn off heat, run cold water into pot, drain. Run more cold water into pot and drain off all excess water. Set aside. This step should be done 1 hour before further preparation to ensure dryness. Occasionally loosen the sprouts with chopstick, to help drying.

2.   Heat a wok over high heat for 1 minute. Add the peanut oil and coat sides of wok with spatula. When a wisp of white smoke appears, add the salt and ginger. When the ginger turns light brown, add the chives. Stir well, about 30 seconds, or until the chives turn bright green. Add the bean sprouts, stir well, cook for 1 minute. Turn off heat. Transfer to a serving dish and serve immediately.

RED
AROUND
TWO
FLOWERS

————

Seung Far
Bun Hung

雙
叉
花
伴
红

This seems to be a good deal of imagery for what is essentially a mixed vegetable dish, but that is what the Cantonese do sometimes. The two flowers are cauliflower and broccoli; the red around, sweet red peppers.

$1/2$ pound cauliflower, cut into flowerets, $1^1/2$ inches long by $1^1/2$ inches wide
$1/2$ pound broccoli flowers, cut into flowerets $1^1/2$ inches long by $1^1/2$ inches wide
$1^1/2$ tablespoons peanut oil
$1/2$ teaspoon salt
$1^1/2$ teaspoons minced ginger
$1^1/2$ teaspoons minced garlic
$1/4$ cup sweet red peppers, washed, dried, seeded, and julienned
1 tablespoon white wine
5 tablespoons vegetable broth (page 42) mixed with 1 teaspoon of cornstarch

1. Water-blanch cauliflower (page 37). Reserve. Water-blanch broccoli. Reserve separately.

2. Heat wok over high heat for 45 seconds. Add the peanut oil and coat sides of wok with spatula. When a wisp of white smoke appears, add the salt, ginger, and garlic. Stir; when garlic turns light brown, add the reserved cauliflower, broccoli, and red peppers. Stir-fry for 1 minute.

3. Add the white wine by drizzling it around the edge of the wok. Mix well with the vegetables for 30 seconds. Make a well in the center of the mixture, stir the vegetable broth–cornstarch mixture, and pour into the well. Cover the well with the vegetable mixture, then stir all the ingredients together until sauce thickens. Turn off heat, transfer to a heated serving platter, and serve immediately.

BEAN CURD WITH FRESH TOMATOES

番茄蕃薑腐

Fan Keh Chi
Dau Fu

Bean curd is such a versatile food that I thought I would like to try it with fresh tomatoes. As a child, I usually ate fresh tomatoes with fish or beef, but this dish has lightness and flavor and is a bit more adventurous than those early tastes.

3/4 pound fresh tomatoes
  4 cakes fresh bean curd
  2 tablespoons peanut oil
1/2 teaspoon salt
  2 teaspoons minced ginger
1/2 teaspoon sugar
  3 scallions, washed, dried, with both ends trimmed, and cut into 1/2-inch pieces on the diagonal

Make a sauce—combine in a bowl:

2 1/2 teaspoons oyster sauce
 1/2 teaspoon sugar
 1/2 teaspoon light soy sauce
 1/2 teaspoon dark soy sauce
   1 teaspoon sesame oil
   1 tablespoon cornstarch
     Pinch of white pepper
   4 tablespoons Chicken Broth (page 40)

1.   Wash the tomatoes and cut into 1-inch pieces. Reserve. Drain the water from the bean curd cakes, cut into 1-inch cubes. Reserve.

2.   Heat wok over high heat for 45 seconds to 1 minute. Add the peanut oil and coat sides of wok with spatula. When a wisp of white smoke appears, add the salt and ginger. When the ginger turns light brown, add the tomatoes; stir and cook for 3 to 5 minutes, or until they soften.

3.   Add the sugar to the wok and mix. Add the bean curd and stir and mix well, cooking for 3 more minutes. Add the scallions and stir and mix thoroughly for 30 seconds. Make a well in the center of the mixture. Stir the sauce and pour into well. Stir all the ingredients together well, about 1 minute, or until the sauce bubbles and thickens. Turn off heat. Remove from wok, transfer to a preheated serving dish, and serve immediately with cooked rice. This dish is especially good with rice because of the tomato taste.

LETTUCE
WITH
OYSTER
SAUCE

———

*Ho Yau
Sahng Choi*

This is a quick, easy, delicious example of Cantonese cooking, using one vegetable that is a Canton staple: lettuce.

1 pound iceberg lettuce leaves. (Only the light green leaves of the lettuce are used for this dish. Discard the outer dark green leaves, as they are usually old and will be tough. Separate the light green leaves individually until you reach the white ones. Do not use white leaves or any of the heart of the lettuce. A 2-pound head should yield enough leaves to weigh a pound.)

Make a sauce—combine in a bowl:

1 1/2 tablespoons oyster sauce
1 teaspoon sesame oil
1 1/2 teaspoons dark soy sauce
3/4 teaspoon sugar
1 1/2 tablespoons cornstarch
Pinch of white pepper
1/2 cup Chicken Broth (page 40)

8 cups cold water
1/2 teaspoon baking soda
2 tablespoons peanut oil
1 teaspoon minced ginger

1.   Wash lettuce leaves several times; break each into 3 pieces with your hands. Drain and reserve. Make the sauce and reserve.

2.   Place the water in a large pot with the baking soda, and bring to a boil. Drop the lettuce leaves into the water, turning them to make certain all are immersed. Cook for 1 minute, until the leaves soften and turn bright green. Place pot under cold running water to cool. Drain. Loosen the leaves with chopsticks and dry them thoroughly by allowing them to drain in the strainer. Reserve.

3.   Heat wok over high heat for 45 seconds and add the peanut oil. Using a spatula, coat the wok with the oil. When a wisp of white smoke appears, add the ginger. When the ginger turns light brown, add the lettuce leaves and stir. Cook for 1 to 1½ minutes. Make a well in the center of the lettuce leaves, stir the sauce, and pour it into the well. Stir and cook until the sauce thickens and turns brown. Remove to a preheated serving dish and serve immediately with fresh rice.

SPINACH AND BEAN THREAD SOUP

Bor Choi Fun
See Tong

This is a soup familiar to every Cantonese farmer. Bean threads are available everywhere, spinach is plentiful, and there are so many shrimp in the waters around Canton that netting them and setting them out to dry in the sun is commonplace. This is a dish not found in restaurants—it is home cooking.

½ of a (2-ounce) package of dried mung bean threads
3 tablespoons dried shrimp
8 cups water
1 tablespoon salt
½ teaspoon baking soda
¾ pound fresh spinach, thoroughly washed and drained, leaves broken in half and set aside

2 tablespoons peanut oil
2 teaspoons minced ginger
2 teaspoons minced garlic
5 cups Chicken Broth (page 40)
1 teaspoon Shao-Hsing wine or sherry

1. Soak the bean threads in hot water for ½ hour. Remove from water, drain, cut into 4-inch strands, and reserve.

2. Soak the shrimp in hot water for ½ hour. Drain and dry thoroughly with paper towels. Reserve.

3. In a large pot, place the 8 cups water, salt, and baking soda. Bring to a boil and add the spinach. Stir and make certain the spinach is covered by the water. When the spinach turns bright green, remove pot from heat, run cold water into pot, drain, and set aside.

4. Heat a large pot over high heat and add the peanut oil. When a wisp of white smoke appears, add the ginger and garlic and stir, using chopsticks or wooden spoon. When the garlic browns, add the shrimp. Stir for 45 seconds, then add the chicken broth and wine. Cover pot and bring to a boil. Lower heat and allow the broth to simmer for 10 minutes.

5. Raise heat and add the spinach and bean threads. Bring to a boil, then remove from heat. Place the soup in a preheated tureen and serve immediately.

JADE
FLOWER
BROCCOLI

—————

*Yuk Far Sah
Lud*

天
花
沙
律

The Chinese regard the green broccoli flowers as a symbol of jade, and jade itself as a symbol of youth and rebirth. Broccoli therefore is served at virtually every New Year meal and at birthday meals. What better thoughts to have about a salad?

8 cups water
2 slices ginger, ¼-inch thick
3 garlic cloves, peeled
1 teaspoon baking soda
1 pound broccoli, separated into flowerets about 1½ inches
    in diameter
3 tablespoons peanut oil
1 teaspoon salt
2 teaspoons minced ginger

1. In a large saucepan, combine the 8 cups of water, the ginger slices, 2 of the garlic cloves, and the baking soda. Bring to a boil over high heat. Add the broccoli and cook until it turns bright emerald green, about 2 minutes. Drain and rinse under cold running water. Drain well and set aside.

2. Mince the remaining clove of garlic. Heat wok over high heat for 45 seconds. Add the peanut oil and with a spatula coat the sides of the wok with the oil. Add the salt, minced ginger, and minced garlic. Stir-fry until the garlic turns brown, about 30 seconds. Add broccoli and stir-fry until crisp and tender, 1½ to 2 minutes.

3. Transfer the broccoli to a serving dish. Let cool to room temperature before serving.

⤳ This salad can be prepared a day ahead. Let stand at room temperature for several hours, or cover and refrigerate for longer keeping.

CUCUMBER
SALAD

*Tseng Gua
Sah Lud*

As early as the fifth century the Chinese were growing the cucumber, which to them is simply a form of melon. In Canton there are two kinds of cucumber, yellow and green. Unfortunately, the word for yellow is *wong*, and people with that name object to being referred to as "yellow squashes," so the green cucumber, or *tseng gua*, is more popular. Eaten in a salad, they are most refreshing, but on occasion, as a taste highlight, a few pieces of pickled cucumber salad may be added to stir-fried meat dishes.

  2 cucumbers, about 2 pounds
  1 teaspoon salt
2½ teaspoons sugar
2½ teaspoons white vinegar
1½ teaspoons sesame oil
  2 tablespoons julienned sweet red peppers

1. Peel, wash, and dry the cucumbers. Cut in half lengthwise, and remove seeds with a spoon or grapefruit knife. Slice into ¼-inch pieces.

2. In a bowl, mix the cucumber slices thoroughly with the salt, and allow to rest for 1 hour. This helps to remove excess water from the cucumbers. Drain off the water, then add the sugar, white vinegar, and sesame oil. Mix well. Add the julienned red peppers and toss together. Allow to marinate, covered and refrigerated, overnight. Serve cold.

CAULIFLOWER SALAD

———

Yeh Choi Far Sah Lud

椰菜花少律

10 cups cold water
1 slice fresh ginger, ¼-inch thick
1 clove of garlic, peeled
1½ pounds fresh cauliflower, cut into 1½-inch flowerets

In a large bowl, make a marinade:

2 small hot red chili peppers, sliced into ¼-inch pieces
1 tablespoon sugar
3 tablespoons white vinegar
1 teaspoon salt
1 teaspoon sesame oil
   Pinch of white pepper

1. In a large pot, place the cold water, ginger, and garlic and bring to a boil. Add the cauliflower and stir. Allow to cook for 2 to 3 minutes, until the cauliflower becomes slightly translucent. Do not overcook. Turn off heat and run cold tap water into the pot. Drain, then fill pot again with cold water and drain again. Allow all excess water to strain off. Reserve.

2. Place the cooled cauliflower in the marinade, mix well to coat, cover, and refrigerate overnight. It may then be eaten, or it will continue to improve for about 3 days. If it is kept for that time, it should be mixed occasionally. Serve cold.

SWEET POTATO SALAD

———

Fan Sui Sah Lud

蕃薯薯少律

This is my variation on a traditional Chinese salad preparation in which a vegetable is thinly cut, or julienned, and then marinated overnight in a mixture of vinegar, sugar, and salt. I use this dressing with turnips, white radishes, and young ginger.

1¼ pounds sweet potatoes or yams
3 tablespoons white vinegar
1 teaspoon sesame oil
1½ tablespoons sugar
1 teaspoon salt
1 teaspoon chopped fresh coriander
4 radicchio leaves

1. Peel, wash, and dry the sweet potatoes. Cut into 2-inch-by-¼-inch julienne strips. Place in a large bowl and add the vinegar, sesame oil, sugar, and salt. Stir to mix thoroughly, cover, and refrigerate overnight.

2. Before serving, remove the salad from refrigerator, add the chopped coriander, and toss together. Arrange the radicchio leaves on individual plates and add a mound of the marinated sweet potato pieces to each. Serve cool.

SOUR
TURNIP

———

Soon Law Bak

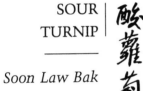

This Cantonese salad is very special. It is served at memorable occasions such as weddings and at the birthdays of one's grandparents. It is especially fine for children, who look forward to eating it as a snack during family gatherings. Nibbling on *soon law bak* does not ruin one's appetite!

2 pounds white turnip, with both ends cut off, peeled, washed, dried, and cut in half lengthwise
1 teaspoon salt
2½ teaspoons sugar
2½ teaspoons white vinegar
⅛ teaspoon white pepper

1. Partially cut each piece of turnip at ⅛-inch intervals along the length, but do not cut completely through. After this process, cut each sliced half into 2-inch segments.

2.   Place the turnips in a bowl with the salt and allow to stand for an hour to let excess water drain out. Remove the water and add the sugar, white vinegar, and white pepper. Mix thoroughly and place in refrigerator, covered with plastic wrap, for 4 hours. Then serve immediately, cold.

GINGER
PICKLE
—
*Wor Mei Dzi
Geung*

Ginger Pickle is a versatile preparation. It is eaten as a snack, is used as an ingredient in many dishes, and is also a garnish. The Cantonese use only fresh young ginger to make these pickles. Young ginger is occasionally difficult to find, since it is available only twice each year in Canton, in summer and late fall. It can be recognized by its creamy white interior, with a pinkish cast, and green shoots protrude from the root. Ginger Pickle is also available in jars, but I prefer the taste of freshly made pickles, with the sweetness contrasting nicely with the subtle hotness of the ginger.

  8 cups water
  1 teaspoon baking soda
1½ pounds fresh young ginger (wash thoroughly and the outer thin brown bark-like coating will come off; but leave skin on), cut into ⅛-inch slices, with shoots retained

Make a marinade:

1¼ teaspoons salt
⅝ cup white vinegar
 1 cup sugar

1.   In a large pot, bring the water and baking soda to a boil. Add the ginger and boil for 30 seconds. Remove from heat. Add cold water to reduce the temperature. Drain.

Add cold water a second time and drain. Repeat a third time and allow ginger to sit in cold water for 10 minutes. Then drain well and place the ginger in a bowl.

2.   Add the marinade to the ginger. Mix well. Cover and refrigerate for at least 24 hours before serving. Serve cold. Ginger Pickle, placed in a tightly closed jar, will keep in the refrigerator for at least 3 months.

CAULIFLOWER PICKLES

和味椰菜花

*War Mei Yeh
Choi Far*

    3   quarts water
    5   cloves garlic, peeled
    1   slice fresh ginger, at least 1 inch thick
3½   pounds fresh cauliflower, cut into 1½-inch flower-
          ets, washed, and drained
1¾   cups sugar
1¾   cups white vinegar
5½   cups cold water
    4   teaspoons salt

1.   In a large pot, bring the 3 quarts water to a boil with the garlic and ginger. Add the cauliflower and water-blanch (page 37) for 30 to 45 seconds. Do not overcook! Turn off heat, remove from heat, and run cold water into pot. Drain. Fill pot with cold water and allow cauliflower to sit in cold water for 15 minutes, then drain.

2.   In an oversized glass jar (a jar with plastic screw top is preferred; if unavailable, place piece of plastic wrap over top before closing), place the sugar, white vinegar, 5½ cups water, and salt. Stir with wooden spoon to ensure that sugar and salt are completely dissolved. Add the cauliflower, ginger, and garlic and stir. Cover and refrigerate for at least 24 hours before serving. Serve cold. The cauliflower will keep, covered and refrigerated, for 2 to 3 months.

PICKLED
PEACHES 酸
呣
——— 桃

Soon Tim Toh

This is a most popular pickle, and the Cantonese hasten to make it as soon as peaches become available, usually in May or June. Peaches are highly regarded as symbols of long life and are always served at birthdays. There is even a steamed bun, pink-colored, in the shape of a peach, *sao bau*, which means "long life bun," served at birthdays during the months when peaches are not available. But in season it is fresh peaches, and pickled peaches, that are eaten.

3 pounds fresh peaches, very hard, but with color indicating they are ripening (about 11 or 12)
3 cups white vinegar
5 cups cold water
1 cup sugar
4 teaspoons salt

1.   Wash the peaches well. Dry thoroughly. Reserve.

2.   In an oversized glass jar sufficiently large to hold all the peaches plus the pickling ingredients, place the vinegar, water, sugar, and salt. Mix well with wooden spoon until all the sugar and salt is dissolved. This is important. They must be completely dissolved.

3.   Add the peaches and stir well. Cover tightly. (A jar with a plastic screw top is preferred. If unavailable, place a piece of plastic wrap on top before closing the jar.)

4.   Refrigerate for 3 days, untouched, before serving. The peaches will keep, in the covered jar, refrigerated, for 3 to 4 months. Serve cold.

◢   The peaches have a pleasant sweet and sour taste, which the Cantonese call *war mei*, or "even taste." If your taste runs more to sweet things, add 2 more tablespoons of sugar to the pickling mixture. But this must be done at preparation time. Sugar should not be added later because it will not penetrate into the peaches properly.

PICKLED
PEARS

———

*Soon Tim Sah
Leh*

酸
甜
沙
梨

These pickled pears are very popular during the summer months. Many different kinds of pears grow in Canton and throughout China. For pickling, only the pear called *sah leh*, or "sand pear," is used. It is almost round, almost apple-shaped, and has a consistency quite like the Bosc pear, with skin like it as well. So for this recipe use Bosc pears.

    3 pounds Bosc pears, very hard, barely ripening (about
         7 or 8)
    2 cups white vinegar
    2 cups cold water
  3/4 cup sugar
    1 tablespoon salt

1. Peel, wash, and dry pears. Reserve.

2. In an oversized glass jar large enough to hold all the pears plus the pickling ingredients, place the vinegar, water, sugar, and salt. Mix with wooden spoon until the sugar and salt are completely dissolved—this is important.

3. Place the pears in jar, mix thoroughly, then close the jar. (A jar with a plastic screw top is preferred; if unavailable, place piece of plastic wrap on top of the jar, then close.)

4. Leave at least 3 days, untouched, in the refrigerator to ensure that the pears absorb the pickling. Covered, they will keep 3 to 4 months, refrigerated. Serve cold.

Fish and Seafood 魚類和海鮮

If you would wish to see fish in as close to their natural state as possible—fresh fish, live fish—then the winding Ching Ping Market in Canton or the teeming markets of Yau Ma Tei and Sam Sui Po on the Kowloon side of Hong Kong are the places to visit. The Cantonese must have fresh fish, fish that are swimming when they are bought, and in these markets sit huge square galvanized-metal vats and tanks filled with live carp, silver carp, bass, eels, trout, flatheads, dace, and the long and special catfish of Asia, as well as shrimp, lobsters, prawns, cuttlefish, and squid.

Go out to the floating fish restaurants in Hong Kong's Aberdeen and you may select live the fish you wish to eat, rare fish such as *fung mei,* the fish the Chinese call "phoenix eyes" because its eyes, almond-shaped, resemble those of a woman, as well as flounder, *garoupa* (a fish native to the South China Sea), bass, and crayfish, crabs, shrimp, scallops, and oysters, all still in their shells.

The Cantonese live with the water and the fruits of the sea. Canton itself, a deepwater port, is split by the wide Pearl River and is less than three hours up the Pearl from Hong Kong, which is surrounded by the South China Sea. Fish to the Cantonese are, after rice, the staple of their diet. Fish are called *hoi sin* by the Cantonese, words that mean "ocean fresh," which all fish must be, or they are ignored.

118

One need only watch a Cantonese woman shop in the fish market to see the reverence in which fish are held, and the extreme care with which they are selected. She will stand in the market looking into one of those huge tanks of water, and when she is satisfied with the fish she desires, she will point. The fishmonger will reach in either with a net or with his hands, snare her fish, and bring it out. The woman will look at the fish carefully to see that it moves vigorously, that its scales are un-damaged by hooks. She will nod and the fish is hers.

And if lunch is to be more than 2 hours hence, she will not permit the fish to be killed. She will have it placed, with water, in a plastic bag and will take it home to prepare herself. Fresh to a Cantonese means *fresh*.

STEAMED
SEA BASS

———

*Ching Jing Sek
Bon*

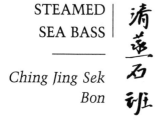

No fish preparation illustrates the Cantonese kitchen like a fish fresh from the sea, steamed. Steaming preserves the flesh of the fish and retains its flavor, even its shape. A steamed fish is virtually always part of an important banquet, almost always served to an important guest, always part of a New Year dinner celebration. The Cantonese steam any fish, but a sea bass is particularly suited to steaming because it is very meaty and has fewer bones than other fish. There are many variations of the steamed fish. Often it is accompanied by shredded mushrooms, often by shredded pork, by black beans, by ginger and scallions. What I have done is an original. The oil used in the marinade, and to finish the sea bass, is my Scallion Oil. The aroma it imparts and its subtle taste are unique.

1 (2-pound) whole fresh sea bass, scales, gills, and intestines removed (page 46)

Make a marinade—combine in a bowl:

  2 tablespoons Scallion Oil (page 22)
  2 tablespoons light soy sauce
  2 tablespoons white wine
  1½ teaspoons sesame oil
  1½ teaspoons white vinegar
  ½ teaspoon salt
  ⅛ teaspoon white pepper

1 tablespoon Scallion Oil
2 scallions, washed, dried, with both ends trimmed, and finely sliced
1 tablespoon finely chopped fresh coriander

1.   Clean the fish well, remove the membranes, and wash inside and out. Make 3 cuts with a sharp knife into the side of the fish to, but not through, the bone. Repeat on other side. Dry the fish well with paper towels and place in a heatproof dish.

2. Pour the marinade over the fish and rub into the fish with your hands. Be certain to rub well into the cuts. Allow to stand for 10 to 15 minutes.

3. Place dish in a steamer and steam (page 38) for about 30 minutes, or until the flesh seen in the cuts turns white and is firm. Turn off heat. Pour the remaining Scallion Oil over fish. Sprinkle with the scallions and coriander and serve immediately.

FLOUNDER
ROLL
WITH
BLACK
BEANS

___

*Jing Long Lei
Tong*

The actual name for this preparation is *chongsan jing long lei tong*, which translates into "steamed dragon's tongue of Chongsan." Chongsan is the birthplace of Dr. Sun Yat-sen and is justly famed for its seafood, particularly flounder and oysters. Usually the recipe is made with fish and oysters, but I realize that in certain parts of the country fresh oysters are a rarity, so I have adapted the traditional dish and filled the rolled flounder with shrimp. The taste, to my husband for one, is better.

1 pound flounder, filleted into 6 pieces (3 fish)
½ pound shrimp (12 shrimp), shelled, deveined, washed, dried, and cut into quarters lengthwise
1 scallion, washed, dried, with both ends trimmed, cut into 3½-inch sections, and julienned, divided into six equal portions
1½ tablespoons Scallion Oil (page 22)

Marinade ingredients:

       4 large cloves garlic
       2 tablespoons black beans, washed, drained
       2 tablespoons white wine
       2 tablespoons light soy sauce
       2 tablespoons Scallion Oil
       4 tablespoons finely sliced scallions
       1 teaspoon sesame oil
       1 teaspoon white vinegar
    $\frac{1}{8}$ teaspoon salt
       1 teaspoon sugar
         Pinch of white pepper
    $1\frac{1}{2}$ teaspoons finely chopped fresh coriander

1.   Trim each of the six fish fillets into roughly rectangular shapes about 5 to $5\frac{1}{2}$ inches long and about $3\frac{1}{2}$ inches wide. Set aside.

2.   Make the marinade. Crush the garlic cloves with the broad blade of the cleaver, remove skin. Place in a sturdy bowl with the black beans and mash into a paste (page 46). Add all other marinade ingredients to bowl and combine thoroughly. Reserve.

3.   Place 1 length of shrimp and a portion of the julienned scallions, then another length of shrimp side by side, starting 1 inch from one end of the flounder fillet. Make certain that the tails of the 2 shrimp lengths are at opposite sides. Roll the flounder into a cylinder.

4. Place the flounder roll in a heatproof porcelain dish, with the end of the roll underneath and the smooth side facing up. Repeat with the other fillets. Pour the marinade over the flounder rolls.

5. Place the dish in a steamer and steam (page 38) for 8 to 10 minutes, until the fish turns white and firm. If you use a metal dish to hold the rolled fillets, the steaming time will be 4 to 5 minutes.

6. When done, remove from heat, pour the 1½ tablespoons Scallion Oil over the fillets, and serve immediately.

⚮ To make the dish in the tradition of Chongsan, you may use oysters, if they are available fresh and can be shucked easily. If the oysters are small, place 2 in each fillet; if large, then one will suffice. All the other ingredients and preparations remain the same.

JADE
FLOWER
FISH

———

*Long Chong
Yuk Shih*

This is a Hong Kong variation on the traditional rolled fish from Chongsan. The translation of the Chinese words is "jade trees hidden in the dragon tongue," which refers to the broccoli rolled into the flounder. This adaptation illustrates quite well the breadth and inventiveness of the Cantonese kitchen.

1 pound flounder, thinly filleted into 8 pieces
8 broccoli flowerets, 2½ inches long by 1½ inches wide
2 tablespoons julienned Smithfield ham (page 23)

Make a marinade—combine in a bowl:

½ teaspoon ginger juice mixed with 2 teaspoons white wine
¼ teaspoon salt
¾ teaspoon sugar
1 teaspoon white vinegar
2 teaspoons light soy sauce
½ teaspoon sesame oil
1 tablespoon Scallion Oil (page 22)
Pinch of white pepper

1 tablespoon Scallion Oil

1.   Trim the 8 fish fillets into rectangles 1¾ inches wide by 3 inches long. Set aside.

2.   Water-blanch the broccoli quickly, about 5 or 10 seconds only, until the color changes to bright green (page 37). Reserve.

3.   Place the flounder fillets in the marinade for about 5 minutes, then follow this method, one at a time: place the fillet in a clean dish. Place a broccoli floweret in the middle of the fillet, the stem crosswise on the fillet, the broccoli flower over the edge. Add one eighth of the ju-

lienned ham atop the stem and roll the fillet so that a
cylinder emerges with a tiny treelike flower sticking out
from one end. Repeat with the other 7 fillets.

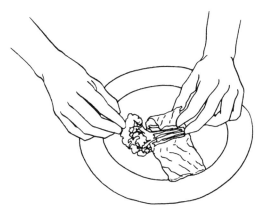

4. Place the rolls seam down, smooth side up, in a heatproof porcelain dish with any remaining marinade poured
over them. Steam (page 38) for 3 to 5 minutes, until fillets
become white and firm. Remove from steamer, pour 1
tablespoon of Scallion Oil over them, and serve immediately. If a metal dish is used, the steaming time will be
a maximum of 3 minutes.

BAKED
GRASS
CARP

Guk Wan Yue

The grass carp is the most highly prized fish in Canton. Some carp are golden, some nearly orange, some silvery gray. The grass carp is blackish gray and comes in many sizes, from 5 to 10 pounds. The Cantonese say that it is a pure fish, for it lives in freshwater, eats only plant life, and is more fleshy, with fewer bones, because it is large. The best is from 6 to 8 pounds. Grass carp is usually available in Asian markets and should be asked for by that name. If it is unavailable, ask for regular carp, also quite large, and have a 1-pound piece cut from the center of the fish's body.

1 pound grass carp (middle portion of a large fish)

Make a marinade—mix in a bowl:

½ teaspoon white vinegar
1½ teaspoons white wine
1 teaspoon light soy sauce
2 teaspoons peanut oil
¼ teaspoon salt
⅛ teaspoon white pepper

Make a sauce—combine in a bowl:

1½ teaspoons minced Chinese bacon (uncooked bacon may be used)
1 tablespoon egg white, beaten
3 tablespoons catsup
1 teaspoon minced garlic
2 teaspoons minced ginger
4 teaspoons finely sliced scallions
2 tablespoons minced onions
¼ teaspoon salt
Pinch of white pepper
½ teaspoon sugar
1 tablespoon Chicken Broth (page 40)

1.   Preheat oven to 400°F.

2.   Wash the fish, remove the membranes, and clean thoroughly. Cut 3 slits in one side of the flesh to, but not into, the backbone. Place in an ovenproof glass dish. Combine the marinade ingredients, pour over the fish, and rub well into the flesh on both sides with hands. Allow the fish to sit for 10 minutes.

3.   Pour the sauce over the fish and again rub the sauce into the flesh and into the slits by hand, until it is well coated.

4.   Place the fish, slit side up, in the oven and bake for 30 to 35 minutes. The fish flesh will become white. Test by gently pushing a chopstick into the flesh; if it goes in easily, the fish is done. Remove from oven and serve in the baking dish, spooning sauce over each portion. This is best served with cooked rice, in order to enjoy the delicious sauce.

BLUEFISH
WITH
FRESH
TOMATOES

———

Fon Keh Ju Yue

In Canton this traditional dish is prepared with fresh carp. Carp is available in Asian and Chinese seafood markets, and if it is convenient you might use it. I have experimented by using different fish in the recipe and have concluded that bluefish is the best. It is fleshy, meaty, and a bit oily, like carp, but is more widely available.

1 pound fresh bluefish, cut from the center of the fish

Make a marinade—mix in a bowl:

1½ teaspoons white vinegar
 2 teaspoons white wine
½ teaspoon salt
    Pinch of white pepper

4½ tablespoons peanut oil
2 slices fresh ginger, each ½ inch thick
2 teaspoons minced ginger
2 teaspoons minced garlic
1 pound fresh tomatoes, washed, dried, and cut into
   ½-inch cubes
2 scallions, washed, dried, with both ends trimmed,
   and finely sliced

Make a sauce—combine in a bowl:

2 teaspoons oyster sauce
¼ teaspoon salt
1 teaspoon sugar
1 teaspoon sesame oil
Pinch of white pepper
1 teaspoon dark soy sauce
1 tablespoon cornstarch
5 tablespoons Chicken Broth (page 40)

1. Clean, wash, and dry the fish. With a sharp knife, make a cut into the center of each side of the fish to, but not through, the bone.

2. Place the fish in a dish, add the marinade, and rub it into the fish with your hands. Allow to rest for 20 minutes.

3. Dry the fish with paper towels. Heat wok over high heat for 30 to 45 seconds. Add 3 tablespoons of the peanut oil and coat wok with spatula. When a wisp of white smoke appears, add the 2 slices of ginger. When the ginger browns, push it aside with spatula and place the fish in wok, then allow the ginger to slide back into the oil. Lower heat and pan-fry the fish for 3 minutes. Turn the fish over and fry for 5 minutes more, until the fish begins to turn white. Remove the fish from wok and set aside. Turn off heat.

4. Empty oil from wok. Wash wok and spatula and dry. Heat wok over high heat for 30 to 45 seconds. Add the remaining 1½ tablespoons peanut oil. When a wisp of smoke appears, add the minced ginger and garlic. When the garlic turns light brown, add the tomatoes. Stir for 1 minute, then lower heat and cook for 2 minutes, until the tomatoes soften.

5. Add the sauce. Stir together. Return the fish to wok. Spoon the sauce and tomato mixture over the fish and allow to simmer for 2 to 3 minutes. Turn off heat. Add the scallions and mix gently. Transfer the fish to a preheated serving dish and serve immediately with cooked rice.

CRISP
FLOUNDER

―――

*Choi Pei Lung
Lei*

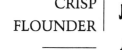

Here is another Cantonese favorite, another use for the wide flounder, the fish called the "dragon's tongue." You will find this fried fish quite different from any other you've ever had. It is fried thoroughly, so crisply that even the small fin bones are crisp, edible, and delicious—like chips. Nor is the fish at all greasy. It is a somewhat special preparation, a change of pace from the usual Cantonese methods of steaming or stir-frying fish.

1 (1½-pound) flounder, scales, gills, and intestines removed (page 46)

Make a marinade—combine in a bowl:

1½ tablespoons white wine
1¼ teaspoons salt
1½ teaspoons white vinegar
⅛ teaspoon white pepper

6 cups peanut oil
1 extra-large egg, beaten
3/4 cup flour
2 tablespoons finely sliced green portions of scallions

1. Wash the fish and remove the membranes. Dry thoroughly with paper towels. Place in a large dish and pour the marinade over it. Rub in the marinade with your hands, coating the fish well. Allow to sit for 15 minutes.

2. Dry fish thoroughly with paper towel. Heat wok over high heat for 1 minute. Add the peanut oil. As the oil heats, coat the fish with the beaten egg. Spread the flour on a sheet of waxed paper and place fish on it. Coat the fish thoroughly with the flour and shake off the excess.

3. The oil should now be heated to 375°F. Place the fish on a Chinese strainer and lower it into the oil. Deep-fry for 3 minutes. Reduce heat and allow oil temperature to lower to 350°F. Fry the fish for another 4 to 6 minutes, until it turns light brown. (If temperature is carefully regulated, the fish will not burn.) Turn off heat, place the fish in strainer over a large bowl, and allow the oil to drain off and the fish to cool to room temperature.

4. Reheat oil to 350°F. Place the fish in the strainer back in the oil and deep-fry for another 5 to 7 minutes, or until the fish is golden brown and very crisp. Turn off heat. Place strainer over large bowl and allow the fish to drain for 1 minute. Transfer it to a preheated platter, sprinkle the scallions on top, and serve immediately.

FISH
AND
LETTUCE
SOUP

生菜魚片湯

*Sang Choi Yue
Pin Tong*

In Canton we use fresh carp, filleted, in this dish. Carp is widely available in Asian markets in the United States. However, the soup is just as tasty when made with sole, flounder, or sea bass. If you use carp, use the back portion of the fish; for other fishes, use the meaty portions.

1/2 pound fresh fish, thinly sliced

Make a marinade—combine in a bowl:

1/4 teaspoon salt
1/2 teaspoon sugar
  1 teaspoon sesame oil
1/4 teaspoon cornstarch
  1 teaspoon ginger juice mixed with 1 teaspoon white
      wine
  1 teaspoon light soy sauce
      Pinch of white pepper

3 cups Fish Broth (page 41)
1 slice ginger, 1/2 inch thick
1 clove garlic
1 head iceberg lettuce, shredded, to make 5 cups
1 tablespoon Scallion Oil (page 22)

1.   Marinate the fish slices in a bowl for 10 minutes. Reserve.

2.   Bring the fish broth, diluted with 1 1/2 cups water, to a boil, with the ginger and garlic. Add the lettuce, stir, bring back to a boil. Add reserved fish and marinade, stir, and bring to a boil again. Turn off heat, add the Scallion Oil, stir, then remove from heat and serve from a pre-heated tureen.

STEAMED
OCEAN-FRESH
WINTER
MELON
SOUP

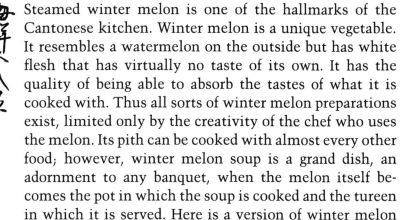

———

*Hoi Sin Dong
Gua Jung*

Steamed winter melon is one of the hallmarks of the Cantonese kitchen. Winter melon is a unique vegetable. It resembles a watermelon on the outside but has white flesh that has virtually no taste of its own. It has the quality of being able to absorb the tastes of what it is cooked with. Thus all sorts of winter melon preparations exist, limited only by the creativity of the chef who uses the melon. Its pith can be cooked with almost every other food; however, winter melon soup is a grand dish, an adornment to any banquet, when the melon itself becomes the pot in which the soup is cooked and the tureen in which it is served. Here is a version of winter melon soup that uses the tastes of the sea; hence its name, *hoi sin*, or "ocean-fresh."

1 winter melon (about 10 pounds)
2 cups Fish Broth (page 41), mixed with 1 cup cold water
2 tablespoons dried shrimp, soaked 30 minutes in hot water, drained, and cut in half
2 tablespoons silk squash, peeled, green portion only, cut into ¼-inch pieces
¼ cup fresh lotus seeds (if unavailable, use ⅛ cup, dried, soaked 1 hour in hot water, then boiled in 3 cups water for 1 hour until tender)
2 fresh water chestnuts, peeled, dried, cut into ¼-inch dice
2 tablespoons diced bamboo shoots
3 Chinese mushrooms, soaked in hot water for 30 minutes, with stems discarded, and cut into ¼-inch pieces
½ teaspoon salt
Pinch of white pepper
1 tablespoon Scallion Oil (page 22)
¼ cup crab meat, picked over
¼ pound fresh shrimp (6 shrimp), shelled, deveined, washed, dried, and cut into ½-inch pieces

¼ pound bay scallops
1 teaspoon sesame oil

1.   Prepare all the ingredients and reserve.

2.   Place the melon in a heatproof glass mixing bowl (Pyrex dish). With a pencil, mark melon about 2 inches from the top. Cut straight across at the mark and discard the top. Using a grapefruit knife, remove the seeds and pulp. Cut a serrated edge around the top.

3.   The melon will be cooked in a clam steamer. Place 10 cups of water in the bottom section of the clam steamer and bring to a boil. Meantime, place the melon in its glass bowl in the top section. To the melon cavity, add the broth-and-water mixture, the dried shrimp, silk squash, lotus seeds, water chestnuts, bamboo shoots, mushrooms, salt, pepper, and Scallion Oil. Place the top section of the steamer atop the bottom section and steam for 1½ to 2 hours.

4.   After 1 hour and 10 minutes add the crab meat, shrimp, and bay scallops, and continue steaming until the melon softens. During the steaming process have boiling water on hand to replenish what evaporates.

5.   When done, remove the melon from the top of clam steamer. Stir in the sesame oil. Serve with a ladle, shaving pieces of the winter melon off the sides and serving with the other ingredients in individual bowls.

⭳   If a clam steamer is unavailable, use a large pot that will accommodate the glass bowl (Pyrex dish) that holds the winter melon. Place a cake rack on the bottom of the pot, add 2 to 3 inches of water, cover pot, and bring water to a boil. Turn off heat, place bowl and melon on rack, turn heat on again, and steam as above.

⤸   The silk squash is an odd, cucumber-shaped vegetable, with ridges along its length. These ridges must be pared off before the silk squash is used. The meat of the silk squash is quite sweet and was a treat for me as a girl because it was available for only two months, May and June. Now it is available the year round.

SEAFOOD HOT POT

Hoi Sin Dah Pin Lo

The hot pot, contrary to what most people believe, is not the sole property of China's northernmost provinces and Mongolia. Shanghai has its hot pot, and so does Canton. In the north the hot pot is a filling, very thick broth based on lamb and mutton. In Shanghai there are a variety of ingredients, but the hot pot is eaten with a large variety of different condiments and sauces. In Canton the hot pot is almost always of fish, usually of firm, fleshy dace. What I have created is a version of the Cantonese hot pot that includes not only fish, but scallops, clams, and oysters as well. I expect it might even be appreciated in the South of France.

1 pound fresh sea scallops, sliced ½ inch thick
¾ pound shrimp (20 shrimp), shelled, deveined, washed, and dried
24 oysters, removed from their shells
24 clams, removed from their shells
¾ pound fillet of halibut, thinly sliced
4 ounces bean thread noodles (2 packages, soaked in hot water for 30 minutes, then cut into 6-inch strands)
6 cakes fresh bean curd, cut into ¼-inch slices
1 pound fresh spinach, old leaves removed, stalks separated, washed 3 or 4 times to remove all sand, and drained
2 bunches watercress, washed and drained

4 cups Fish Broth (page 41)
4 cups cold water
1 piece fresh ginger, 2 inches by 1½ inches
2 large garlic cloves, peeled

1.   Each ingredient—seafood, noodles, bean curd, or vegetable—should be placed in its own plate or bowl, arranged around a hot pot (available in Asian markets) or an electric frypan.

2.   Heat 2 cups of the fish broth and 2 cups of the water together in frypan. Add the ginger and garlic. Bring to a boil.

3.   Then you may eat as eclectically as you wish, placing the fish, seafood, or vegetable of your choice in the broth and cooking it. The use of strainerlike spoons fashioned of wire is suggested. These spoons are available in Asian markets. If they are unavailable, then you may use an ordinary slotted spoon. Eat at will, dipping your cooked foods in either of two sauces, Ginger Soy (page 162) or Vinegar Soy (page 142).

4.   Keep replenishing the fish broth and water. When the seafood and vegetables have been consumed, spoon the remaining broth into small bowls and drink it, as the final taste of the hot pot.

◢   Another suggestion I have is to put 1 tablespoon Scallion Oil (page 22) and 2 teaspoons sesame oil into the boiling mixture just as the first morsels of food are placed there. The combination of the two will give off a fine aroma.

SHARK FIN
SOUP

———————

Yue Chi Tong

The dorsal fin of the shark has long been considered a luxury food in China. Important banquets always include a shark fin dish, usually a soup, although shark fin is also cooked with braised vegetables. In Canton and Hong Kong, where it is particularly prized, shark fin is available in many grades based on quality and rarity, and the shark fin is prepared in a long and often tedious soaking and steaming process. But shark fin is also available already processed and dried, and it is not difficult to sample this important dish. The uses of shark fin in soups are many, but what I have developed is a relatively easy and very tasty soup. When properly cooked, with some patience, the shark fin is a mass of vermicelli-like noodle strands that take on the tastes of the ingredients with which it is cooked.

4   ounces (1½ to 2 cups) dried shark fin
3   cups cold water
2   tablespoons white vinegar
2   tablespoons white wine
3   scallions, washed, dried, with both ends trimmed, and
        cut in half crosswise
1   slice fresh ginger, 1 inch thick
1   piece pork fat, trimmed from a piece of fresh pork,
        about 3 ounces
6   cups Chicken Broth (page 40)
1   cup shredded snow peas
1   teaspoon sesame oil

1.   Soak the shark fin until it becomes soft, about 3 hours, then wash and rinse through a fine strainer. (It is important to use a fine strainer so that you will not lose any of the strands.) Soak in the water and white vinegar overnight. Strain again through a fine strainer and place in a heatproof dish with the wine, scallions, ginger, and pork fat and steam for 30 minutes in 2 cups of the Chicken Broth. Discard the scallions, ginger, and pork fat, strain off the liquid, and reserve the shark fin.

2. In a pot, bring the remaining 4 cups Chicken Broth and the shark fin to a boil, cover, lower heat, and simmer for 20 minutes. Bring back to a boil and add the snow peas. Stir, and let the soup come back to a boil. Then turn off heat, add the sesame oil, stir, and pour into a preheated tureen and serve.

FANTAIL SHRIMP 凰尾蝦

Fung Mei Har

The shrimp is thought to be a happy food. The reason is simply because the Cantonese word for shrimp is *har*, which is the sound of laughter.

1 pound large shrimp, shelled, deveined, washed, thoroughly dried, and butterflied (about 20 to 24 shrimp)

For a batter:

- ³/₄ cup cornstarch
- ³/₄ cup flour
- 1³/₄ tablespoons baking powder
- 1 cup plus 1 tablespoon cold water
- 1 tablespoon peanut oil
- ¹/₂ teaspoon salt

4–5 cups peanut oil for frying

Make a curry sauce—mix in a bowl:

- 1 cup Chicken Broth (page 40)
- 1¹/₂ tablespoons cornstarch mixed with 1¹/₂ tablespoons cold water
- 2¹/₂ teaspoons curry powder mixed with 2¹/₂ teaspoons cold water

1.   Make the batter: place the cornstarch, flour, and baking powder in a bowl. Pour in the cold water gradually, stirring clockwise with chopsticks, until the mixture is smooth. Add the peanut oil and salt and blend well. Set aside.

2.   Heat wok over high heat, add the 4 to 5 cups peanut oil, and heat the oil to 350°F., at which point a wisp of white smoke should be seen. Dip the shrimp into the batter (holding it by its tail) and gently place in the oil. Cook for 30 seconds, then, using tongs, turn over, and keep turning until golden brown. Cook 3 or 4 at a time. Once it is cooked, place in an oven set at "warm" to keep heated.

3.   To a saucepan, add all the curry sauce ingredients. Over medium heat, stir constantly until the sauce thickens and begins to bubble. Pour into gravy boat and serve with shrimp.

SHRIMP
WITH
YELLOW
CHIVES

———

*Gau Wong
Chau Har*

This is a very familiar dish in Canton. Yellow chives are highly prized by the Cantonese for their mild, delicate flavor, far more subtle than that of the pungent green variety. Until a few years ago yellow chives were unavailable outside Asia, but that is no longer the case. This dish, of shrimp and those chives, is the essence of Cantonese cooking: simple, easy, and light.

½ pound shrimp, shelled, deveined, washed, and dried

Make a marinade—mix in a bowl:

1½ teaspoons peanut oil
  1 tablespoon egg white, beaten
  1 teaspoon oyster sauce
  ½ teaspoon light soy sauce

^{1}/$_2$ teaspoon sugar
Pinch of white pepper
1^1/$_2$ teaspoons cornstarch

1^1/$_2$ tablespoons peanut oil
2 teaspoons minced ginger
1 teaspoon minced garlic
1^1/$_2$ teaspoons Shao-Hsing wine or sherry
1 fresh water chestnut, peeled, washed, dried, and julienned

Make a sauce—combine in a bowl:

1 teaspoon light soy sauce
1^1/$_2$ teaspoons oyster sauce
^{1}/$_2$ teaspoon sugar
1 teaspoon cornstarch
Pinch of white pepper
2 tablespoons Chicken Broth (page 40)

1 cup yellow chives, washed, dried, with ^{1}/$_8$ inch cut off from end, then cut into 1-inch pieces
^{1}/$_2$ teaspoon sesame oil

1. Marinate the shrimp in the marinade for 30 minutes. Reserve.

2. Heat wok over high heat for 45 seconds to 1 minute. Add the peanut oil; coat wok with spatula. When a wisp of white smoke appears, add the ginger and garlic. Stir, and when garlic turns light brown, add the shrimp with their marinade.

3. Spread the shrimp in a single layer, and cook for 1 minute. Add the Shao-Hsing wine by drizzling it into the wok along the sides. Turn the shrimp over and cook for 30 seconds more, or until the shrimp turn pink and begin to curl. Then add the water chestnut, and stir and mix together.

4. Make a well in the center of the mixture, stir the sauce, and pour into well. Cover with shrimp and water chestnuts and mix well. When the sauce thickens, add chives and mix well. Turn off heat. Add the sesame oil and stir all the ingredients together. Transfer to a preheated serving dish and serve immediately.

SHRIMP
WITH
MINCED
GARLIC

蒜茸炒蝦

*Seun Yung
Chau Har*

This is a new, and simple, Cantonese dish from Hong Kong. Usually minced garlic is an ingredient among many others in a stir fry, or in a sauce or marinade. Here it is the prime ingredient to complement the shrimp.

½ pound large shrimp (12 shrimp), shelled, deveined,
        washed, and dried with paper towels
1 tablespoon peanut oil
2 teaspoons minced garlic

Make a marinade—combine in a bowl:

1 teaspoon light soy sauce
¼ teaspoon sugar
½ teaspoon sesame oil

Make a sauce—combine in a bowl:

1 teaspoon oyster sauce
½ teaspoon Shao-Hsing wine or sherry
1½ teaspoons cornstarch
    Pinch of white pepper
4 tablespoons Chicken Broth (page 40)

Sprigs of fresh coriander (for a garnish)

1. Marinate the shrimp in the marinade for 30 minutes. Reserve.

2.   Heat wok over high heat for 45 seconds. Add the peanut oil; coat wok with spatula. When a wisp of white smoke appears, add the minced garlic.

3.   When the garlic turns light brown, add the shrimp with their marinade. Shrimp should be in a single layer. Cook for 1 minute, or until shrimp turn pink and begin to curl; then turn them over. Cook for another minute.

4.   Make a well in the center of the shrimp. Stir the sauce and pour into well. Mix all the ingredients thoroughly. When the sauce thickens and begins to bubble, turn off heat. Remove the shrimp to a preheated serving dish and serve immediately, garnished with sprigs of fresh coriander.

BOILED
SHRIMP
CANTONESE

白灼海蝦

*Bok Chuk Hoi
Har*

A favorite in the city of Canton, where these shrimp, prepared under the name of "scalded ocean shrimp" are served in many restaurants and hotels, particularly at banquets. The shells are left on, and the fun of eating the shrimp is much the same as at a Louisiana shrimp boil.

³⁄₄ pound medium shrimp (20 to 22 shrimp)
 3 cups cold water

1.   Squeeze each shrimp ½ inch from the top and the vein will pop out. Gently pull the vein out, then wash each shrimp well, drain off water, and set aside.

2. In a large heavy pot (cast-aluminum preferred for its heat retention), bring the water to a rolling boil over high heat. Add the shrimp and bring back to a boil. Cover pot, turn off heat, and allow the shrimp to sit for 3 to 5 minutes, until they turn pink and curl.

The shrimp are best served with the following sauce, prepared as the shrimp are coming to a curl.

Make the sauce—mix in a bowl:

2 teaspoons minced chili peppers (red preferred)
2 tablespoons light soy sauce
1 tablespoon Scallion Oil (page 22)
2 tablespoons Chicken Broth (page 40)
1 tablespoon finely sliced scallions

When the sauce is ready, divide it equally into 4 small sauce dishes. Remove the shrimp from the pot to a preheated serving dish and eat, peeling the shrimp with the fingers and dipping into the sauce.

Following is an alternate sauce I have created for the boiled shrimp. I call it *See Cho Yau*, or Vinegar Soy Oil. It is a sauce, not an oil, but reflects the use of hot oil as an ingredient.

Make the sauce—mix in a bowl:

2 tablespoons Chicken Broth (page 40)
1 tablespoon dark soy sauce
1 tablespoon light soy sauce
1 tablespoon white vinegar
½ teaspoon hot oil (page 18)
1 tablespoon finely sliced scallions

As with the first sauce, divide the sauce into 4 small sauce dishes and serve, for dipping, with the boiled shrimp.

DRUNKEN
SHRIMP

Joi Har

This very special preparation is usually made with live shrimp. In China, the marinating liquor, usually a potent rice liquor, is poured over the live shrimp in a bowl. They ingest it, thus marinating themselves from the inside. The shrimp are then cooked, flambé fashion, by ladling ignited liquor through them until they are cooked. Since live shrimp are rare in most parts of the North American continent, I have adapted the recipe to use fresh, but not live, shrimp. Similarly, I use Cognac instead of the Chinese liquor because Cognac has become very much the drink of choice in many parts of China, and because the taste is superb.

3/4 pound medium shrimp (about 20 to 24 shrimp)
 6 tablespoons Cognac

Make a sauce—combine in a bowl:

    3 small fresh hot peppers, washed, dried, and minced
    2 tablespoons light soy sauce
    2 teaspoons white vinegar
    2 teaspoons sesame oil
    1 tablespoon Chicken Broth (page 40)
 1/2 teaspoon sugar
1 1/2 tablespoons finely sliced green portions of scallion

1. Cut the shrimp shells along back vein from end to just before the tail, leaving shells and tails on. Clean the veins under cold running water. Drain the shrimp and dry thoroughly with paper towels.

2. Place 4 tablespoons of the Cognac in a bowl and add the shrimp. Mix together well until the shrimp are coated. Allow to marinate for 2 hours.

3. As the shrimp marinate, make the sauce and reserve.

4. Heat wok over high heat for 1 minute. Add the remaining 2 tablespoons of Cognac. With spatula, coat the wok sides with Cognac. When it is quite hot, light a match and ignite the Cognac. Add the shrimp together with the Cognac marinade to wok and stir-fry until the shrimp turn pink, about 4 to 6 minutes.

5.   Transfer to a heated platter and serve. Pour the sauce into individual small dishes for dipping.

STEAMED
LOBSTER
WITH
GINGER

———

*Geung Chung
Jing
Lung Har*

This is a simple and elegant dish. There are several versions of steamed lobster in Canton. Often lobsters are steamed with black beans; occasionally they are steamed in the Shanghai fashion, with fresh lemon; they are often steamed in combination with scallops. The large, clawless lobsters found off China, the so-called dragon shrimp, are quite different from the Maine lobster, but the meat is as sweet, and the Cantonese dote on them.

1 (2-pound) lobster, fresh-killed

Make a marinade—combine in a bowl:

    2 tablespoons white wine
    1 tablespoon light soy sauce
    2 tablespoons Scallion Oil (page 22)
  1/4 teaspoon salt
    1 teaspoon sugar
  1 1/2 teaspoons sesame oil
       Pinch of white pepper
    1 teaspoon grated ginger

3 tablespoons finely shredded ginger
2 scallions, white portions only, cut into 1 1/2-inch lengths,
       then shredded
6 sprigs fresh coriander (for a garnish)

1.   Have your fishmonger kill the lobster, or kill it yourself: hold the lobster head, and with your other hand plunge a boning knife into the chest cavity and cut back to the tail. Pull apart firmly. Remove the vein and the inedible interior portions (which resemble a black pouch). Then, with a cleaver, cut the body in half.

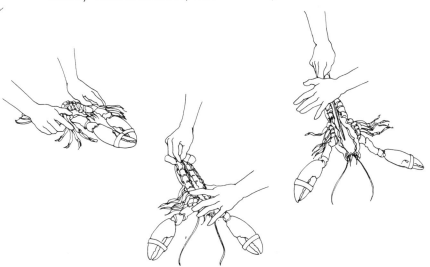

2.   With the cleaver, cut the head and claws off, cut the tail section into bite-size pieces, and cut the claws into pieces. Marinate the lobster pieces in the marinade for 30 minutes.

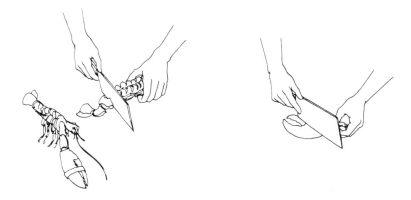

3.   In a heatproof dish, place the cut-up lobster. Pour the marinade over it. Sprinkle the shredded ginger and scallions over the lobster and steam for 20 minutes (page 38), or until the lobster shells turn red and the meat turns white. Garnish with the sprigs of coriander and serve with cooked rice.

FAR
JIU
LOBSTER

———

*Far Jiu Guk
Loong Har*

A wonderful example of the inventiveness of the Cantonese kitchen, this dish is flavored with a very special Chinese wine. It is called Far Jiu, in Cantonese; Hua Tiao, in Mandarin. The reason I give you both names is to avoid some confusion. The wine is one of the several grades of Shao-Hsing wine. Some of them are quite like sherries, and these are what many of my recipes call for. This wine is the best grade of Shao-Hsing. It is lighter, smoother, and very much like a light Cognac in taste. It imparts a different taste to foods. I was served this lobster preparation at a banquet in Hong Kong and I became determined to share its wonderful taste.

1 (2-pound) lobster, fresh-killed (not boiled), deveined, with inedible interior parts removed (page 145)

Make a marinade—combine in a bowl:

1 teaspoon ginger juice mixed with 1 tablespoon of
Far Jiu wine or Cognac (see note below)
1½ teaspoons light soy sauce
1 tablespoon oyster sauce
¾ teaspoon salt
1¼ teaspoons sugar
Pinch of white pepper
2 teaspoons sesame oil

3 tablespoons peanut oil
2 tablespoons shredded ginger
2 scallions, washed, dried, with both ends trimmed, and cut into 1/2-inch pieces on the diagonal, white and green portions separated
2 cloves garlic, minced
1 1/2 tablespoons Far Jiu wine or Cognac (see note below)
1 teaspoon cornstarch
6 sprigs fresh coriander (for a garnish)

1.   With a Chinese cleaver, cut lobster into bite-size pieces. Place in the marinade and allow to marinate for 20 minutes. Remove the lobster from marinade and reserve. Also reserve the marinade.

2.   Heat wok over high heat for 1 minute. Add the peanut oil and coat wok with spatula. When a wisp of white smoke appears, add the shredded ginger. Stir for 10 seconds, then add the white portions of the scallions. Stir for another 10 seconds, then add the garlic. When the garlic turns light brown, add the lobster pieces, spread in a single layer, and allow to cook for 2 minutes.

3.   Stir all the ingredients in the wok thoroughly. Add the Far Jiu wine by drizzling it into the wok along the sides. Mix well. Add the green portions of the scallions and stir well. Add half of the reserved marinade and stir all the ingredients thoroughly.

4.   Cover the wok and cook for about 2 minutes, or until the lobster shells turn red and the meat whitens. Stir the cornstarch into the remaining marinade and pour into wok. Continue to stir until the sauce thickens. Turn off heat. Transfer to a preheated serving platter and serve immediately, garnished with sprigs of coriander.

↘   I have used the Cantonese pronunciation of Far Jiu throughout because that is the way the dish is referred to in Cantonese Hong Kong. When you buy the wine, it will usually be in odd-shaped brown crockery bottles that look like gourds, pinched in the middle and canted to the side. The gold paper label of the bottle reads "Shao-Hsing Hua Tiao Chiew," which is Mandarin for "Shao-Hsing Hua Tiao Wine." This grade of Shao-Hsing also comes in bottles. Read the label carefully. As I have noted, if this wine is unavailable, do not use the sherry-like Shao-Hsing; use Cognac, to get the best taste.

STEAMED
SCALLOPS
WITH
SMOKED
HAM

金華玉帶子

*Gum Wah Yuk
Dai Ji*

In Canton the smoked ham used is from Yunnan. It is perhaps the most famous salted and smoked ham in all of China. It comes from the province of Yunnan, west of Canton, and below Sichuan. Cooks throughout China use it alone or in combination with other foods. This dish is a perfect illustration of the Cantonese concept of complementary tastes: the strong flavor of the ham with the delicate flavor of the scallops, and steamed so the purity of neither is lost. Yunnan ham is unavailable in the United States, and I find Smithfield ham to be a fine stand-in for it.

12 scallops, 1 inch thick by 1½ inches wide
12 slices Smithfield ham, 1½ inches long, 1 inch wide,
⅛ inch thick, prepared for cooking use (page 22)

Make a sauce—combine in a bowl:

1 tablespoon white wine
1 tablespoon light soy sauce
1 tablespoon Scallion Oil (page 22)
¾ teaspoon sugar
½ teaspoon sesame oil
Pinch of white pepper

    1 tablespoon peanut oil
 ¼ teaspoon salt
    1 slice ginger, ¼ inch thick
1½ cups broccoli flowerets, 1½ by 1½ inches, washed
        and drained
    2 teaspoons white wine

1. Using a sharp knife, make a slanting cut across the top of each scallop, about ½ inch deep. Place the scallops in the center of a heatproof dish, in a circle.

2. Insert a ham slice into each cut.

3. Stir the sauce well and pour over the scallops. Place the dish in a steamer and steam for 3 to 4 minutes (page 38), or until the scallops become white and firm. Do not oversteam, because the scallops will toughen.

4. While the scallops steam, cook the broccoli. Heat wok over high heat for 45 seconds to 1 minute. Add the peanut oil; coat wok with spatula. When a wisp of white smoke appears, add the salt and ginger. Cook for 20 seconds, then add the broccoli. Stir well and mix for 1 minute. Add the wine by drizzling it down the sides of the wok. Mix well. Cook for 2 more minutes, or until the broccoli turns bright green. Turn off heat.

5. Remove dish containing the scallops from steamer and arrange the broccoli flowers around the scallops. Serve immediately.

STEAMED
CLAMS AND
SCALLOPS
WITH
BLACK
BEANS

莫
鼓
蒸
双
鲜

*Dau See Jing
Seung Sin*

This is another of those Hong Kong Cantonese chef creations. In Cantonese the preparation can be translated,
poetically, to mean "black beans with double ocean-fresh,"
and that is exactly what it is.

12 Cherrystone clams, on the half shell
 2 teaspoons fermented black beans, washed and drained
 4 sea scallops, 1½ inches wide by 1 inch thick, each
     cut into 3 medallions
 1 tablespoon Scallion Oil (page 22)

Make a sauce—combine in a bowl:

 3 tablespoons light soy sauce
 1 tablespoon Shao-Hsing wine or sherry
 1 tablespoon sugar
 1 tablespoon white vinegar
 1 tablespoon sesame oil
     Pinch of white pepper

1.   Have fishmonger open the clams, leaving them on
the half shell. Place the opened clams on heatproof dish
and divide the black beans among them, atop each clam.

2.   In a bowl, toss the scallop medallions with the Scallion Oil. Place a medallion atop each bean-topped clam.
Mix the sauce and pour over the clams and scallops.

3.   Steam for 2 to 3 minutes (page 38). Avoid oversteam-
ing, because both clams and scallops will be tough if they
are steamed too long. Turn off heat and serve in the dish
you steamed them in, with plain rice.

MUSSELS
IN
BLACK
BEAN
SAUCE

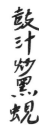

*See Jop Chau
Hak Hin*

In Cantonese, mussels are called *hak hin*, which means "black clams"; it is an altogether sensible and accurate description. There is no word in Cantonese for "mussel." But words aside, this is one of the most popular of Cantonese preparations. I don't know of anyone who does not like these "black clams."

2 pounds fresh mussels

Mussel boil ingredients:

10 cups water
 1 piece ginger, 1 inch wide, slightly smashed with cleaver
 2 teaspoons white vinegar
 1 tablespoon salt

Make a sauce—combine in a bowl:

 1 teaspoon white vinegar
 1 teaspoon sugar
 1 teaspoon dark soy sauce
1½ tablespoons oyster sauce
 1 teaspoon Shao-Hsing wine or sherry
 1 teaspoon sesame oil
 4 teaspoons cornstarch
   Pinch of white pepper
 1 cup Fish Broth (page 41)

2 tablespoons black beans, washed twice and drained
2 cloves garlic
2 tablespoons peanut oil
3 tablespoons sliced scallions

1. Clean the mussels. Remove sand and beards, and wash at least 4 times, until thoroughly clean. Set aside.

2.   In a large pot, place the boil ingredients over high heat. Cover and bring to a boil. Add the mussels and stir. When the mussels open, use a pair of tongs to remove them from pot and place in a large bowl.

3.   While the water comes to a boil, make the sauce and reserve.

4.   Make a paste: place the black beans in a stainless-steel bowl. Smash the garlic cloves with cleaver, remove skins, and add the garlic to the black beans. Mash together into a paste with cleaver handle (page 46). Reserve.

5.   Heat wok over high heat for 45 seconds to 1 minute. Add the peanut oil and coat wok with spatula. When a wisp of white smoke appears, add the bean-garlic paste, using spatula to loosen it. When the garlic turns light brown, stir the sauce, pour into wok, mix well, and lower heat.

6.   Add the reserved mussels, return heat to high, and stir, making certain the mussels are well coated with the sauce, about 2 to 3 minutes, until sauce thickens. Turn off heat, sprinkle the mussels with the sliced scallions, transfer to a preheated serving dish, and serve immediately, with cooked rice, to enjoy the sauce.

STIR-FRIED
MUSSELS
WITH
GINGER
AND
SCALLIONS

薑蔥炒黑蜆

*Geung Chung
Chau
Har Hin*

Here is another dish using those Cantonese "black clams." Although you will find the cooking process similar to that of the previous recipe, the taste is very different.

2 pounds mussels

Mussel boil ingredients:

10 cups water
 1 piece ginger, 1 inch wide, slightly smashed with cleaver
 2 teaspoons white vinegar
 1 tablespoon salt

Make a sauce—combine in a bowl:

1½ tablespoons oyster sauce
1½ teaspoons dark soy sauce
 ¼ teaspoon salt
 1 teaspoon sugar
 1 teaspoon white vinegar
 1 teaspoon sesame oil
 1 teaspoon Shao-Hsing wine or sherry
 4 teaspoons cornstarch
   Pinch of white pepper
 1 cup Fish Broth (page 41)

1½ tablespoons peanut oil
 3 tablespoons shredded ginger
 1 cup scallions, washed, dried, with both ends trimmed, and cut into 1-inch pieces

1. Clean mussels. Remove sand and beards, and wash at least 4 times, until thoroughly clean. Set aside.

2. Make the sauce and reserve.

3. In a large pot, place the boil ingredients over high heat. Cover and bring to a boil. Add the mussels and stir.

When the mussels open, use a pair of tongs to remove them from the pot and place them in a large bowl. Reserve.

4.   Heat wok over high heat for 45 seconds to 1 minute. Add the peanut oil; coat wok with spatula. When a wisp of white smoke appears, add the ginger and stir for 30 seconds. Turn off heat. Stir the sauce and pour into wok. Turn heat back up and stir sauce. Add mussels and mix until they are thoroughly coated, about 2 to 3 minutes, and sauce thickens. Add scallions and mix all the ingredients well. Turn off heat, transfer to a preheated serving dish, and serve with cooked rice.

EGG HORNS |

———

Jin Don Gok

This is a fine example of Cantonese home cooking, and wonderfully suited to today's table. These small filled egg pancakes, which have the delightfully illustrative name "egg horns," are usually served as the first course in a larger meal. However, they also make a delicious snack. I remember them as rewards my grandmother made for me when I had run an errand for her or done a job well.

¹/₄ pound shrimp, shelled, deveined, washed, and dried

Make a marinade—mix in a bowl:

2 scallions, washed, dried, with both ends trimmed, and finely sliced
2 fresh water chestnuts, peeled, washed, dried, and cut into ¹/₈-inch dice
1 tablespoon egg, beaten
¹/₂ teaspoon ginger juice, mixed with ¹/₂ teaspoon white wine

2 teaspoons peanut oil
1 teaspoon sesame oil
$^{1}/_{8}$ teaspoon salt
$^{1}/_{2}$ teaspoon sugar
$^{1}/_{2}$ teaspoon light soy sauce
1 teaspoon oyster sauce
2 teaspoons cornstarch
Pinch of white pepper

Ingredients for pancakes:

3 extra-large eggs
2 tablespoons Chicken Broth (page 40)
2 teaspoons peanut oil
$^{1}/_{8}$ teaspoon salt
$^{1}/_{2}$ teaspoon sugar
2 teaspoons cornstarch
Pinch of white pepper

Peanut oil for cooking pancakes

1.   Chop the shrimp into a paste. Place in a bowl with the marinade and mix and blend, stirring in one direction only. Refrigerate for 2 hours.

2.   While the shrimp marinate, make the pancake batter. In a large bowl, place all the pancake ingredients and beat together, by hand, with fork or chopsticks, until well blended.

3.   Divide the marinated shrimp paste into 16 portions.

4.   Make the pancakes. Use a wok because it is easier to keep the size of the pancakes in the well of a wok to a little more than 2 inches in diameter. This control is not possible in a small pan, because the batter is thin and will run.

Heat wok over high heat for 30 seconds. Add 1 teaspoon of peanut oil, coat wok with spatula. When white smoke appears, stir the batter and pour 1 tablespoon pancake batter into the well of the wok. Lower heat and jiggle wok from side to side so pancake becomes firm.

5.   Place a portion of filling in the center of the pancake while it is in the wok. Using spatula, fold the pancake over the filling, creating a half-moon shape. Press the edges with blade of spatula to seal, then turn over. When the pancake sets, remove from the wok. (A good guide is that about $2^{1}/_{2}$ minutes will have elapsed from the time you put the oil in the wok until you remove the finished pancake, now an egg horn.)

6.   Repeat until 15 egg horns have been made. Stir batter each time before pouring into wok, and add about $^{1}/_{2}$ teaspoon oil each time, if needed. As each egg horn is made, remove from wok and place in a heatproof dish in an oven turned to "warm." When all are done, serve immediately.

⤙   This dish may be made with chopped fish, such as halibut, with lean ground beef, or with lean ground pork. The marinade and all cooking instructions remain the same, except for the pork. As the pork egg horns are made, they should go into the warm oven, but when all are made they should be placed in a preheated 325°F. oven for 15 minutes to ensure that the pork filling is thoroughly cooked. This will not dry out the egg horns.

Poultry | 鷄
鴨

The importance of fowl, of poultry, in the Cantonese diet cannot be overestimated. Chickens, ducks, geese, and pigeons, as well as game birds such as partridge, quail, and pheasant, are dietary musts, though ducks and chickens are the birds eaten most often. And the various, inventive ways of cooking them are exhilarating. They are baked, roasted, steamed, fried, cooked wrapped in lotus leaves, or encased in salt or clay, and they are of course used as the bases for flavorful stocks and cooking broths.

Fowl are shredded and tossed in warm salads, cut up and stir-fried with vegetables or with seafood; they are cooked in wine; their meat is minced and served in lettuce leaves, or diced and ground and added to other preparations.

An indication of how birds are regarded in the Chinese kitchen can be obtained by looking at the menu of a typical imperial meal served to Emperor Ch'ien Lung more than two centuries ago.

As related in a fine and scholarly book, *Food in Chinese Culture*, by K. C. Chang, the Emperor that particular day dined on "a dish of fat chicken, pot-boiled duck"; on another course of swallows' nests and julienned smoked duck; on julienned pot-boiled chicken; on smoked fat chicken, salted duck, and "court style fried chicken."

Except for some bean curd and vegetables, some dumplings and rice cakes, that was the entire menu.

In this chapter you will find chicken and duck, roasted, boiled, braised, steamed, and stir-fried with vegetables, nuts, fruit, and pickled vegetables. In the Hakka and Chiu Chow section you will discover the art of salt baking and long simmering. Nor is just the flesh of birds eaten. Organ meat is minced for inclusion in steamed soups; duck eggs are cured and eaten as garnishes with other dishes. Even chicken feet, stewed with cinnamon and other spices, then steamed, are served as staples of the Cantonese *dim sum* table.

CANTONESE
CRISPY
CHICKEN

炸
子
鷄

Jah Ji Gai

In Canton there is a very famous restaurant, Bun Kai, also called Pan Xi, that has been in business since I was a young girl. I remember being taken there by my aunts, and I also remember that one of my favorite dishes there was *Jah Ji Gai*. On a recent visit to Canton I went to the restaurant, and one of Canton's, and China's, more famous chefs, Fan Hawn Hung (referred to in his kitchen as Uncle Number Seven), shared his recipe for this crisp chicken dish with me. It is a dish that finds its way to most Cantonese banquets. I have modified his recipe slightly to suit the Western kitchen, but essentially it is his, and it is delicious.

1 whole chicken, about 3 pounds
3 pieces eight-star anise
1/4 whole dried tangerine peel
3 cinnamon sticks, 2 inches long
1 slice ginger, 1 inch thick, slightly smashed
10 cups cold water
2 tablespoons salt
2 tablespoons sugar
1/2 cup white wine
1 whole nutmeg

To coat chicken, mix in a bowl:

1 tablespoon honey melted with 2 tablespoons boiling water
1 teaspoon Shao-Hsing wine or sherry
1 teaspoon white vinegar
1/2 teaspoon cornstarch

6 cups peanut oil

1.   Clean the chicken: remove all fat and membranes and wash with cold water. Sprinkle salt on the outside of the chicken and rub well into the skin. Rinse under cold running water. The chicken must be drained of all excess water. Place the chicken in a large strainer, in a seated position, and place strainer over a bowl, to drain.

2. Combine all the ingredients from the anise to the nutmeg in a large pot (an oval Dutch oven preferred) and bring to a boil. Cover pot, lower heat, and simmer for 20 minutes.

3. Turn up heat to high and bring to a boil again, then place the chicken in pot, breast side up. Cover. When pot begins to boil, lower heat immediately and simmer for 10 minutes. Turn the chicken over and repeat this process.

4. Turn off heat and allow the chicken to sit for 10 minutes with pot cover on. Then remove chicken, and discard all ingredients from the pot. Place the chicken on a cake rack that has been set on a large platter. As it drains, pierce the chicken with a cooking fork to help the process.

5. With a pastry brush, coat the chicken thoroughly with the coating mixture. Allow the coated chicken to dry thoroughly, about 6 hours. During this period turn the chicken, being careful not to disturb the coating, several times. (The use of an electric fan can reduce the drying period to about 3 hours.)

6. Heat wok over high heat for 1 minute. Add the peanut oil and heat to 375°F. Using a large Chinese strainer, lower the chicken into the oil, breast side up, and deep-fry for 3 minutes. Use a ladle to pour the oil over the chicken to ensure uniformity of frying. Turn the chicken over by inserting a wooden spoon into its cavity, then fry for another 3 minutes, ladling the oil over as before. Repeat until the whole chicken is golden brown.

7. Turn off heat. Remove the chicken and allow to drain, then place on a chopping board and chop into small, bite-size pieces (page 45) and serve immediately with roasted spice salt (recipe follows).

Roasted Spice Salt

    2 teaspoons salt
  ½ teaspoon five-spice powder
  ½ teaspoon whole Sichuan peppercorns

Heat wok over high heat, 45 seconds to 1 minute. Lower heat and add all the ingredients. Dry-roast, stirring, until the five-spice powder turns black. Remove and strain off the peppercorns; discard them. Place the spice salt in a small dish and serve with the chicken.

The spice salt can be made 2 or 3 days in advance, then, when cool, placed in a tightly sealed jar, unrefrigerated.

WHITE 白
CUT 切
CHICKEN 雞

─────

Bok Chik Gai

This favorite of the Cantonese must be made with fresh chicken, preferably fresh-killed. It is best made with chicken that has not been refrigerated. I know that fresh-killed poultry is less and less available these days, but the taste of this preparation is enhanced considerably if you can find one.

  10 cups water
    3 scallions, washed, dried, with both ends trimmed, cut
         in half crosswise
    1 tablespoon salt
    2 tablespoons sugar
    1 whole (3½-pound) chicken, with fat and membranes
         removed, washed and cleaned thoroughly, and
         drained

1. In a large pot (an oval Dutch oven preferable), place the water, scallions, salt, and sugar and bring to a boil. Place the chicken in pot, breast side up, cover, and bring back to a boil. Lower heat and simmer for 15 minutes.

Turn the chicken over, using wooden spoon and fork in cavities. Cover pot again and simmer for another 15 minutes. Turn off heat.

2.   Allow the chicken to sit in the pot, with cover on, for another 30 minutes.

3.   Remove from pot and drain well. Make certain water is removed from cavity. Place on a chopping board and cut into bite-sized serving pieces (page 45).

Ginger Soy Sauce

White Cut Chicken is served best with this dipping sauce of mine. I make this sauce in various ways so that it blends well with the food I serve it with. This is perfect for White Cut Chicken.

Mix in a bowl:

    1 tablespoon dark soy sauce
    1 tablespoon light soy sauce
    2 tablespoons Chicken Broth (page 40)
    1 tablespoon minced ginger
    2 tablespoons minced scallions, white portions only
    2 teaspoons sesame oil
    $\frac{1}{2}$ teaspoon sugar

Divide the sauce into individual small sauce dishes and serve with the chicken, which should be eaten at room temperature.

SESAME
CHICKEN
———
Ji Mah Gai See

Sesame seeds are very special in Canton. There is, of course, the fine, scented oil from pressed sesame seeds that gives so much fragrance to cooked dishes. But the seeds themselves are fragrant, particularly after they have been roasted. When they are sprinkled on food, they impart a special nutty aroma. There is a Cantonese aphorism that says that sesame seeds are excellent for the spirit, like motor oil for an engine.

4 cups cold water
2 scallions, washed, dried, with both ends trimmed, and cut in half crosswise
1 slice ginger, 1/4 inch thick
3/4 pound chicken cutlet, whole

Make a sauce—combine in a bowl:

1 tablespoon light soy sauce
1 teaspoon white vinegar
1 teaspoon Shao-Hsing wine or sherry
2 teaspoons sesame oil
1/2 teaspoon sugar
2 tablespoons Chicken Broth (page 40)
Pinch of white pepper

2 tablespoons thinly sliced scallions
1 1/2 teaspoons black sesame seeds
2 cups shredded iceberg lettuce

1. In a large pot, add the cold water, scallions, and ginger, and bring to a boil. Boil for 3 minutes. Add the chicken cutlet, bring to a boil, and boil for 2 minutes. Turn off heat, cover, and allow to cool to room temperature.

2. Remove the chicken from pot, place on a chopping board, and hit smartly with the broad side of cleaver blade. This will break the fabric of the meat. Then with your hands pull the meat apart, shredding it.

3. Place the shredded chicken in the bowl with the sauce and mix together well. Add the sliced scallions and mix well again. Reserve.

4. Dry-roast the sesame seeds (page 39). When done, allow to cool, then pour into bowl with the chicken and sauce. Mix well together. Prepare a serving dish by making a border of the shredded lettuce. Then pour the chicken into the center of the dish and serve immediately.

BRAISED
CHICKEN
IN
BLACK BEAN
SAUCE

———

Dau See Gai

This dish is justly famous in Canton. There is not a chef who does not fancy himself the best at preparing it. The combination of fresh chicken and pungent black beans and garlic is irresistible.

1 (3½-pound) chicken, freshly killed, cut into larger than bite-size pieces (page 45), washed well, with bones, fat, and membranes removed, drained, and dried thoroughly
3½ tablespoons water chestnut powder (page 25)
5 cups plus 2 tablespoons peanut oil

Make a paste—mash together:

4–6 garlic cloves, peeled
5 tablespoons fermented black beans, washed several times to remove salt, and drained well

Make a sauce—combine in a bowl:

2½ tablespoons oyster sauce
1½ teaspoons sugar
½ teaspoon salt
1 tablespoon dark soy sauce

3 tablespoons white wine

¾ cup Chicken Broth (page 40), or more

Sprigs of fresh coriander (for a garnish)

1. Coat the chicken pieces with the water chestnut powder. In wok over high heat, heat 5 cups of the peanut oil to 375°F., until the oil smokes. Deep-fry the chicken pieces by lowering them into the oil with a Chinese strainer. Fry 45 seconds to 1 minute, or until the red blush is gone from the skin. Remove the chicken, drain, and reserve. Remove oil from wok and wipe wok dry.

2. Place the remaining 2 tablespoons peanut oil in wok over high heat, and when a wisp of white smoke appears, add the garlic-bean paste. Break up paste with spatula. When the garlic turns light brown, add the chicken pieces and mix well all the contents of wok. Add the white wine by drizzling it down the sides of the wok, and mix briefly.

3. Stir the sauce and pour into wok; mix until the chicken is well coated. Turn off heat.

4. Transfer chicken to a pot. Pour ¾ cup of the Chicken Broth into wok to help collect all the juices and sauces, then pour into pot over chicken. Cover pot and cook over low heat until the chicken is tender, 30 to 40 minutes, stirring every 10 minutes. If the sauce thickens too much (as in a puree) add a little more broth, 1 to 2 tablespoons at a time.

5. Remove the chicken and sauce from pot and transfer to a preheated serving dish. Garnish with sprigs of fresh coriander and serve with freshly cooked rice.

CANTONESE
STEAMED
CHICKEN

———

Lop Cheung
Jing Gai

Only the Cantonese steam chicken with other foods in this manner, a process that creates a complex flavor for the chicken. This is a happy aspect of the Cantonese kitchen, putting several foods and many different flavors and spices together to create something truly unique.

$3/4$ pound chicken cutlets, with fat and membranes removed, and cut into 1-inch cubes

2 Chinese sausages, washed, dried, and sliced diagonally into $1/4$-inch pieces

12 small Chinese black mushrooms, soaked in hot water for 30 minutes, washed, squeezed dry, with stems discarded, and cut into $1/4$-inch pieces ($1/2$ cup cut)

1 teaspoon ginger juice mixed with 1 tablespoon white wine

$1/4$ teaspoon salt

1 teaspoon sugar

1 teaspoon sesame oil

2 teaspoons light soy sauce

2 teaspoons peanut oil

$1/2$ tablespoon oyster sauce

2 teaspoons cornstarch
Pinch of white pepper

3 tablespoons Chicken Broth (page 40)

6 sprigs fresh coriander (for a garnish)

1. Place all the ingredients except the coriander in a large mixing bowl and mix together thoroughly. Allow the mixture to marinate for 20 minutes.

2. Transfer to a heatproof dish, place in a steamer, and steam (page 38). After 5 minutes, turn the chicken pieces and sausage sections over and steam for another 5 to 10 minutes, or until the chicken turns white.

3. Turn off heat. Remove dish from steamer, garnish the chicken and sausages with the coriander, and serve immediately with cooked rice.

CHICKEN
STEAMED
WITH
FRESH
LEMON

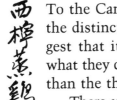

To the Cantonese, *sai ling* means "foreign lemon," and the distinction is made with this particular dish to suggest that it is best made with lemons that come from what they called "Golden Mountain," or California, rather than the thicker-skinned lemons of Canton.

There are many versions of this combination of chicken and lemon, almost all of them called "lemon chicken." In most, even in China, chicken is coated and fried and then a thickened yellow lemon-flavored sauce is poured over it. I prefer to steam the chicken with fresh lemon, which imparts delicacy and style to a fine dish.

Sai Ling Ching
Gai

¾ pound chicken cutlets, cut into 1-inch cubes

Make a marinade—combine in a bowl:

2 teaspoons fresh lemon juice, squeezed from ½ fresh lemon
Squeezed half of the lemon, cut into 4 (1-inch) pieces
½ teaspoon ginger juice mixed with 2 teaspoons white wine
1½ teaspoons light soy sauce
2½ teaspoons oyster sauce
½ teaspoon salt
1½ teaspoons sugar
1 teaspoon sesame oil
2½ teaspoons peanut oil
Pinch of white pepper
2 teaspoons cornstarch

Sprigs fresh coriander (for a garnish)

1. Add the chicken pieces to the marinade and toss well. Allow to marinate for 20 minutes.

2. Place the chicken with its marinade in a heatproof dish. Place dish in a steamer and steam (page 38) for 15 minutes, or until the chicken turns white. Halfway through the steaming process, turn the chicken over.

3.   Turn off heat. Remove the chicken from steamer and serve either from the heatproof dish or in a preheated serving dish, with the sauce poured over it. Garnish with fresh coriander and serve with cooked rice, so that you may enjoy the sauce.

STIR-FRIED
CHICKEN
AND
MELON

———

*Mut Gua Chau
Gai Pin*

This recipe, one of Canton's favorite summer preparations, contains both honeydew and cantaloupe, which the Cantonese call by the same name, *mut gua*, literally, "honey melon." For the dish to be at its best, the melons should be ripe and sweet but very firm. Use the flesh of the melon closest to the seeds; it will be sweeter.

$^1\!/_2$ pound skinless, boneless chicken breasts, trimmed
and cut thinly across the grain on the diagonal
into 2-inch slices, $^1\!/_4$ inch thick

Make a marinade—combine in a bowl:

  2 teaspoons oyster sauce
$1^1\!/_2$ teaspoons white wine
  1 teaspoon light soy sauce
  1 teaspoon sesame oil
$^3\!/_4$ teaspoon grated ginger
  2 teaspoons cornstarch
$^3\!/_4$ teaspoon sugar
$^1\!/_2$ teaspoon salt
    Pinch of white pepper

  3 tablespoons peanut oil
$^1\!/_4$ teaspoon salt

½ cup snow peas, with strings removed, and each pod
      cut crosswise on the diagonal into 3 pieces
4 scallions, white portions only, cut into ½-inch pieces
½ honeydew melon, cut into 1-inch-square slices, ¼
      inch thick (about 1¼ cups)
½ cantaloupe, cut into 1-inch-square slices, ¼ inch thick
      (about 1¼ cups)
1 tablespoon minced garlic

1. Add the chicken to the marinade, stir well, and allow to marinate at room temperature for 1 hour.

2. Place wok over high heat for about 45 seconds. Add 1 tablespoon of the peanut oil. Swirl it around with spatula to coat sides of wok. Add the ¼ teaspoon salt and heat until a wisp of white smoke appears. Add the snow peas and scallions. Cook, stirring, until the snow peas turn bright green, about 1 minute. Add the honeydew and cantaloupe and stir-fry until just hot, about 1 minute. Remove from wok and set aside.

3. Wash the wok and spatula in hot water. Wipe dry. Reheat wok over high heat. Add the remaining 2 tablespoons peanut oil and coat sides of wok with it, using spatula. Heat until a wisp of white smoke appears. Add the garlic and stir-fry until it is light brown, about 30 seconds.

4. Add the chicken, spreading it out in a thin layer. Cook without stirring for 1 minute. Turn the chicken over, stir, and cook until the flesh is white, 30 to 60 seconds. Add the reserved melons and vegetables and stir-fry until well mixed and hot, about 30 to 60 seconds. Serve immediately.

MANGO
CHICKEN

———

Heung Mong
Chau
Gai Pin

香
杧
炒
雞
片

Here is another of the summer favorites of Canton. Mangoes are a most popular fruit, and plentiful, and they are eaten sweet and soft, in desserts, as slightly sour pickles, and stir-fried. To be stir-fried they must be sweet but firm, and as they cook, their wonderful fragrance is released. Thus the name of this dish, "fragrant mango cooked with chicken."

1/2 pound chicken cutlets, cut into slices 2 inches long, 1/2 inch wide, 1/4 inch thick

Make a marinade—combine in a bowl:

1/2 teaspoon ginger juice mixed with 1 teaspoon white wine
1/4 teaspoon salt
1/2 teaspoon sugar
1/2 teaspoon sesame oil
2 teaspoons oyster sauce
1 teaspoon light soy sauce
1 teaspoon cornstarch
Pinch of white pepper

2 1/2 tablespoons peanut oil
2 teaspoons minced ginger
1/2 cup mango, peeled and sliced into pieces 1 inch long, 1/2 inch wide, 1/4 inch thick
1/2 cup scallions, white portions only, cut on the diagonal into 1/2-inch pieces
2/3 cup sweet green peppers, seeded, washed, dried, and cut into pieces 1/2 inch wide, then diagonally into 1/2-inch lengths
1/4 cup fresh water chestnuts, peeled, washed, dried, and cut into 1/8-inch slices
1 teaspoon minced garlic
1 1/2 teaspoons cornstarch mixed with 3/8 cup Chicken Broth (page 40)

1. Marinate the chicken in the marinade for $\frac{1}{2}$ hour. Set aside.

2. Heat wok over high heat for 45 seconds to 1 minute. Add 1 tablespoon of the peanut oil; coat sides of wok with spatula. When a wisp of white smoke appears, add the ginger. Cook for 30 seconds, then add the mango, scallions, peppers, and water chestnuts and stir-fry for 1 minute, or until the peppers turn bright green. Turn off heat, remove from heat, and set aside. Wash and dry wok and spatula.

3. Heat wok over high heat for 45 seconds, add the remaining $1\frac{1}{2}$ tablespoons peanut oil; coat wok with spatula. When white smoke appears, add the garlic. When the garlic turns light brown, add the chicken and its marinade and spread in a thin layer. Cook for 1 minute, then turn over and cook for another minute, until chicken turns white. Add the vegetables and mango and stir-fry for $1\frac{1}{2}$ minutes.

4. Make a well in the center of the ingredients, stir the cornstarch–Chicken Broth mixture and pour into well. Quickly cover and mix together thoroughly, cooking for $1\frac{1}{2}$ minutes more, or until the mixture thickens. Turn off heat, transfer to a preheated dish, and serve immediately.

CHICKEN
STIR-FRIED
WITH
GINGER
PICKLE
AND
PINEAPPLE

紫
薑
雞
片

———

Ji Law Gai Pin

6 ounces chicken cutlet, thinly sliced into pieces 1 by 2¹/₂ inches

Make a marinade—combine in a bowl:

¹/₄ teaspoon ginger juice mixed with ¹/₂ teaspoon white wine
 2 teaspoons oyster sauce
¹/₈ teaspoon salt
¹/₂ teaspoon sugar
¹/₂ teaspoon sesame oil
¹/₂ teaspoon light soy sauce
   Pinch of white pepper
 1 teaspoon cornstarch

 2 tablespoons peanut oil
¹/₄ cup fresh mushrooms, washed, dried, and cut into ¹/₄-inch slices
¹/₃ cup fresh pineapple, cut into pieces ¹/₂ by 1 inch and ¹/₄ inch thick
 2 tablespoons scallions, white portions only, cut into ¹/₂-inch diagonal slices
¹/₃ cup sweet red peppers, washed, dried, seeded, and cut into 1-inch cubes
¹/₃ cup green peppers, washed, dried, seeded, and cut into 1-inch cubes
 2 tablespoons ginger pickle, cut into ¹/₂-inch strips (page 114)
 1 teaspoon minced garlic
 1 teaspoon cornstarch dissolved in 4 tablespoons Chicken Broth (page 40)

1.   Marinate the chicken in the marinade for ¹/₂ hour. Reserve.

2.   Heat wok over high heat for 45 seconds to 1 minute. Add 1 tablespoon of the peanut oil and coat sides of the wok with it, using spatula. When a wisp of white smoke appears, add the mushrooms, pineapple, scallions, peppers, and ginger pickle and stir-fry together for 1½ minutes. When the green pepper turns bright green, turn off heat, remove the vegetables, and reserve.

3. Wash and dry wok and spatula. Heat wok over high heat for 45 seconds to 1 minute, add the remaining 1 tablespoon oil, and coat wok with spatula. When white smoke appears, add the minced garlic and stir-fry. When the garlic turns light brown, add the chicken with marinade in one layer and cook for 1 minute, then turn over and cook for another minute.

4. When the chicken turns white, add the vegetables and stir-fry all together for 1½ to 2 minutes. Make a well in the center and, after stirring cornstarch and Chicken Broth mixture, pour it into the well, and cover it with the food. Stir-fry all ingredients together for 1 to 1½ minutes, or until mixture thickens. Turn heat off, transfer the contents of the wok to a preheated serving dish, and serve immediately.

ROAST
DUCK

——————

Siu Op

The Cantonese regard roast duck as a most important preparation, particularly when they entertain. Westerners are perhaps more familiar with Peking Duck, a dish that has become known worldwide, and rightly so. But a well-roasted duck in the Cantonese fashion can be as elaborate to prepare and is as satisfying as any duck from the court of Peking. My version simplifies the traditional method of roasting duck.

> 1 freshly killed (4-to-5-pound) duck
> 3 tablespoons white wine
> 1 tablespoon salt
> 1 tablespoon sugar
> $3/4$ teaspoon white pepper
> 1 slice ginger, 1 inch thick, slightly smashed
> 2 scallions, washed, dried, both ends trimmed, and halved crosswise
> $1^1/_2$ teaspoons chopped fresh coriander
> 1 piece star anise
> 1 cinnamon stick, about 3 inches long

1.   Preheat oven to 400°F. for 20 minutes.

2.   Wash the duck thoroughly, removing all the membranes. Drain well. Rub the body and cavity of the duck with the white wine. Sprinkle the salt over the outside and in the cavity and rub it in with your hands. Repeat with the sugar. Sprinkle the white pepper in the cavity. Place the ginger inside the duck cavity along with the scallions, coriander, star anise, and cinnamon.

3.   Line a shallow baking pan with heavy-duty aluminum foil. Place the duck on a roasting rack, breast side up, and put it in the oven. Roast for 15 minutes, turn over, and cook for another 15 minutes. Turn the duck breast side up again, and pierce the skin all over with a fork. Roast for another 20 to 30 minutes, or until cooked. Remove the duck from the oven and let it cool completely.

4. Cut into bite-size pieces (page 45) and serve with Cucumber Salad (page 111).

DUCK
AND
MELON
SALAD
———
*Mut Gua Op
Sah Lud*

蜜瓜鴨少律

This summer preparation using roast duck is a fine example of the creativity of the Cantonese kitchen in Hong Kong. I first tasted a version of the dish in Hong Kong several years ago, and I enjoyed the mix of flavors so much that I was determined to devise my own version. Here it is.

³/₄ cup Roast Duck meat (page 174) julienned
1¹/₂ tablespoons crushed dry-roasted peanuts (page 39)
³/₄ cup julienned cantaloupe
¹/₄ cup julienned celery
¹/₃ cup julienned carrot
¹/₄ cup julienned sweet red peppers
¹/₄ cup julienned scallions, white portions only
¹/₂ teaspoon salt
1 teaspoon sugar
³/₄ teaspoon light soy sauce
1 teaspoon sesame oil
1¹/₄ teaspoons white vinegar
¹/₂ teaspoon Shao-Hsing wine or sherry
Pinch of white pepper
Oranges (for a garnish)

Place all the ingredients except the oranges in a large mixing bowl. Mix together thoroughly. Cover and refrigerate for 4 hours. Serve, cool, in a dish garnished with half-moon slices of fresh oranges arranged in scallops around edge of serving dish.

DUCK
WITH
PISTACHIO
NUTS

———

*Op Yuk Boon
Hoi
Sum Guor*

Roast duck is used as an ingredient in other dishes, usually stir-fried or in different soups. Here is a recipe, using roast duck, that I created for the Wine Institute, Winegrowers of California. The Cantonese name for pistachios, *hoi sum guor*, translates into "open heart nut." The words *hoi sum* mean "happy," all of which means good things for this mixed dish based on roast duck.

2½ tablespoons peanut oil
½ teaspoon salt
2 teaspoons minced ginger
¾ cup sweet red peppers, cut into ½-inch cubes
½ cup celery, cut into ½-inch cubes
¾ cup string beans, washed, with ends trimmed, and cut into ½-inch pieces
¼ cup bamboo shoots, cut into ½-inch cubes
¼ cup scallions, white portions only, cut into ½-inch pieces
2 fresh water chestnuts, peeled, washed, dried, and cut into ¼-inch cubes
2 teaspoons minced garlic
1 cup Roast Duck meat (page 174), cut into ½-inch cubes

Make a sauce—combine in a bowl:

¾ teaspoon light soy sauce
¾ teaspoon sesame oil
¼ teaspoon salt
½ teaspoon sugar
2 teaspoons cornstarch
Pinch of white pepper
3 tablespoons Chicken Broth (page 40)

½ cup pistachios, shelled, with inner skin left on

1. Heat wok over high heat for 45 seconds. Add 1½ tablespoons of the peanut oil. Using spatula, coat the sides of the wok. When a wisp of white smoke appears, add the salt and ginger. When the ginger turns light brown, add all of the vegetables except the garlic and stir-fry for $1\frac{1}{2}$ to 2 minutes, or until the string beans turn bright green. Remove the ingredients from the wok and reserve.

2.   Clean wok and spatula and dry thoroughly. Reheat wok over high heat. Add the remaining 1 tablespoon peanut oil and coat the wok. When a wisp of smoke appears, stir in the minced garlic. When the garlic turns light brown, add the duck meat. Stir-fry for $1\frac{1}{2}$ minutes, or until the duck meat is hot. Add the reserved vegetables to wok and mix well with the duck meat, about 1 minute.

3.   Make a well in the center of the mixture, stir the sauce, and pour into well. Mix thoroughly, and when the sauce thickens, turn off heat, add the pistachios, stir together well, then transfer to a heated serving dish and serve immediately, with cooked rice.

ROAST
DUCK
AND
PICKLES
SALAD

子桃梨鴨少律

———

Ji Toh Lei Op
Sah Lud

Here is another preparation using Cantonese roast duck, in this instance a combination of pickled fruit and ginger, the strong tastes of which complement the taste of the roast duck perfectly.

¾ cup Roast Duck meat (page 174) julienned
1 tablespoon dry-roasted white sesame seeds (page 39)
½ cup julienned Pickled Peaches (page 116)
½ cup julienned Pickled Pears (page 117)
2 tablespoons julienned Ginger Pickle (page 114)
1 cup julienned sweet red peppers
¼ cup julienned scallions, white portions only
1 teaspoon light soy sauce
¼ teaspoon salt
½ teaspoon sugar
1 teaspoon Shao-Hsing wine or sherry
1 teaspoon sesame oil
12 cherry tomatoes (for a garnish)

Place all the ingredients except the tomatoes in a large mixing bowl, and mix together well. Cover and refrigerate for 4 hours and serve, cool, on a platter decorated around the edge with 12 halved cherry tomatoes, placed cut side down.

Meat | 肉類

Historically, to the Cantonese, meat is pork. Old cookbooks, old writings on food, when giving instructions for the cutting, preparation, and serving of meat, mean pork. When Confucius wrote his careful instructions for the proper cutting of vegetables and meat, he meant pork. To this day, for many older Cantonese people, meat means only pork. There are different reasons for this.

First, many Cantonese are Buddhists, and while some of them refrain from eating any meat at all, none will eat beef. In addition, beef in China was not always as plentiful as pork. Third, the strong aroma and taste of lamb are traditionally not to the liking of many Cantonese.

Of course, things have changed somewhat. Beef is more plentiful today, and people are less religious than in the time of my grandmother. Lamb is eaten in Canton these days, though to a lesser degree than beef, and in infinitesimal amounts when compared to the consumption of pork. In recent years the Cantonese have begun to eat veal as well, and though it, too, is somewhat alien to their taste, there is a growing acceptance of it. Truly, however, it is with pork, that most versatile of meats, that the Cantonese kitchen shines.

A significant market exists for roast suckling pig. A wedding feast must include suckling pig, and so must an engagement feast, and the traditional banquet that is held by every family to celebrate the first-month birthday of a family's first child. The Dragon Boat Festival in Canton and Hong Kong each spring is an occasion for roast pig, as is the arrival of the Lunar New Year.

The Cantonese also barbecue pork, roast it, stir-fry it, broil it, steam it in soup, braise it, and make dumplings containing it. Pork livers are steamed, and other organ meats are often cooked in a rich stock quite like that of the *lo soi* preparations of the Chiu Chow people. Pork responds well to stewing, to marinades, and to aromatic sauces. And who among us has not had spare ribs cooked in and basted with a sauce sweetened with sugar or fresh honey?

HONEY
ROAST
PORK

窜汁叉烧

Mut Jop Char
Siu

This method of flavoring and roasting pork is a Cantonese specialty. Traditionally, after the pork has been roasted, it is dipped in a wash of honey. Instead, I use the honey as an integral part of the marinade, which in my opinion gives it a finer taste.

5 pounds boneless pork loin

Make a marinade—combine in a bowl:

3 tablespoons dark soy sauce
3 tablespoons light soy sauce
5 tablespoons honey
3 tablespoons oyster sauce
2 tablespoons blended whiskey
3 tablespoons hoisin sauce
1/8 teaspoon white pepper
3 tablespoons preserved bean curd (see note below)
    mixed with some of the liquid from the jar,
    enough to form a paste
1 teaspoon five-spice powder

1. Cut the pork into strips 1 inch thick. With a small knife, pierce the meat repeatedly at 1/2-inch intervals to help tenderize it.

2. Line a roasting pan with aluminum foil. Place the pork in a single layer in the bottom of the pan. Pour the marinade over the pork and allow to marinate for at least 4 hours, or overnight.

3. Preheat the oven to broil. Place the roasting pan in the oven and roast the pork for 30 to 50 minutes. To test the degree of doneness, remove one strip after 30 minutes and slice it to see if it is cooked through. During the roasting period, the pork should be basted 5 or 6 times and turned 4 times. If the sauce dries, add 1 to 2 tablespoons of water to pan.

4. When the meat is cooked, allow it to cool, then refrigerate until you are ready to use it. Honey Roast Pork can be made in advance of use. It can be refrigerated for 4 to 5 days, and can be frozen for 1 month. If it is frozen, allow it to defrost before using.

↘   Wet preserved bean curd comes in both jars and cans. That in cans is larger than that in jars. I prefer it in jars because the ingredient is easier to manage and to measure.

HONEY
PORK
WITH
SCALLIONS
———
*Yung Chung
Chau Char Siu*

In Canton, Honey Roast Pork is used in many ways after it has been prepared. It can, of course, be eaten immediately, but in Canton it is most often combined with vegetables and noodles in stir-fried dishes. It is also used in soups and cooked with rice. It is as versatile as it is delicious.

    3 tablespoons peanut oil
  ¼ teaspoon salt
    2 bunches scallions, with both ends trimmed, washed, dried, and cut into sections, white and green portions separated
    2 cloves garlic, minced
    2 cups Honey Roast Pork (page 181) thinly sliced
2½ tablespoons Honey Roast Pork marinade (see page 181)

1. Heat wok over high heat for 45 seconds. Add 2 tablespoons of the peanut oil and the salt. When a wisp of white smoke appears, place the white portions of scallions in wok and stir-fry for 20 seconds. Add the green portions and stir-fry until they turn bright green. Turn off heat and remove all the scallions from wok. Set aside.

2. Wash wok and spatula and dry. Heat wok over high heat for 45 seconds and add the remaining 1 tablespoon peanut oil, coating wok with spatula. Add the minced garlic. When the garlic turns light brown, add the pork. Stir-fry for about 1 minute, until pork is very hot.

3. Add the pork marinade and stir until mixed thoroughly. Add the reserved scallions and mix well. Turn off heat, remove contents of wok to a preheated serving dish, and serve immediately.

HONEY
ROAST
PORK
WITH
VEGETABLES

又
烧
菘

This is another favorite spring and summer dish for the Cantonese. It illustrates all that is best and most typical of Cantonese cooking: fresh vegetables and ingredients, quick stir-frying, and the preservation of all of the natural tastes.

Char Siu Sung

2 tablespoons peanut oil
1/2 teaspoon salt
1 1/2 teaspoons minced ginger
1/2 cup string beans, washed, dried, with both ends trimmed, and cut into 1/2-inch pieces
2 fresh water chestnuts, peeled, washed, and cut into 1/4-inch dice
1/4 cup bamboo shoots, cut into 1/4-inch dice
1/3 cup celery, washed, dried, and cut into 1/2-inch dice
1/2 cup sweet red peppers, washed, dried, seeded, and cut into 1/2-inch dice
1/4 cup scallions, white portions only, washed, dried, and cut into 1/4-inch pieces
1 teaspoon minced garlic
1 cup Honey Roast Pork (page 181), cut into 1/2-inch dice
1/3 cup dry-roasted peanuts (page 39)
1/2 teaspoon sesame oil

1. Heat wok over high heat for 30 to 45 seconds. Add 1 tablespoon of the peanut oil and coat sides of wok with spatula. Add the salt. When a wisp of white smoke appears, add the minced ginger and stir. When the ginger turns light brown, add the string beans and stir. One by one, add each of the following, and stir: water chestnuts, bamboo shoots, celery, peppers, and scallions. Cook for 1½ minutes, or until the string beans turn bright green. Turn off heat and remove vegetables from wok. Reserve.

2. Wipe wok and spatula with paper towels. Heat wok over high heat again for 30 seconds, add the remaining 1 tablespoon peanut oil, and coat wok with spatula. When white smoke appears, add the minced garlic and stir. When the garlic turns light brown, add the diced pork and stir-fry for 1 minute. Add the reserved vegetables and mix well for 1 minute, until hot.

3. Turn off heat, add the dry-roasted peanuts, and toss, mixing thoroughly. Add the sesame oil and mix well. Transfer to a preheated serving dish and serve immediately.

THE SOUP
OF PLENTY
(LOTUS ROOT
SOUP
WITH
PORK)

蓮
藕
湯

Lin Ngau Tong

This soup is a Lunar New Year tradition, and a play on words is what makes the tradition. The words for "lotus root" are *lin ngau*, which arc almost identical to *lin yau*, which to the Cantonese means that each year one should achieve more. Thus the soup is a New Year greeting. The Cantonese also believe that the holes in the lotus root indicate that one should think things through. A meaningful soup indeed.

  1¼ pounds fresh lotus root, washed thoroughly and left whole
   8 cups cold water
   1 slice ginger, ½ inch thick
   1 clove garlic, peeled
  1½ pounds fresh pork butt, left whole
  1–1½ teaspoons salt
   2 scallions, washed, dried, with both ends trimmed, and finely chopped

1. Place the lotus root in pot with the water, add the ginger and garlic, and bring to a boil. Reduce heat, cover pot, and allow to cook slowly for 30 minutes.

2. Add the pork. Allow to cook for 1 hour. At this point the lotus root should be tender. Test by inserting the end of a chopstick into the root. If it is cooked, the chopstick will enter the root easily. Add the salt and stir until dissolved.

3. Remove the lotus root and pork from the soup. Reserve.

4. Serve the soup hot in bowls garnished with chopped scallions.

5. Cut the lotus root lengthwise in half, then slice it. Slice the pork as well and arrange both on a serving platter.

Two different sauces are suggested for the lotus root and the pork:

Make the first sauce for the lotus root—mix together:

1 tablespoon light soy sauce
1 tablespoon red vinegar
$\frac{1}{2}$ teaspoon sugar
1 teaspoon minced scallions
$\frac{1}{2}$ teaspoon minced hot chili peppers

Make the second sauce for the pork—mix together:

1 tablespoon Chicken Broth (page 40)
$1\frac{1}{2}$ tablespoons light soy sauce
1 teaspoon minced scallions
1 teaspoon sesame oil

Place each in a dish for dipping and serve with the lotus root and pork as a second course following the soup.

DICED PORK WITH CASHEW NUTS

Eyu Guor Yuk Ding

The Cantonese call cashew nuts *eyu guor*, or "kidney-shaped fruit." Cashews, in Canton, were once rare and expensive, and when I was a child I used to volunteer to help my aunt cook this dish so I could steal the cashew nuts after they had been roasted.

¹/₂ pound pork loin, or 4 rib pork chops, boned, cut into ¹/₄-inch dice

Make a marinade—combine in a bowl:

¹/₂ teaspoon ginger juice mixed with 1 teaspoon Shao-Hsing wine or sherry
¹/₄ teaspoon salt
³/₄ teaspoon sugar
1 teaspoon light soy sauce
1 tablespoon oyster sauce
1 teaspoon sesame oil
Pinch of white pepper
2 teaspoons cornstarch

¹/₃ cup cashew nuts
2¹/₂ tablespoons peanut oil
1 teaspoon minced ginger
¹/₂ cup string beans, washed, dried, with both ends trimmed, and cut into ¹/₄-inch pieces
¹/₂ cup sweet red peppers, washed, dried, and cut into ¹/₄-inch dice
¹/₃ cup green peppers, washed, dried, and cut into ¹/₄-inch dice
2 tablespoons scallions, white portions only, washed, dried, and cut into ¹/₄-inch pieces
1 teaspoon minced garlic
1 tablespoon Shao-Hsing wine or sherry

1. Marinate the pork in the marinade for ¹/₂ hour. Reserve.

2. Dry-roast the cashew nuts (page 39). Reserve.

3. Heat wok over high heat for 30 to 45 seconds. Add 1 tablespoon of the peanut oil; coat wok with spatula. When a wisp of white smoke appears, add the minced ginger. When the ginger turns light brown, add the string beans, peppers, and scallions. Stir together well for 1 to 1½ minutes, or until the string beans turn bright green. Turn off heat. Remove the vegetables from wok. Set aside.

4. Wipe off wok and spatula. Heat wok for 45 seconds. Add the remaining 1½ tablespoons oil. Coat wok with spatula and, when white smoke appears, add the garlic. When the garlic turns light brown, add the pork, spreading it in a thin layer. Cook for 1 minute. Add the wine by drizzling it down the sides of the wok. Turn the pork over, mix, cooking for 1 more minute, or until the pork becomes white.

5. Add the vegetables and mix all the ingredients well. Turn off heat. Add the cashews and combine all the ingredients well. Transfer the contents of the wok to a preheated serving dish and serve immediately.

BOK CHOY
WITH
CHINESE
BACON

———

*Bok Choy Chau
Lop Yuk*

Bacon in China was not always available, as I remember, for we generally ate our pork fresh. What there was, was cured and made available only during two months of the year, December and January. I recall we used to buy it and have it with many dishes during the New Year period, when it was very special. These days, of course, it is always available. Enjoy it!

⅔ cup Chinese bacon (thinly sliced), with fatty portions separated from portions striped with meat
1 slice ginger, ¼ inch thick
¼ teaspoon salt
1¼ pounds *bok choy*, washed, dried, leaves and stalk pieces separated, and cut into 1-inch pieces

Make a sauce—combine in a bowl:

1¹/₂ teaspoons oyster sauce
1 teaspoon dark soy sauce
¹/₃ cup Chicken Broth (page 40)
1 tablespoon cornstarch

1. Heat wok over high heat. Place the fatty portion of the bacon in wok and cook for 1 minute. Add the remainder of the bacon. Cook for 1 or 2 minutes. Remove all the bacon, leaving the liquid fat in wok.

2. Raise heat; add the ginger and salt. When the ginger turns light brown, add the white stalk portions of the *bok choy* and stir for about 1 minute. Add the *bok choy* leaves and stir-fry. If too dry, sprinkle a little cold water on the leaves. The leaves should turn bright green.

3. Make a well in the center of the *bok choy.* Stir the sauce and pour into the well, then mix all the ingredients thoroughly until the sauce thickens and becomes dark brown.

4. Add the reserved bacon, mix well until hot, and serve in a preheated serving dish.

STEAMED "HAIRY MELON" SOUP

Tsee Guah Chung

These zucchini-like melons, which when ripe have a kind of peach fuzz on their skins, are called *tsee guah.* They are quite versatile, and the Cantonese eat them steamed, boiled, baked, and stuffed. The best are relatively small, about 3 inches in diameter and about 1 foot in length, and bright green. As they get older they become larger, more rounded, and yellowed at one end, and they also become less firm. Thus the younger the better for this preparation, which duplicates on a small scale the large banquet-size soup tureens of winter melon, which is the larger sister of the hairy melon. Like the winter melon, the hairy melon assumes the tastes of the ingredients with which it is cooked.

3 hairy melons, at least 12 inches long, even a bit larger, and at least 3 inches in diameter
1 thick slice Smithfield ham (usually sold in ³/₄-pound to 1-pound pieces)
4 cups water
2 fresh water chestnuts, peeled, washed, dried, and minced
1 Chinese black mushroom, about the size of a silver dollar (1½ inches in diameter), soaked in hot water for 30 minutes, with stem removed, and minced
3 cups Chicken Broth (page 40)
2 teaspoons green portions of scallions, finely sliced

1.   Wash the melons. Cut in half, across, then with a grapefruit knife scoop out the seeds and center core of all 6 halves. Wrap the base of each half in a cloth and wedge it into a small heatproof dish, so that it sits securely.

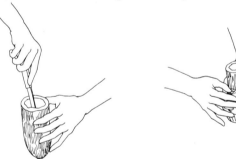

2.   Cook the slice of ham: place the ham in the water and bring to a boil. Boil, partially covered, for 45 minutes to 1 hour to remove the salt. Remove the ham from the water and mince enough to make 6 tablespoons. Reserve the remainder for a future use.

3.   Into each melon place one sixth of all the ingredients except the scallions. Place heatproof dishes in a steamer or a clam pot, and steam (page 38) for about 1½ hours, or until the melons soften, but do not lose shape.

4. Remove from steamer, sprinkle with the sliced scallions, and serve individually. Eat with a small spoon, shaving scallops of the melon meat from the insides as you progress.

⊾ The entire 3 cups Chicken Broth may not be used, depending upon the size of the melons. The use of Smithfield ham duplicates the taste of the ham of Yunnan quite effectively. Yunnan ham is a rare, much-sought-after ingredient in China. Its preparation and taste is similar to that of Smithfield ham.

HONEY
SPARE
RIBS
_____

*Mut Jup Pai
Guat*

蜜汁排骨

A specialty of Cantonese chefs whose expertise is roasting. This is truly an art in Canton, and even the best of Shanghai chefs will not make this dish as well as a Cantonese—but you can.

1 (3-to-3½-pound) rack spare ribs

Make a marinade—combine in a bowl:

1 tablespoon brown bean sauce (see note below)
2 tablespoons oyster sauce
2½ tablespoons hoisin sauce
1½ tablespoons light soy sauce
1½ tablespoons dark soy sauce
3 tablespoons honey
1½ tablespoons whiskey
Pinch of white pepper

1. Remove the flap and the extra fat from the rack of ribs, then with a sharp knife score the ribs all over.

2. Line a baking pan with foil and lay the rack of ribs inside. Using your hands, rub the marinade into the meat. The ribs must marinate for at least 6 hours, or overnight. You may prepare the ribs and marinate them in the refrigerator overnight, but they must be at room temperature at the time of broiling.

3. Preheat oven to broil for 15 to 20 minutes. Place pan in oven and broil the ribs for approximately 30 to 50 minutes. You may have to add a little water if the sauce begins to evaporate. During the broiling process, baste the ribs several times and turn over the rack several times as well.

4. When the ribs are done, remove from pan and separate with a cleaver. Serve immediately, with the basting sauce as an accompaniment.

⌦ Brown bean sauce is the thick portion of the soybean mixture that settles to the bottom of the vat during the fermentation process. It comes in cans and jars. Once a can is opened, the sauce should be transferred from can to jar. It will keep, covered and refrigerated, for six months.

BEEF
SATAY

———

*Sah Deh Ngau
Yuk*

This is an excellent example of how the Cantonese accept the tastes of another cuisine and by subtly changing it make it their own. The satay is widely known throughout Indonesia, Singapore, Malaysia, and Thailand and was brought to China by traders. In Canton and Hong Kong there are many versions of this curry-enhanced preparation. I have several versions myself; this is one that I favor for its particular strong aroma and flavor.

- ½ cup dark soy sauce
- 2 tablespoons curry powder, preferably Madras
- ⅛ teaspoon white pepper
- 5½ tablespoons honey
- 2 pounds flank steak, cut into 1-inch cubes
- 3 tablespoons peanut oil

1. Mix well 2½ tablespoons of the dark soy sauce with the curry powder, then set aside. Place the white pepper and honey in a large bowl, add ¼ cup of the dark soy, stir, then add the curry mixture. Add the remainder of the soy sauce and mix well. Place the beef cubes in the mixture, and allow to stand for at least 8 hours, or preferably overnight, in the refrigerator, covered with plastic wrap.

2. Place the peanut oil in a shallow frypan. Remove cubes with slotted spoon, place in oil and brown the beef cubes for 1 minute on each side, until they become light brown in color. Remove with a slotted spoon to a baking pan, and place them in a single layer. Add the pan juices and the marinade.

3. Place the baking pan in a preheated broiler and broil 3 to 7 minutes, according to your meat preference—rare, medium, or well done. Remove and serve immediately.

This satay can be prepared ahead and reheated in the oven, after refrigeration. It can be frozen as well. Before reheating, allow to defrost and come to room temperature.

FILLET
OF BEEF
ROASTED
IN SATAY
SAUCE

咖喱牛柳肉

*Gah Lei Ngau
Lau Yuk*

This is another version of satay. Here I do not cut up the beef; rather, I use a piece of tenderloin. However, once it is cooked, it retains the flavor of Southeast Asia. It is quite adaptable to the Western kitchen. It can be served hot or cold.

2 pounds center-cut beef tenderloin, 9 to 10 inches long
½ cup dark soy sauce
2½ tablespoons curry powder, preferably Madras
    Pinch of white pepper
⅓ cup honey
2 tablespoons peanut oil

1. With the back of a knife, make 6 equally spaced marks crosswise on the beef fillet to divide it into equal portions. With a sharp knife or Chinese cleaver, cut two thirds of the way through the meat at the markings.

2. In a small bowl, mix together the soy sauce, curry powder, white pepper, and honey.

3. Place the beef in a shallow roasting pan and pour the marinade over it. With your hands, rub the marinade into the meat on the outside and in the cuts. Cover with plastic wrap and refrigerate overnight. About 1 hour before cooking, remove the meat from refrigerator and let stand, basting frequently with the marinade as the meat returns to room temperature.

4. Preheat the oven to 500°F. Rub the beef with the peanut oil and roast, basting with the marinade in the pan every 5 minutes for 15, 20, or 25 minutes depending upon your preference for rare, medium, or well-done meat. Add 2 tablespoons of water to the pan if the sauce begins to dry out.

5. Serve. Cut the meat into the slices indicated by the cuts and pour a little sauce on each. Serve the remaining sauce in a boat on the side.

SNOW
PEAS
WITH
BEEF

雪
荳
炒
牛
肉

*Seut Dau Chau
Ngau Yuk*

Snow peas are among the most popular of Cantonese vegetables. Oddly, when I was a child in Sun Tak, I remember they were referred to as *hor lan dau*, which translates into "Holland beans." Presumably, those first seedlings came from Europe. Now, however, they are referred to as *seut dau*, or "snow peas." In France, Belgium, and parts of England they are *mange-touts*, which caused a little confusion for me when first I entered a kitchen in England's Lake District. So *much* history for such a little pod—but they *are* delicious.

1/2 pound London broil, thinly sliced against the grain
into pieces 2 inches long and 1/2 inch wide

Make a marinade—combine in a bowl:

1/2 teaspoon ginger juice mixed with 1 teaspoon
Shao-Hsing wine or sherry
1/4 teaspoon salt
3/4 teaspoon sugar
1 1/2 teaspoons oyster sauce
1 teaspoon dark soy sauce
1/2 teaspoon sesame oil
1 teaspoon cornstarch
Pinch of white pepper

2 tablespoons peanut oil

1 teaspoon minced ginger

2 cups snow peas, with strings removed, washed, dried, and each cut into 3 pieces on the diagonal

1 teaspoon minced garlic

Make a sauce—combine in a bowl:

1 teaspoon oyster sauce

$1/2$ teaspoon dark soy sauce

$1/8$ teaspoon salt

$1/4$ teaspoon sugar

$1/4$ teaspoon sesame oil

$1^{1/2}$ teaspoons cornstarch

$1/3$ cup Chicken Broth (page 40)

Pinch of white pepper

1.   Marinate the beef for 30 minutes. Reserve.

2.   Heat wok over high heat for 30 to 45 seconds. Add 1 tablespoon of the peanut oil; coat sides of wok with spatula. When a wisp of white smoke appears, add the minced ginger. When the ginger turns light brown, add the snow peas. Stir-fry for 30 to 45 seconds, or until the snow peas turn bright green. Turn off heat; remove. Reserve.

3.   Wipe off wok and spatula with paper towels. Heat wok over high heat for 30 to 45 seconds. Add the remaining 1 tablespoon peanut oil and coat wok. When white smoke appears, add the minced garlic. When the garlic turns light brown, add the beef with its marinade. Spread the beef in a thin layer; cook 1 minute, until the beef changes color. Turn over and stir-fry for 30 to 45 seconds. Add the snow peas and mix thoroughly, cooking for 30 seconds.

4.   Make a well in the center, stir the sauce, and pour into the well. Mix together well, and cook for 1 minute, or until sauce thickens. Turn off heat, transfer to heated serving platter, and serve immediately.

GINGER
PICKLE
BEEF
WITH
ASPARAGUS

紫蘆炒牛

———

*Ji Loh Chau
Ngau*

This dish of springtime, when asparagus is in season, is an excellent illustration of the Cantonese way of mixing contrasting textures and tastes. There is the beef, the ginger pickle, and finally the fresh, crisp asparagus, all combined, yet each retaining its character.

$^{1}/_{2}$ pound London broil, sliced across the grain into pieces 1 by 2 inches

Make a marinade—combine in a bowl:

$^{1}/_{2}$ teaspoon ginger juice mixed with 1 teaspoon Shao-Hsing wine or sherry
 1 teaspoon peanut oil
$^{1}/_{2}$ teaspoon sesame oil
 2 teaspoons oyster sauce
$^{1}/_{2}$ teaspoon dark soy sauce
 1 teaspoon cornstarch
$^{1}/_{8}$ teaspoon salt
$^{3}/_{4}$ teaspoon sugar
   Pinch of white pepper

 2 tablespoons peanut oil
 1 cup asparagus, washed, dried, and, using the tender shoots and tips, cut into $^{1}/_{2}$-inch diagonal pieces
$^{1}/_{2}$ cup red sweet peppers, cut on the diagonal into $^{1}/_{2}$-by-1-inch pieces
 2 tablespoons julienned Ginger Pickle (page 114)
$^{1}/_{4}$ cup scallions, white portions only, washed, dried, and cut into $^{1}/_{2}$-inch diagonal pieces
 1 teaspoon minced garlic
 1 teaspoon cornstarch dissolved in 4 tablespoons Chicken Broth (page 40)

1. Marinate the beef in the marinade for 30 minutes. Reserve.

2. Heat wok over high heat for 45 seconds to 1 minute. Add 1 tablespoon of the peanut oil; coat the sides of the wok with oil, using a spatula. When a wisp of white smoke appears, add the asparagus; stir-fry for 1 minute. Then add the peppers, Ginger Pickle, and scallions and stir-fry for another minute. Turn off heat, remove the vegetables from wok, and reserve.

3. Wash and dry wok and spatula. Heat wok over high heat for 45 seconds to 1 minute, add the remaining 1 tablespoon peanut oil and coat wok with spatula. When white smoke appears, add the garlic and stir-fry. When the garlic turns light brown, add the beef with its marinade. Cook in a thin layer for 1 minute, then turn over and cook for 30 seconds.

4. When the beef changes color, add the reserved vegetables and mix all the ingredients together. Cook for 2 minutes, then make a well in the center and, stirring the cornstarch–Chicken Broth mixture, pour it into the well. Cover it with the food in the wok and mix. When the sauce thickens, turn off heat, remove the food from the wok to a preheated serving dish, and serve immediately.

STIR-FRIED
BEEF
WITH
LEEKS

大蒜炒牛肉

———

*Dai Seun Chau
Ngau Yuk*

Occasionally I am asked by surprised students of mine how it is that leeks exist in China, because, they say, leeks are French, are they not? Well, of course they are not *only* French; leeks are well known and well eaten, and in Canton they are particularly big and fat, and their taste is strong and distinctive. They go well with strong-flavored meats such as beef and lamb. But since lamb is rarely eaten in Canton, I have combined leeks with beef for this recipe.

½ pound London broil, thinly sliced against the grain
into pieces 2 inches long and ½ inch wide

Make a marinade—combine in a bowl:

1½ teaspoons peanut oil
1½ teaspoons oyster sauce
 1 tablespoon egg white, beaten
 ½ teaspoon ginger juice mixed with 1 teaspoon Shao-
Hsing wine or sherry
 ½ teaspoon dark soy sauce
 ½ teaspoon sesame oil
 ⅛ teaspoon salt
 ½ teaspoon sugar
Pinch of white pepper
1½ teaspoons cornstarch

2 tablespoons peanut oil
1 cup leeks, with outer green layer of stalk removed,
washed well to remove sand, dried, and cut into
½-inch pieces, on the diagonal
2 small hot red chili peppers, minced
2 teaspoons minced ginger

Make a sauce—combine in a bowl:

 ½ teaspoon dark soy sauce
1½ teaspoons oyster sauce
 ½ teaspoon sugar
 1 teaspoon cornstarch
 3 tablespoons Chicken Broth (page 40)
Pinch of white pepper

1 teaspoon sesame oil

1. Marinate the beef in the marinade for 30 minutes.
Reserve.

2.   Heat wok over high heat for 45 seconds to 1 minute. Add 1 tablespoon of the peanut oil; coat sides of wok with spatula. When a wisp of white smoke appears, add the leeks and minced chilis and stir-fry for 1½ to 2 minutes. Turn off heat, remove, and set aside.

3.   Wipe off wok and spatula with paper towels. Heat wok over high heat, add the remaining 1 tablespoon peanut oil, and coat wok. When white smoke appears, add the minced ginger. When ginger turns light brown, add the beef with its marinade. Spread the beef in a thin layer and cook for 45 seconds, then turn over and stir-fry for another 45 seconds. Add the reserved leeks and chilis, and stir-fry together for 1 minute.

4.   Make a well in the center of the mixture, stir the sauce, and pour into the well. Cover well and stir together thoroughly for 1 minute, or until the sauce thickens. Turn off heat, add the sesame oil, and mix well. Remove to a preheated serving dish and serve immediately.

BEEF
WITH
BROCCOLI

*Yuk Far Chau
Ngau*

This is a favorite dish of Westerners; I am asked to give a recipe for it quite often. Although it happens to be a staple in virtually every Cantonese restaurant—and in non-Cantonese restaurants as well—it is difficult for a working chef to give a recipe for something that is cooked without measurement. Here is a recipe that you will enjoy and that I believe to be foolproof.

½ pound London broil, thinly sliced against the grain into pieces 2 inches long and ½ inch wide

Make a marinade—combine in a bowl:

½ teaspoon ginger juice mixed with 1 teaspoon Shao-Hsing wine or sherry
¼ teaspoon salt

½ teaspoon sugar
1½ teaspoons oyster sauce
½ teaspoon dark soy sauce
½ teaspoon sesame oil
1 teaspoon cornstarch
   Pinch of white pepper

½ pound broccoli flowerets, cut into 2-inch-long pieces,
   washed, and drained
1½ tablespoons peanut oil
2 teaspoons minced ginger
1 teaspoon minced garlic
2 teaspoons Shao-Hsing wine or sherry

Make a sauce—combine in a bowl:

1½ teaspoons oyster sauce
½ teaspoon dark soy sauce
¼ teaspoon salt
½ teaspoon sugar
½ teaspoon sesame oil
1½ teaspoons cornstarch
   Pinch of white pepper
¼ cup Chicken Broth (page 40)

1. Marinate the beef in the marinade for 30 minutes. Reserve.

2. Water-blanch the broccoli flowerets (page 37) for about 5 to 10 seconds, or until the flowerets turn bright green. Remove and drain. Reserve.

3. Heat wok over high heat for 30 to 45 seconds. Add the peanut oil; coat sides of wok with spatula. When a wisp of white smoke appears, add the ginger and garlic. When the garlic turns light brown, add the beef with its marinade. Spread the beef in a thin layer and cook for 1 minute. Turn over and stir-fry for 30 seconds. Add the broccoli flowerets and mix well, cooking for 1 more minute. Add the Shao-Hsing wine or sherry by drizzling it down the sides of the wok, then stir and mix thoroughly.

4. Make a well in the center of the mixture. Stir the sauce and put in the well. Cover quickly and stir together for 1 to 1 1/2 minutes, until the sauce thickens. Turn off heat, transfer to a preheated serving platter, and serve immediately.

STEAMED
BEEF
WITH
SZECHUAN
MUSTARD
PICKLE

*Ja Choi Jing
Ngau Yuk*

The Cantonese call these preserved vegetables by several names (see mustard pickle, page 20) but most often it is referred to as Szechuan mustard pickle. It is a popular vegetable in Canton and Hong Kong, where, steamed with beef, it is the perfect change of taste from the stir-fry. It is rarely served in restaurants; this is a dish for the home.

1/2 pound London broil, cut across the grain into
        pieces 2 inches long by 1 inch wide, and
        quite thin
2 1/2 tablespoons Szechuan mustard pickle, julienned
1/4 cup white portions of scallions, washed, dried,
        and julienned
1 tablespoon julienned ginger
1 tablespoon peanut oil
1 1/2 teaspoons sesame oil
1/2 teaspoon ginger juice mixed with 1 1/2 teaspoons
        Shao-Hsing wine or sherry
2 teaspoons oyster sauce
1/2 teaspoon dark soy sauce
1/2 teaspoon light soy sauce
1/2 teaspoon sugar
    Pinch of white pepper
2 teaspoons cornstarch
3 tablespoons Chicken Broth (page 40)

Ingredients to be added before serving:

2 tablespoons white portions of scallions, julienned
$^1/_2$ teaspoon sesame oil

1. In a mixing bowl, combine all the ingredients except those to be added before serving, until thoroughly mixed. Place in a heatproof dish, then place dish in a steamer and steam for 6 to 8 minutes (page 38). For those who prefer meat somewhat rare, steam for 4 minutes.

2. Remove from steamer, add the julienned scallions and sesame oil, and toss together. Serve immediately with plain cooked rice.

STEAMED
BEEF
WITH
CHINESE
MUSHROOMS

*Dung Gu Jing
Ngau Yuk*

This is truly a dish for the home, one rarely if ever found in a restaurant. Even in the family setting, it is rare, and is regarded as a change of pace from the usual steamed preparations: pungent black mushrooms and beef instead of lighter steamed vegetables with chicken, perhaps, or seafood. This is a hearty dish, well suited to cooler weather.

$^1/_2$ pound London broil, thinly sliced against the grain into pieces 2 inches long and $^1/_2$ inch wide
6 Chinese black mushrooms, soaked in hot water for 30 minutes, with stems discarded, cut into $^1/_4$-inch pieces (use mushrooms of medium size, about the diameter of a half dollar, or 1$^1/_4$ inches)
$^1/_4$ cup scallions, white portions only, shredded into 2-inch lengths
1 tablespoon shredded ginger

Make a marinade—combine in a bowl:

$1/2$ teaspoon ginger juice mixed with $1 1/2$ teaspoons
    Shao-Hsing wine or sherry
 1 tablespoon peanut oil
 2 teaspoons oyster sauce
 1 teaspoon dark soy sauce
 1 teaspoon light soy sauce
$1/2$ teaspoon sesame oil
$1/2$ teaspoon sugar
    Pinch of white pepper
 2 teaspoons cornstarch
 3 tablespoons Chicken Broth (page 40)

Ingredients to be added before serving:

 2 tablespoons scallions, white portions only, cut into
    2-inch pieces and shredded
 2 teaspoons shredded ginger
$1/2$ teaspoon sesame oil

1. In a heatproof dish place the beef, mushrooms, scallions, and ginger. Pour the marinade over, mix well, and allow to stand for 30 minutes.

2. Place dish in steamer and steam for 5 to 6 minutes (page 38). At 6 minutes the beef will be close to well done, so if you prefer it a little more rare, steam less. After 2 minutes of the steaming process, turn beef over.

3. Turn off heat. Sprinkle the steamed mixture with the scallions, ginger, and sesame oil and toss well with chopsticks or wooden spoon. Remove from steamer and serve in its dish with cooked rice, to enjoy the sauce.

TOMATO,
POTATO,
AND
BEEF
SOUP

Dong Ting Tong

Most people are surprised when I serve this soup and inform them that it is pure Cantonese. They always ask if Canton grows tomatoes and potatoes, and I assure them that they are indeed products of the farms there, and widely used in cooking. This is a dish for winter. Of course, winter in Canton usually means temperatures in the forties and fifties Fahrenheit, but that, I remember, was cold to us. This soup is called, in fact, "winter soup."

6 ounces ground beef, chuck preferred

Make a marinade—combine in a bowl:

1 1/2 teaspoons oyster sauce
1 teaspoon light soy sauce
3/4 teaspoon sugar
1/2 teaspoon salt
1/2 teaspoon blended whiskey
3/4 teaspoon cornstarch

2 tablespoons peanut oil
1 teaspoon salt
1 slice ginger, 1/4 inch thick
1 clove garlic, minced
3 cups fresh tomatoes, peeled, cut into 1/2-inch cubes (see note below)
2 cups potatoes, peeled, cut into 1/4-inch cubes
4 cups cold water

1. Place the ground beef in the marinade and allow to marinate for 1 hour.

2. Heat wok over high heat; add the peanut oil and salt, ginger, and garlic. When a wisp of white smoke appears, add the tomatoes and potatoes and stir-fry for about 1 to 1 1/2 minutes.

3.   Remove from wok and place in a pot. Add the cold water and bring to a boil. Cover pot and simmer over low heat for $^1/_2$ hour, until the potatoes are softened.

4.   Raise heat and add the beef with its marinade, breaking up the beef with a fork. Bring the mixture to a boil again, then turn off heat. Pour the soup into a preheated tureen and serve.

⅃   Tomatoes are peeled best after they have been blanched. Place them whole into boiling water for 2 to 3 minutes. Remove and place immediately into cold water. Allow to cool, then peel.

STIR-FRIED
VEAL
WITH
FRESH
TOMATOES

*Keh Chau Ngau
Jai Yuk*

The Cantonese for veal is *ngau jai yuk,* which means literally, "meat of the suckling cow." It is virtually unheard of in Canton and eaten only rarely in Hong Kong, where it is always stir-fried with various vegetables. I have created a veal stir fry using fresh tomatoes, mushrooms, snow peas, and peppers. It is not only innovative but colorful and tasty as well.

$^1/_2$ pound veal, the tenderest cutlet or thigh meat, thinly sliced into pieces 1 inch by $2^1/_2$ inches

Make a marinade—combine in a bowl:

1 tablespoon egg white, beaten
2 teaspoons peanut oil
2 teaspoons oyster sauce
$^3/_4$ teaspoon sesame oil
1 teaspoon light soy sauce
$^1/_8$ teaspoon salt
$^1/_2$ teaspoon sugar
1 teaspoon Shao-Hsing wine or sherry

   1 tablespoon cornstarch
      Pinch of white pepper

   3 tablespoons peanut oil
   2 teaspoons minced ginger
$\frac{1}{3}$ cup snow peas, peeled, washed, dried, and each sliced
        into 3 pieces on the diagonal
$\frac{1}{2}$ cup fresh mushrooms, cut into $\frac{1}{4}$-inch slices
$\frac{1}{3}$ cup fresh tomatoes, minced
$\frac{1}{4}$ cup scallions, white portions only, cut into
        $\frac{1}{4}$-inch pieces
   1 teaspoon minced garlic

Make a sauce—combine in a bowl:

   1 teaspoon light soy sauce
   1 teaspoon Shao-Hsing wine or sherry
$\frac{1}{8}$ teaspoon salt
$\frac{1}{2}$ teaspoon sugar
   1 teaspoon oyster sauce
$\frac{1}{2}$ teaspoon sesame oil
   1 teaspoon cornstarch
      Pinch of white pepper
   4 tablespoons Chicken Broth (page 40)

2 tablespoons sweet red peppers, minced

1. Marinate the veal in the marinade for 30 minutes. Reserve.

2. Heat wok over high heat for 30 to 45 seconds. Add 1 tablespoon of the peanut oil and coat wok with spatula. When a wisp of white smoke appears, add the minced ginger. Stir; when the ginger turns light brown, add the snow peas, and stir and cook for 30 seconds. Add the mushrooms and stir together, cooking for another 30 seconds. Add the tomatoes and scallions. Cook and stir for another 20 seconds. Turn off heat. Remove from wok and set aside.

3. Wash and dry wok and spatula. Heat wok over high heat for 30 to 45 seconds. Add the remaining 2 tablespoons peanut oil and coat wok with spatula. When white smoke appears, add the minced garlic. Stir, and when the garlic turns light brown, add the veal with its marinade. Spread the veal in a thin layer and cook for 45 seconds. Turn the veal over and stir-fry, adding the reserved vegetables. Make a well in the center of the mixture, stir the sauce, and pour it into the well. Cover and mix all the ingredients thoroughly.

4. When the sauce thickens, add the minced sweet peppers and combine them well. Turn heat off, transfer to a preheated serving dish, and serve immediately.

VEAL
STEW

*Ngau Jai Kau
Yuk*

This is another invention of mine: cooking veal by the traditional Cantonese braising method. I wonder what my grandmother would have thought of this?

1 pound fresh veal, cut into 1½-inch cubes
2 tablespoons cornstarch
4 cups peanut oil
¼ cup onions, diced into ¼-inch pieces
¼ cup shallots, diced into ¼-inch pieces
1 clove garlic, minced
1½ tablespoons Shao-Hsing wine or sherry

Make a sauce—combine in a bowl:

1 teaspoon sesame oil
2 teaspoons light soy sauce
2 teaspoons dark soy sauce
2 tablespoons catsup
¼ teaspoon salt

1½ teaspoons sugar
1½ tablespoons oyster sauce
    Pinch of white pepper

½–¾ cup Chicken Broth (page 40)
    ¾ cup green peppers, cut into 1½-inch cubes
    ¾ cup sweet red peppers, cut into 1½-inch cubes

1.   Coat the veal with the cornstarch. Shake off excess.

2.   Heat wok over high heat. Add the peanut oil and heat to 350°F. Oil-blanch the cubes of veal by placing them in a Chinese strainer and lowering them into the hot oil for 45 seconds to 1 minute, or until the cubes turn light brown. Turn off heat. Remove from wok and place strainer over a bowl so oil drains. Reserve the veal.

3.   Pour the oil from the wok, then return 2 tablespoons to it. Heat over high heat until a wisp of white smoke appears. Add the onions and shallots and cook for 2 to 3 minutes. Add the garlic, stir all the ingredients together, and cook for 30 seconds. Add reserved veal and mix well. Drizzle the Shao-Hsing wine into the wok down the sides and combine it well.

4.   Stir the sauce and pour into wok. Mix all the ingredients thoroughly, making certain the veal is well coated. Turn off heat.

5.   Transfer the contents of the wok to a pot (heavy aluminum preferred). Pour ½ cup of the Chicken Broth into the wok, and with a spatula swish it around to gather all the remaining sauce. Pour into the pot.

6.   Cover pot and bring to a boil over medium heat. Stir the contents. Lower heat and simmer for about 1 hour, until the veal is tender. Stir from time to time to avoid sticking. If needed, add the remaining ¼ cup Chicken

Broth, a little at a time. Raise heat to high, add all the peppers, and mix well into the stew. Turn back heat to medium and allow to return to a boil. Turn off heat. Transfer to a preheated serving bowl and serve with cooked rice.

The Chiu Chow and the Hakka 潮卅和客家

The Cantonese kitchen is sufficiently large and all-encompassing to include the cooking of two nearby cuisines, those of the Chiu Chow and the Hakka, both in southern Guangdong Province. Although neither is extensive enough or varied enough to be considered a school of cookery, there are regional peculiarities that make them important aspects of the cooking of Canton.

The Hakka, the so-called guest people of China, have been that vast country's traditional wanderers. Dynasties ago they lived well in the north, but because they were different—taller, with pronounced cheekbones—they became the object of varying degrees of prejudice and thus began a forced migration that took them south as far as Canton and the New Territories between China and Hong Kong. There they came to rest. They are easily recognizable by their black cotton pajamalike clothes and the wide-brimmed fringed hats they wear.

An industrious group, the Hakka are farmers, fishermen, and laborers, and the men and women can often be seen working on construction projects in Hong Kong proper. They are also an adventurous lot, and it is the Hakka, along with other Cantonese and southern Chinese, who were the first Chinese to emigrate to Hawaii. In later years they became very wealthy merchants, traders, and businessmen.

The Hakka kitchen is quite like that of the Cantonese. In fact it *is* Cantonese. What differences exist are of style rather than of substance. Because they were wanderers, the Hakka picked and caught as they moved, and ate what they gathered. They wasted nothing. A fish would be caught and eaten and its bones rendered to make a stock that could be carried along. A pig would be killed and every inch of its body eaten in some form. A well-known Hakka dish is the spinal nerve of a calf stir-fried with vegetables. They cook in the simplest of ways. Only a few spices and no heavy oils are utilized in their foods. They dote on vegetables and bean curd, and stuff both, often with minced fish or shrimp, before eating. Yet the Hakka have contributed one great dish to the vast Chinese kitchen: Salt-Baked Chicken, wherein a chicken is encased in sea salt and baked until tender, with the salt in the bed of a hole in the ground, its "oven."

Another and different aspect of the Cantonese kitchen is provided by the Chiu Chow people, also referred to as Chao Chou, whose ancestral home is the southern Chinese region around Swatow and Fukien, one of the first regions to be opened to European traders in the nineteenth century.

The Chiu Chow people live near the sea, and their cooking therefore inclines heavily toward seafood. They like sharp flavors with their foods and so they simmer ducks, geese, and chickens in a most pungent sauce they call *lo soi*, or "old water," a sauce that is never used up but remains as a sort of master sauce or starter which is constantly replenished and which becomes more intense. The Chiu Chow also eat equally rich soups, almost daily, based on rich stocks, and they enhance other foods by dipping them into sauces of tangerine oil, red vinegar, and sweet purees of tangerines and plums.

They also dip foods in a thin fish sauce, which is quite like those of the countries of Southeast Asia. In fact it is probably these southern Chinese from Fukien, from Swatow, these Chiu Chow, who brought much of the Chinese kitchen to those other parts of Asia.

The Chiu Chow eat stir-fried preparations, roasts, and smoked foods, most of which they have absorbed from the Cantonese repertoire. Yet the Chiu Chow have a history of cooking that is more than seven centuries old, and they have traditionally been the street food peddlers and the food stall proprietors in Hong Kong, Singapore, and Malaysia. (Chiu Chow restaurants abound throughout Asia and in Hong Kong.)

They are experts in the preparation of seafood, and their shark fin soup and bird's nest soup are highly regarded, though their methods of preparing those dishes do not differ to any degree from the Cantonese versions of the same dishes. The Chiu Chow are famed for vegetable carving. They, as well as the Hakka, use a spice called sand ginger, dried or powdered, a strong root known as *kaempferia galanga*, and they preserve vegetables like kale and squash for use with meats in stir fries.

In Hong Kong there are many Chiu Chow restaurants, most of which have been in business for decades. There are fewer Hakka restaurants, but they are not rarities. And virtually all of Hong Kong's Cantonese restaurants offer a few Chiu Chow and Hakka dishes, because they recognize good tastes.

CHIU
CHOW
LO
SOI
DUCK

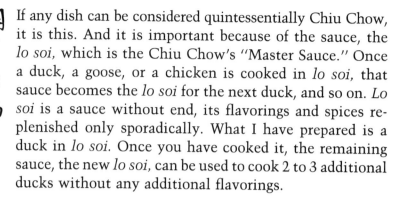

Chiu Chow Lo
Soi Op

If any dish can be considered quintessentially Chiu Chow, it is this. And it is important because of the sauce, the *lo soi*, which is the Chiu Chow's "Master Sauce." Once a duck, a goose, or a chicken is cooked in *lo soi*, that sauce becomes the *lo soi* for the next duck, and so on. *Lo soi* is a sauce without end, its flavorings and spices replenished only sporadically. What I have prepared is a duck in *lo soi*. Once you have cooked it, the remaining sauce, the new *lo soi*, can be used to cook 2 to 3 additional ducks without any additional flavorings.

4 pieces eight-star anise
4 pieces cinnamon stick, each 3 inches long
½ tablespoon fennel seed
½ teaspoon Sichuan peppercorns
6 pieces sand ginger (see note below)
½ dried tangerine peel
6 pieces licorice root, each 1½ inches long
1 whole nutmeg
½ teaspoon whole cloves
1 piece ginger, 2 inches long, slightly smashed
4 cloves garlic, peeled
3 scallions, washed, dried, with both ends trimmed, and cut into 3-inch pieces

2 cups dark soy sauce
2 cups light soy sauce
5 cups Chiu Chow Stock (page 216)
5 cups cold water
¾ cup *fen chiew*, or gin (see note below)
1 pound rock sugar or light brown sugar
1 (5-to-5½-pound) freshly killed duck

1. Fold a piece of cheesecloth, 10 inches by 10 inches, in half, then in half again. You will then have a square 5 inches by 5 inches. Sew 2 of the 3 open sides closed, creating a "pillow."

2. Place the ingredients from the eight-star anise to the scallions in the pillow, and sew it closed.

3. In a pot, preferably a large stockpot, place the soy sauces, Chiu Chow Stock, water, *fen chiew* (or gin), rock sugar (or brown sugar), and the sewn bag of spices. Cover pot and over high heat bring to a boil. Lower heat and simmer for 1 hour. Stir occasionally to make certain the sugar is dissolved.

4. While the *lo soi* simmers, prepare the duck: wash it thoroughly inside the cavity and out; remove the membranes. Drain off the water. Cut off first 2 joints of both wings. Reserve the duck.

5. Place a low cake rack in the pot. Lower the duck, breast side down, onto the rack. Turn heat to high and bring the *lo soi* back to a boil. Then immediately lower heat and simmer the duck, covered, for 2 hours, if the head is on. If the head is off, simmer for about 1½ hours. Ladle the sauce over the duck if it is not completely covered. Make certain heat is low, so the duck skin will not split open.

6. Turn off heat. Allow the duck to rest in the *lo soi* for 1 hour. Then remove to a chopping board, cut the duck with a cleaver into bite-size pieces (page 45), and serve immediately on a preheated platter.

⌇ *Fen chiew* (page 16) is a strong distilled grain spirit that has been a component of Chinese cookery for fifteen hundred years. It is distilled from sorghum and is 130 proof. It is usually available in liquor stores in Asian neighborhoods. If it is unavailable, gin may be used in its place.

⌇ Sand ginger, or *kaempferia galanga,* as it is often labeled (page 21), is a root that is often utilized in Chinese herbal medicines. It comes, sliced, dry, in small packages. The Chiu Chow people use it for its fragrance.

⤳ The identical recipe can be used to cook a chicken. The chicken should be about 3½ pounds and should be simmered for 30 to 40 minutes, and turned over once during the process.

CHIU
CHOW
STOCK
_____

*Chiu Chow
Seung tong*

潮
州
上
湯

For the Chiu Chow the making of stock is a gigantic undertaking. Families make it in enormous quantities because they use it almost daily for their special soups. Chefs use their stock in virtually everything they cook. Because it is made in such huge amounts, it is not unusual for a stockpot to contain whole chickens, pounds of lean pork, whole Yunnan ham shank bones. Chiu Chow stock is so special that it is called *seung tong*, or "the best soup," from which all soups proceed. I have made a version of Chiu Chow stock that you will find rich and satisfying, and a fine base for soups, and I have reduced the amounts of ingredients to manageable levels.

    4 pounds pork neck bones
    3 pounds chicken bones
    2 pounds chicken wings
1½ pounds shank bone of Smithfield ham, or ham bones
 ½ pound piece of fresh ginger, lightly smashed
    6 quarts water
    2 tablespoons salt

1. In a very large stockpot, place all the bones and parts and the ginger, add the cold water, cover, and bring to a boil over high heat. Add the salt, lower heat, and simmer, uncovered, for 7 hours. Skim off the residue on the surface during the simmering.

2. Turn off heat, allow to cool, strain off bones. The recipe makes about 3½ quarts stock. Place in containers for use.

3. The stock may be refrigerated for 3 to 4 days in a covered container. It may be frozen for up to 2 months.

CHIU
CHOW
RICE
NOODLE
SOUP

潮
州
粿
條

*Chiu Chow
Guor Tiu*

This is the most famous of Chiu Chow preparations and is based on the Chiu Chow Stock and cooked fettucini-like rice noodles called *guor tiu,* or "rice sticks." The best of these noodles are made in Thailand and come dried, in packages, labeled "Rice Noodles, Banh Pho." This soup is inexpensive and hearty and is the luncheon of choice of virtually all the Chiu Chow people. Occasionally made in the home, using the rich stock, it is more often eaten in restaurants and is accompanied by glasses of steaming-hot strong tea.

  8 cups cold water
  6 ounces rice noodles
  2 cups Chiu Chow Stock (page 216)
1½ tablespoons Tianjin preserved vegetable (see note below), minced
  8 large shrimp, shelled, deveined, and washed
  8 Fish Balls (page 218) or Shrimp Balls (page 220)
  2 cups finely sliced iceberg lettuce

1. Place the cold water in a pot over high heat and bring to a boil. Add the rice noodles, and with a wooden spoon stir and make certain the noodles are submerged in the water. Cook, stirring, 3 minutes, until the noodles are cooked *al dente. Do not* overcook. Turn off heat, run cold water into pot, drain, and reserve the noodles.

2. Place the Chiu Chow Stock in a pot with the Tianjin preserved vegetable and bring to a boil, covered. Add the shrimp and Fish or Shrimp Balls and bring back to a boil.

Cook for 30 to 45 seconds, or until the shrimp turn pink and curl. Add the lettuce and the reserved noodles, stir, and bring again to a boil. Turn off heat, transfer to a preheated tureen, and serve immediately.

⤳ This Chiu Chow soup tastes best with minced Tianjin preserved vegetable (page 25). However, there is no substitute for it, so if it is unavailable, use nothing in its place, except perhaps a minced clove of garlic. An added note: 2 to 3 teaspoons of the minced vegetable added to stir-fried dishes add a fine piquancy to their taste. Try it.

FISH
BALLS

_____

*Chiu Chow Yue
Yuen*

潮
州
魚
丸

½ pound filleted carp (see note below)
2 tablespoons egg white, beaten
2 teaspoons oyster sauce
1 teaspoon sesame oil
1 teaspoon peanut oil
½ teaspoon light soy sauce
¾ teaspoon sugar
½ teaspoon white vinegar
1½ teaspoons white wine
Pinch of white pepper
8 cups cold water

1. Place the carp fillet on a chopping board. Cut the fish into 1-inch pieces, then, using a cleaver, chop the fish into a paste.

2. Place the chopped fish in a bowl and add all the other ingredients except the cold water. Mix together with your hands, or in the bowl of an electric mixer, using the flat paddle. If an electric mixer is used, mix for 5 to 7 minutes, until the mixture is firm. To mix by hand, the Chiu Chow way, you must throw the fish mixture repeatedly into the bowl with some force. This lifting-out and throwingin process blends the ingredients well, makes the mixture firm, and ensures that the fish balls will not fall apart.

3. Have a small bowl of water by you to keep your hands moist. Divide the fish mixture into 20 equal parts. Wet your hands and roll each piece into a ball. The wetness will ensure that the fish mixture will not stick to your hands. Continue until 20 fish balls are made.

4. Add the cold water to a pot and bring to a boil. Add the fish balls and bring back to a boil. Cook for 3 to 4 minutes, until the fish balls are firm. Turn off heat. Run cold water into the pot, then drain. Reserve the fish balls.

❧ Carp is the preferred fish for fish balls, for both its taste and consistency, but flounder or sole may also be used. *Do not* use any frozen fish, for the fiber of the fish meat is weakened by freezing.

❧ The fish balls can be made as early as 2 days in advance. Once made they should be kept in a covered container or bowl, refrigerated. Before adding them to the soup, they should be returned to room temperature.

SHRIMP
BALLS

潮
卅
蝦
丸

*Chiu Chow Har
Yuen*

½ pound shrimp, shelled, deveined, washed, and dried
2 tablespoons minced scallions
1½ teaspoons minced Tianjin preserved vegetable (see note below)
2 tablespoons egg white, beaten
¾ teaspoon sugar
  Pinch of white pepper
½ teaspoon light soy sauce
1½ teaspoons oyster sauce
1 teaspoon sesame oil
1 teaspoon peanut oil
1½ teaspoons white wine
8 cups cold water

1.   Place the shrimp on a chopping board. Cut each shrimp into 4 pieces, then with a cleaver chop the shrimp into a paste.

2.   Place the chopped shrimp in a bowl and add all the other ingredients except cold water, than mix either with an electric mixer or by hand. If an electric mixer is used, mix for 4 to 5 minutes, using the flat paddle, until mixture is firm. If by hand, pick up the shrimp mixture and throw it with some force into the bowl. Repeat about 10 times until the mixture is blended and firm.

3.   Have a small bowl of water by you to keep your hands moist. Divide the shrimp mixture into 20 equal parts. Wet your hands and roll each piece into a ball. The wetness will prevent the shrimp mixture from sticking to your hands. Continue until 20 shrimp balls are made.

4.   Add the cold water to a pot and bring to a boil. Add the shrimp balls and bring back to a boil. Cook for 3 to 4 minutes, until the shrimp balls are firm. Turn off heat. Run cold water into the pot, then drain. Reserve the shrimp balls.

⟍   There is no substitute for Tianjin preserved vegetable (page 25), but if it is unavailable, use 1 clove garlic, minced, and a pinch of salt in its place.

⟍   The shrimp balls can be made as early as 2 days in advance. Once made they should be kept in a covered container or bowl, refrigerated. Before adding them to the soup, they should be returned to room temperature.

CHINESE
CHIVES
WITH
SALTED
PORK

———

*Ham Chi Yuk
Chau
Gau Choi*

咸豬肉炒韭菜

A typical dish of the Chiu Chow people. They often poach their food in seawater—everything from duck and chicken to all manner of seafood. The second step, the stir frying, is an aspect of cookery that the Chiu Chow appropriated from the Cantonese kitchen.

1 (1½-pound) piece of fresh bacon
8 cups cold water
2 tablespoons salt
1 tablespoon peanut oil
½ pound fresh chives, washed, with dried portions of stalk removed, both ends trimmed, and cut into 1-inch pieces (if Chinese chives, which have a stronger flavor than Western chives, are unavailable, use the latter)

Make a sauce—combine in a bowl:

2 tablespoons Chicken Broth (page 40)
½ teaspoon cornstarch
½ teaspoon sesame oil

1. Boil fresh bacon in the water, to which the salt has been added (to approximate the taste of seawater): boil the water, place the bacon in the water, bring back to a boil, lower heat, and simmer, partially covered, for 3 to 3½ hours, until it is very tender. The boiling process should leave the bacon fat intact, but remove all greasiness.

2. Remove the salted pork from pot and place in a bowl of cold water. It must be kept cold, so change the water as it becomes warm. Do this for 1 hour. Then remove the pork from bowl and refrigerate for 3 hours, until very cold. Slice the pork thinly. (Use half of the pork; reserve the remainder for future use. See note.) Allow the slices to come to room temperature. Reserve.

3. Heat wok over high heat. Add the peanut oil; coat the sides of the wok with a spatula. When a wisp of white smoke appears, add the chives. Stir-fry for about 1 minute, or until the chives turn bright green. Turn off heat, remove, and reserve.

4. Wipe off wok and spatula with paper towels. Heat wok again. When hot, add the strips of sliced pork and stir-fry until hot. Add the chives and mix together about 1 minute, until hot. Stir the sauce and put into wok and mix thoroughly. When it is well mixed and the sauce thickens, turn off heat. Remove, transfer to a preheated serving dish, and serve immediately.

Place the unused salted pork on a dish, cover with plastic wrap, and refrigerate. It will keep 5 to 7 days refrigerated.

THE
DISH
OF THE
EMPEROR

*Won Tui Gwok
Wu Choi*

This is one of those dishes with a legend attached, the sort of thing that seems to make them all the more tasty. According to Chiu Chow legend, an emperor of the Southern Sung Dynasty was passing through the Chiu Chow area more than seven hundred years ago and was entertained with this dish. Of course, it was made with the cured ham of Yunnan and with the sweet, tender leaves of the sweet potato vine. It pleased the emperor, and he is said to have suggested that it be the "national dish" of the Chiu Chow. Sweet potato vine leaves are rather rare here, but spinach will do nicely. Have a taste of legend!

       8 cups cold water
    1/2 teaspoon baking soda
       1 pound fresh spinach, with 1/2 inch cut from the root
           end of the head so the leaves fall off, washed 3
           to 4 times to remove sand, and with leaves cut
           in half at stem
   2 1/2 tablespoons peanut oil
       8 Chinese mushrooms, about the size of a quarter,
           soaked in hot water for 30 minutes, squeezed
           dry, with stems discarded, and julienned
    1/2 teaspoon salt
    1/2 teaspoon sugar
    1/3 cup julienned Smithfield ham (page 23)

1.   In a large pot place the cold water and baking soda and bring to a boil over high heat. Add the spinach and stir into the water with chopsticks to ensure the leaves are immersed. Cook for 20 to 30 seconds, or until the leaves turn bright green. Turn off heat; run cold water into pot. Drain the spinach through a strainer over a bowl. Reserve.

2.   Heat wok over high heat for 45 seconds. Add the peanut oil, and coat sides of wok with a spatula. When a wisp of white smoke appears, add the mushrooms. Stir for 20 seconds, and add the salt and sugar. Mix well for

30 seconds and add the Smithfield ham. Mix thoroughly for 30 seconds more, then add the reserved spinach. Cook together, stirring, for 45 seconds, or until the mixture is hot. Turn off heat, transfer to a preheated serving dish, and serve immediately.

CHIU CHOW FRIED RICE

潮州炒飯

Chiu Chow Chau Fon

This is one of the most famous of the Chiu Chow dishes. It is unusual in several ways. The rice is cooked but not fried, even though the Chiu Chow refer to it as their "fried rice." Usually the Chiu Chow cook quickly; this dish takes a little more time, and has three steps. This makes it an important dish for the Chiu Chow, and they emphasize its importance by bringing it to the table cooked, but not assembled, then mixing it just before serving. This flourish-like finish they borrowed from the Cantonese, but the small ceremony is a suitable introduction to the taste.

1½ cups extra-long-grain rice
1½ cups cold water
2 tablespoons peanut oil
1½ teaspoons minced ginger
1½ teaspoons minced garlic
¼ pound shrimp, shelled, deveined, washed, dried, and cut into ½-inch pieces
½ cup Roast Duck meat (page 174), cut into ¼-inch dice
⅓ cup Honey Roast Pork (page 181), cut into ¼-inch dice
½ cup broccoli stems, peeled, washed, dried, and cut into ¼-inch dice

¹/₄ cup Chinese mushrooms, soaked in hot water for 30
minutes, washed, squeezed dry, with stems discarded, and cut into ¹/₄-inch dice
¹/₄ cup bamboo shoots, cut into ¹/₄-inch dice
2 teaspoons Shao-Hsing wine or sherry

Make a sauce—combine in a bowl:

2 tablespoons oyster sauce
1 teaspoon dark soy sauce
1¹/₂ teaspoons light soy sauce
³/₄ teaspoon sugar
1 teaspoon Shao-Hsing wine or sherry
1 teaspoon sesame oil
2 tablespoons cornstarch
Pinch of white pepper
1¹/₂ cups Chiu Chow Stock (page 216) or Chicken
Broth (page 40)

2 extra-large eggs

1.   Cook the rice (page 57) in the water.

2.   As the rice cooks, heat the serving dish: place in a
preheated oven at 250° F., a heatpoof glass dish, 10 inches
in diameter, about 2 inches deep or more.

3.   Heat wok over high heat for 45 seconds to 1 minute.
Add the peanut oil, and coat wok with spatula. When a
wisp of white smoke appears, add the ginger and garlic.
Stir, and when the garlic turns light brown, add the shrimp.
Stir-fry for 30 seconds. Add the duck, pork, broccoli stems,
mushrooms, and bamboo shoots. Stir and mix for another
minute. Add the Shao-Hsing wine by drizzling it into the
wok down the sides. Mix well, cooking for 30 seconds.
Turn off heat. Leave the ingredients in the wok.

4.   Stir rice and place in the preheated heatproof bowl
in an even layer. Reserve.

5.   Stir the sauce mixture and add to ingredients in wok; turn heat to medium. Stir constantly with spatula in one direction, mixing thoroughly. When the sauce begins to bubble, add the eggs by breaking them into the wok, as if you were poaching them. Gently stir the sauce, taking care not to break the eggs. When the egg whites become opaque and cooked, turn off heat.

6.   Using a ladle, pick up the wok mixture and the eggs, again taking care the eggs do not break, and pour atop the rice. Bring the bowl to the table and there, using a large spoon, mix all of the ingredients, then serve immediately.

POACHED
FISH
WITH
TWO
SAUCES

———

Chiu Chow
Sang
Lum Yue

The Chiu Chow, as a coastal people, have historically had continual access to the foods of the sea. Like their Cantonese brothers, they steam, poach, and fry their fish; and like the Cantonese, they devise various sauces for fish. Here is an example of a typical Chiu Chow fish preparation, with two very different sauces that may be served with it, simultaneously. One of the sauces contains some of the intense fish-flavored extract sauce that the Chiu Chow people use as a dip, a taste they share with other people of Southeast Asia. The other is a pungent sweet and sour sauce, quite unlike any other you may have tasted, I am sure.

 1 whole (1½-to-1¾-pound) sea bass
10 cups water
 2 tablespoons white vinegar
¼ cup white wine
 1 piece ginger, 1 inch thick, slightly smashed

Ingredients for Ham Sauce:

1½ tablespoons peanut oil
  3 tablespoons julienned Smithfield ham (page 23)
  1 scallion, washed, dried, with both ends trimmed,
       and cut into 1½-inch pieces, then with the
       white portions shredded
  3 tablespoons julienned celery
  2 tablespoons Chinese mushrooms, soaked in hot
       water for 30 minutes, washed, with stems
       discarded, and julienned
  3 tablespoons julienned sweet red peppers

Combine in a bowl (liquid #1):

  1 teaspoon Shao-Hsing wine or sherry
½ teaspoon fish sauce (page 16)
¼ teaspoon salt
¾ teaspoon sugar
   Pinch of white pepper
  1 tablespoon cornstarch
  1 cup Chiu Chow Stock (page 216)
  1 teaspoon sesame oil

Ingredients for Sweet and Sour Sauce:

1½ tablespoons peanut oil
  4 tablespoons scallions, washed, dried, with ends
       trimmed, and cut into ⅛-inch slices
1½ tablespoons Chinese mushrooms, soaked in hot
       water for 30 minutes, rinsed, dried, with
       stems discarded, and cut into ⅛-inch dice
  3 tablespoons sweet red peppers, cut into ⅛-inch
       dice
  2 fresh water chestnuts, peeled, washed, dried, cut
       into ⅛-inch dice
  1 tablespoon Ginger Pickle, cut into ⅛-inch dice
       (page 114)

Combine in a bowl (liquid #2):

> 2 tablespoons Chinese Chinkiang vinegar mixed with
>   2 tablespoons white vinegar (see note below)
> 4 tablespoons sugar
> 3 tablespoons catsup
> 2 teaspoons cornstarch
> 1 teaspoon sesame oil
> $1/_3$ cup cold water

2 tablespoons Scallion Oil (page 22)
8 sprigs of fresh coriander

1.   Prepare the fish (page 46). Or have the fishmonger scale and clean fish and remove intestines and gills. Wash the fish well; remove all membranes. Dry well. Make 2 cuts in each side of the fish—at its thickest part—to, but not through, the bone. Reserve.

2.   In an oval Dutch oven place the water, white vinegar, white wine, and ginger. Cover and bring to a boil over high heat. Boil for 5 minutes. Place the fish in the liquid, cover pot, turn off heat, and allow the fish to rest in the liquid for 10 minutes.

3.   As the water boils, make the Ham Sauce: heat wok over high heat for 30 to 45 seconds. Add the peanut oil; coat wok with spatula. When a wisp of white smoke appears, add the Smithfield ham and all the vegetables. Stir-fry for 30 to 45 seconds. Stir liquid #1 and pour into wok. Mix well until the sauce bubbles and thickens. Turn off heat, transfer the sauce to preheated sauceboat. Reserve.

4.   Wash wok and spatula, and as fish poaches, make the Sweet and Sour Sauce: heat wok over high heat for 30 to 45 seconds. Add the peanut oil; coat wok with spatula. When white smoke appears, add all the vegetables. Stir-fry for 30 to 45 seconds. Stir liquid #2, pour into wok, and mix well until the sauce thickens. Turn off heat and transfer to a preheated sauceboat. Reserve.

5. Remove the fish from the poaching liquid and transfer to a preheated serving platter. Pour the Scallion Oil over it, garnish with fresh coriander, and serve with the two sauces. It should be served with cooked rice so that the sauces may be enjoyed.

◄ Of course, you may wish to make only one sauce. In that case the sauce should be made as the fish poaches.

◄ Chinkiang vinegar (page 16) is quite strong. It has an aroma that resembles balsamic vinegar; in fact, the Cantonese call it "perfumed vinegar." It imparts a wonderful flavor to the Sweet and Sour Sauce. If it is unavailable, then *do not* mix red wine vinegar with white vinegar. Instead, use 4 tablespoons red wine vinegar only.

SALT-BAKED CHICKEN

Yim Guk Gai

This preparation is synonymous with Hakka cooking. In general when it is ordered in restaurants outside of Canton or Hong Kong, what is served is a pallid imitation. Instead of baking the chicken in salt, the bird is passed through heated salt solutions. What this does is make the chicken simply salty boiled chicken, instead of being the delicate and *nonsalty* dish it should be, for baking the chicken in salt does *not* make it salty. Instead, the salt acts as the oven that bakes the chicken and leaves it moist and flavorful as well. Wrapping the chicken in lotus leaves also adds a delicate aroma and taste to it. The use of the salt "oven" is essential to this dish, for it is how the nomadic Hakka cooked, making ovens out of holes in the ground, as they traveled.

1 whole (3-to-3¼-pound) chicken

½ teaspoon powdered sand ginger (page 21) mixed with 1 tablespoon Shao-Hsing wine or sherry

2 scallions, washed, dried, with both ends removed, and each cut into 4 equal pieces and smashed with the flat of the cleaver blade

1 slice ginger, ¼ inch thick

¼ dried tangerine peel, soaked in hot water for 30 minutes

2 lotus leaves, soaked in hot water for 20 minutes until softened, then drained

5 pounds kosher salt

1.   Clean and wash the chicken; remove all fat and membranes. Drain off excess water, and allow the chicken to drain thoroughly, then pat dry with paper towels.

2.   Rub the wine-ginger mixture inside the chicken cavity and outside of the chicken as well. Place the scallions, ginger, and tangerine peel inside of cavity. Place the lotus leaves, smooth sides up, on a flat surface, overlapping them so that no holes can be seen. Place the chicken, breast side up, on the leaves and wrap the chicken by folding the sides and ends over it. (If lotus leaves are unavailable, cheesecloth may be used.)

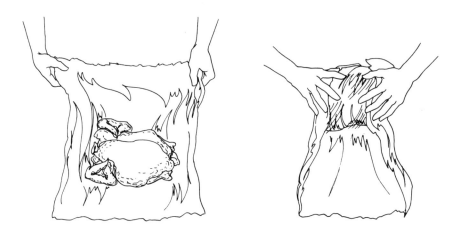

3. Pour half of the salt into the bottom of an oval Dutch oven and place in an oven, preheated to 450°F., for 30 minutes, until the salt is very hot. Meanwhile, heat wok over high heat, pour remainder of salt into it, and dry-roast until very hot, about 30 minutes.

4. Remove Dutch oven from oven, place the chicken on the bed of salt, breast side up, and pour the salt from the wok over it to cover it completely. Return to oven and roast, uncovered, for 1 hour 10 minutes. Remove from oven and allow to sit for 15 minutes.

5. Brush away the salt cover and remove the chicken to a large platter. Unwrap it from the lotus leaves and discard them. Chop the chicken into bite-size pieces (page 45) and serve immediately with the following sauce.

Sauce for Salt-Baked Chicken

- 3 tablespoons light soy sauce
- 2 tablespoons Scallion Oil (page 22)
- 1 teaspoon sesame oil
- 1 teaspoon Chinkiang vinegar (page 16) or red wine vinegar
- 1½ tablespoons finely shredded ginger
- 1½ tablespoons finely shredded white portions of scallions
- Pinch of white pepper

Mix all the ingredients together and serve in small dipping bowls with the Salt-Baked Chicken.

SALT-BAKED
SQUID

——————

Jiu Yim Sin Yau

椒鹽鮮魷

This is a rather famous Hakka dish; it is called salt-baked even though it isn't. The process of water-blanching the squid, then coating it and oil-blanching it, approximates baking to the Hakka taste. In Cantonese, *jiu yim* means "pepper and salt," and those are the flavors that dominate this dish.

1/2 pound fresh squid, meat only (see below)
1/2 teaspoon baking soda
2 tablespoons salt
1/4 teaspoon five-spice powder
3 cups water

Make a marinade—combine in a bowl:

1/2 teaspoon sesame oil
    Pinch of white pepper
1/4 teaspoon salt

2 tablespoons cornstarch
4 cups peanut oil
1 tablespoon fresh hot chili peppers, cut into 1/8-inch
    rounds

Shredded iceberg lettuce (for a garnish)

1. Prepare the squid: pull out the tentacles and intestines. Cut squid open lengthwise, in butterfly fashion.

With a Chinese cleaver, score the squid in a crisscross pattern. Then, with kitchen shears, cut into pieces 2 inches by 1½ inches. Sprinkle the baking soda on them and toss until evenly coated. Allow to stand for 1 hour.

2. Mix the salt and five-spice powder. Heat dry wok over high heat for 45 seconds. Add the salt mixture and stir thoroughly until you smell the spices, about 1 minute. Remove from wok and reserve.

3. Place the water in pot and bring to a boil. Add the reserved squid and return to a boil. Water-blanch the squid for 1 minute (page 37). Turn off heat. Remove. Run cold water over the squid, then drain off all excess water.

4. Marinate the squid in the marinade for 30 minutes.

5. Place the cornstarch on a plate, add the squid, and toss until lightly coated. Shake off excess cornstarch.

6. Heat wok over high heat. Add the peanut oil and heat to 325°F. Place the squid in a Chinese strainer, lower into the oil, and oil-blanch for 1 minute (page 37). Turn off heat. Remove, drain off the oil from the squid, and reserve. Drain wok.

7. Heat wok over high heat. Add the sliced chilis and stir for 30 seconds, then add the squid. Turn off heat, add ½ teaspoon of the five-spice–salt mixture, and stir together quickly until well mixed. Remove the squid from wok and transfer to a preheated platter, garnish with the shredded lettuce, and serve immediately.

❧ The remaining five-spice–salt mixture can be stored in a closed jar for future use. It will retain its strength for 2 weeks, unrefrigerated.

❧ For those who would like different tastes, this recipe

can be made with scallops or shrimp.

Prepare the scallops: 1/2 pound sea scallops, whole, rinsed.

Prepare the shrimp: 12 large shrimp (about 1/2 pound). Remove feelers. Cut shell along vein. Devein, but leave shell on. Wash.

All other preparations remain the same.

| MUSTARD GREENS SOUP | 酸菜湯 | The Hakka people use mustard greens to a greater degree than do the Cantonese. This dish illustrates the Hakka principle of cookery: fresh ingredients, cooked together simply, without complication, used in combination with foods that have been preserved and can be used repeatedly. |

Seun Choi Tong

1 cup mustard greens (page 20)
1/2 pound fresh lean pork butt, cut into pieces 1 1/2 by 1/2 by 1/8 inch

Make a marinade, combine in a bowl:

1 teaspoon ginger juice mixed with 1 teaspoon Shao-Hsing wine or sherry
2 teaspoons peanut oil
1 teaspoon sesame oil
1 teaspoon light soy sauce
1/4 teaspoon salt
1/2 teaspoon sugar
2 teaspoons cornstarch
   Pinch of white pepper

3 cups Chicken Broth (page 40)
1 cup cold water

1 tablespoon fresh lemon juice
1 tablespoon chopped fresh coriander (for a garnish)

1.   Prepare the mustard greens: wash thoroughly to remove sand. Slice into pieces 1½ inches long by ¼ inch wide. Reserve.

2.   Marinate the pork in the marinade for 20 minutes. Reserve.

3.   In a large pot place the Chicken Broth, cold water, and mustard greens and bring to a boil, covered. Boil for 1 minute, then add the lemon juice and stir. Add the reserved pork with its marinade and return to a boil. Allow to boil for 1 minute. Turn off heat. Transfer to a preheated tureen, garnish with the coriander, and serve immediately.

PORK STEW HAKKA
東坡扣肉

―――

Dung Bor Kau Yuk

This is one of the most important dishes of the Hakka kitchen, which utilizes the technique of "long cooking"—or simmering—or stewing—extensively. The Hakka long-cook fresh bacon and various cuts of pork and poultry. The traditional recipe for this dish has fresh bacon, with its skin and fat, coated with soy sauce, deep-fat-fried, then simmered. I make this dish, which the Hakka call *so dung bor*, after an ancient, revered scholar, in a different manner. I use fresh pork butt, and the cooking process is simplified.

1½ pounds fresh lean pork butt, cut into 1½-inch cubes
2 tablespoons cornstarch
6 cups peanut oil
3 tablespoons shallots, peeled and diced into ¼-inch pieces
2 tablespoons black beans, washed and drained
1 tablespoon Shao-Hsing wine or sherry

Make a sauce—combine in a bowl:

> 1 tablespoon dark soy sauce
> 1½ teaspoons light soy sauce
> 1½ teaspoons sugar
> 1 teaspoon sesame oil

> ½–1 cup Chicken Broth (page 40)
> ½ pound spinach, washed several times to remove
> sand, with stems removed
> 8 cups cold water
> ½ teaspoon baking soda

1. Coat the pork cubes with the cornstarch, shake off excess, and spread in a thin layer in a Chinese strainer.

2. Heat the peanut oil in wok to 375° F. Lower the strainer into the hot oil and oil-blanch the pork for 2 minutes, or until the cubes become light brown. Remove, allow to drain over a bowl, and reserve.

3. Pour the oil from the wok. Return 2 tablespoons and turn heat to high. Add the shallots and stir for 1½ minutes. Add the black beans and mix thoroughly, cooking for 30 seconds, until you smell the bean aroma. Add the pork and stir-fry all the ingredients together. Add the wine to wok by drizzling it down the sides and mix well.

4. Stir the sauce and pour into wok. Mix all ingredients until the pork cubes are well coated. Turn off heat. Transfer the ingredients of the wok to a pot (heavy-duty aluminum preferred). Add half the Chicken Broth to the wok and stir to loosen the residue; pour into the pot.

5. Cover pot; bring to a boil over medium heat. Reduce heat, stir the contents of the pot, and allow to simmer for 1 hour, or until the pork is tender. If the sauce is too thick, add some of the remaining Chicken Broth. Stir occasionally to ensure that the stew does not stick to the pot.

6. Just before the pork stew is cooked, water-blanch the spinach. In a large pot place the cold water and baking soda and bring to a boil. Add the spinach and stir, making certain the spinach is covered with water. When the spinach turns bright green, turn off heat. Run cold water into pot. Drain off water, then remove the spinach to a preheated serving platter and spread it out to form a bed.

7. Pour the stew over the spinach and serve immediately with cooked rice.

⅃   This dish can be prepared in advance and can be frozen, except for the spinach. The final steps (steps 6 and 7) must be done just before serving.

HAKKA
BEAN
CURD
CASSEROLE

———

*Hakka Yung
Dau Fu*

客家釀荳腐

Bean curd, *dau fu*, is as important in the Hakka branch of the Cantonese kitchen as it is to the Cantonese themselves. Stuffing hollowed-out cakes of bean curd is a hallmark of the Hakka, and a delicious concept it is. Always use fresh cakes of bean curd. It should be purchased fresh and stored in a sealed container of water, refrigerated. It will remain fresh for 10 days if the water is changed daily.

6 cakes fresh bean curd
6 ounces shrimp, shelled, deveined, washed, and dried

Ingredients for shrimp filling—combine in a bowl:

$1/2$ teaspoon ginger juice mixed with $1^1/2$ teaspoons white wine
$1/2$ teaspoon light soy sauce
1 teaspoon sesame oil
2 teaspoons oyster sauce
$1/4$ teaspoon salt
$3/4$ teaspoon sugar
$1/2$ egg white, beaten
Pinch of white pepper
$1^1/2$ tablespoons cornstarch
3 scallions, washed, dried, with both ends trimmed, and finely sliced

1 tablespoon tapioca flour (page 24)
3 tablespoons peanut oil
2 cups Chicken Broth (page 40)
2 cups iceberg lettuce, broken into pieces 2 by 3 inches

1. Remove the bean curd from its water, place in a strainer over a bowl, and allow to drain for 3 to 4 hours. Pat dry with paper towels.

2. Chop the shrimp into a paste, add to bowl of filling ingredients, and mix thoroughly. Refrigerate, covered, for 2 hours.

3. Cut each cake of bean curd in half diagonally; with a pointed knife, cut out a pocket in each half of the curd.

4. Dust the pocket with tapioca flour, then fill with a tablespoon of the shrimp mixture. Pack smoothly with a knife or with your fingers.

5. Pour the peanut oil into a cast-iron skillet. Heat over high heat until a wisp of white smoke appears. With the stuffed side of the bean curd down, pan-fry over medium heat for 3 minutes. Turn the curds and cook each side for 1 minute.

6. Place the fried bean curds in a heatproof casserole, or large pot. Add the Chicken Broth, to cover. Bring to a boil. Add the lettuce, mix until the lettuce softens, then serve immediately.

STUFFED EIGHT-JEWEL MUSHROOMS

Baht Bo Yung Dung Gu

The name of this Hakka preparation, Eight-Jewel, refers to the many tastes included in it. But the words *baht bo* also mean "eight sons," which to the Hakka is an important message indeed, for sons carry the family name and take over family businesses. The Hakka do not have a dish called Eight Daughters. I wonder why?

3/4-pound fresh pork butt

Ingredients for pork filling—combine in a bowl:

2 tablespoons dried shrimp, soaked for 30 minutes in hot water, drained, and minced
1/4 cup bamboo shoots, cut into 1/8-inch dice
3 fresh water chestnuts, peeled, washed, and cut into 1/8-inch dice
3 scallions, washed, dried, with both ends trimmed, and finely sliced
1/2 teaspoon salt
1 teaspoon sugar
1 teaspoon light soy sauce
1 medium egg white, beaten
2 1/2 tablespoons cornstarch
1 teaspoon sesame oil
Pinch of white pepper

24 Chinese mushrooms, about 1½ inches in diameter, soaked for 30 minutes, washed, squeezed dry, with stems removed
¼ teaspoon salt
1 teaspoon sugar
2 teaspoons dark soy sauce
2 scallions, washed, dried, with both ends trimmed, and cut into thirds
1 ounce fresh chicken fat, or 2 tablespoons peanut oil (chicken fat is much preferred for its taste)
1 slice ginger, ½ inch thick
1½ tablespoons tapioca flour (page 24)

1. Grind the pork, then mix with the ingredients for the pork filling. Refrigerate for 2 hours.

2. Place the mushrooms in a heatproof dish. Add the salt, sugar, and soy sauce and toss with the mushrooms.

3. On top of the mushrooms place the scallions, chicken fat, and ginger. In a steamer, steam them for 30 minutes (page 38), then set aside. Discard the scallions, ginger, and chicken fat.

4. In the cavity of each mushroom lightly sprinkle the tapioca flour to bind the filling to the mushrooms. Pack each mushroom with 1 to 1½ tablespoons of the pork filling. With your finger, smooth the filling and gently press it down to ensure that it will not fall out.

5. Replace the stuffed mushrooms in the heatproof dish that was used to steam them first. Steam for 10 to 12 minutes. Turn off heat and serve in the same dish.

↘ A fine accompaniment to these mushrooms would be Cauliflower Pickles (page 115).

The Last Course

There you have it—the cooking of Canton and of the larger Cantonese community. I will not yield to the temptation that affects some, and call this book complete. It is not a complete book of Cantonese cookery, because there can never be a *complete* book of Cantonese cookery. The cooking of my ancestral home is a living entity that breathes, changes, expands, adapts. It is never still, it is never complete, which of course is why it is so exciting, so fertile.

Let me give you an example. There exist in the Cantonese kitchen no such things as desserts or sweets to follow a meal. In Canton a meal, a dinner, a banquet, no matter how elaborate or festive, is concluded with fresh fruit—with sweet green or yellow apples, with pears, or tangerines, or oranges. It is a custom that remains strong.

Yet we see these days all sorts of Chinese "desserts," complicated efforts that are constructions of candied and preserved fruits, ice creams, even elaborate spongy cakes fashioned after classical European pastries. I have no patience with most of these, for they usually appear to be put together willy-nilly, without thought, simply to provide the sweetness that cooks believe is desired by the Western palate.

There do exist many sweets in the Chinese kitchen, most of them the work of Shanghai chefs who over the

241

years have had to satisfy Western cravings for the sweet. In Canton there are, to be sure, sweet foods—buns, cakes, sweet steamed rices—but most often these are meant to be snacks, to accompany morning *dim sum*, or afternoon tea, or as special culinary offerings to be presented to guests and visitors to one's home at holidays and feasts.

Still, as I have pointed out, the Cantonese kitchen expands, accommodates, and envelops, and so, in very recent years, a few sweets have come to the Cantonese dinner table. Yet, even so, they are not presented, or eaten, the way the Western table would recognize them. They are prepared to *precede* fresh fruit, which is still the dessert of choice. Here are my versions of two of these, Tapioca Melon Soup and Sweet Red Bean Soup, both meant to be served cool, before the fresh fruit.

TAPIOCA
MELON
SOUP

——————

*Mut Gwah Sai
Mai Tong*

This smooth and delicate cool soup, with the combination of tiny pearls of tapioca and small balls of fresh melon, is delightful on a warm day. I prefer it cool from the refrigerator. The tapioca "pearls," as they are called, are fashioned from the residue of the root of the cassava plant after it has been cooked to remove acids. They expand when cooked in liquid and do indeed resemble translucent pearls.

    1 cup tapioca pearls (labeled "Tienley Brand Small Size"—see note below)
1½ cups water, at room temperature
  3 cups cold water
  4 ounces rock sugar, or brown sugar
¼ cup cream of coconut
1¼ cups milk
¾ cup melon

1.   Place the tapioca pearls in a bowl. Add 1½ cups of water at room temperature, and soak for 1½ hours.

2.   To a pot, add the cold water and rock sugar. Raise heat to high and bring to a boil. Lower heat and allow to simmer until the rock sugar is dissolved, about 5 to 7 minutes. Stir occasionally. If you use brown sugar, it will dissolve immediately.

3.   Turn heat back to high. Add the soaked tapioca and stir constantly until the tapioca pearls become translucent. Lower heat, cover, and simmer for 5 minutes, stirring occasionally to avoid sticking.

4.   Add the cream of coconut, raise heat slightly, stir, and allow to come to a boil. Add the milk, stir, allow to come to a boil again, then turn off heat immediately. Transfer contents to a bowl and allow to cool to room temperature. Refrigerate for 4 to 6 hours.

5.   As the tapioca soup cools, prepare the melon (use either honeydew or cantaloupe, or a combination of both, depending upon your preference). Using a small melon scoop, scoop out tiny melon balls. If you do not have a scoop, dice the melon into ¼-inch pieces. Refrigerate the melon.

6. To serve, pour the tapioca soup into a tureen. If it is too thick, thin it slightly with cold milk. It should have a loose porridge consistency. Add the melon balls or pieces, stir together, and serve cold in individual bowls.

⌇ There are several brands of tapioca pearls and two sizes. Use the smallest, which are best. The recipe utilizes the "Tienley Brand Small Size," as noted. There are also on the market almost identical "pearls" that are made from a flour paste from the sago palm tree. They are called "sago pearls" and are more starchy than those of tapioca.

The following recipe is for another brand of tapioca "pearls" that I have used with much success. The brand is labeled "Summit Brand," and along with the Tienley brand, it seems to be the most widely available.

The consistency of the soup made with the Summit brand is slightly different, and the amounts of the ingredients used vary as well. But it is worthwhile to have the second recipe so that you can enjoy the variety. The ingredients for the soup made with Summit brand pearls follow; the cooking instructions are identical to those given above.

¾ cup tapioca pearls (Summit brand)
1 cup water, at room temperature
3¼ cups cold water
3 ounces rock sugar, or brown sugar
⅓ cup cream of coconut
1½ cups milk
1 cup melon

SWEET
RED BEAN
SOUP

紅
荳
沙

———

Hung Dau Sah

This sweet soup is served during the Lunar New Year celebration, at which time it is usually eaten hot or warm. At other times of the year it is served cool. I prefer the latter, particularly in warmer weather, because it is so refreshing.

1/2 pound Chinese red beans (see note below)
7 cups cold water
4 1/2 ounces rock sugar, or brown sugar

1. Place the beans in a pot, cover with cold tap water, and wash 3 times to remove grit. Drain.

2. Place beans back in pot and add the 7 cups of cold water. Turn heat to high, cover pot, and bring to a boil. Stir the beans, lower heat, and allow to simmer 1 1/2 to 2 hours, until the beans are very tender. Allow a small opening between cover and pot during the simmering process. Stir occasionally.

3. When the beans are tender and breaking apart, add the rock sugar or brown sugar. Stir and cook until the sugar dissolves, about 5 to 7 minutes for rock sugar, immediately for brown sugar.

4. Turn off heat. Pour bean soup into large bowl. Allow to cool to room temperature, then refrigerate, covered, for 8 hours. Serve very cool, from a tureen, in individual bowls.

↘ Chinese red beans come in 1-pound packages. They are small, about the size of mung beans. My recipe provides for a soup that is moderately sweet. If you prefer it sweeter, add more sugar to taste.

You will enjoy these desserts, I am certain, because they are not cloyingly sweet and because they are differently refreshing. They are also—and this is significant to me—pertinent examples of the new cooking of Canton, brought to you in the preceding pages of this book. I hope that you will cook from my recipes, that you will enjoy what you cook, and that the recipes will induce you to experiment yourself. And I wish you, in Cantonese, as my father would, *Ho ho sik*, or "Good eating!" . . .

Suggested Wines and Menus

飲
书
食

... And "Good drinking!" The discussion is constant over what should be drunk with Chinese food. It becomes even more pertinent when we talk about what goes well with Cantonese food, for the tastes of the Cantonese kitchen are far more subtle, far more varied than those of any other region of China. The Cantonese generally drink tea with their meals, and the teas are chosen carefully to complement foods or for what the Cantonese consider their internal values. Oolong tea, for example, dark but mild, is a Cantonese favorite, but many people prefer *bo lei*, strong and bitter, because they claim it aids the digestion. Some would rather have jasmine-scented tea with *dim sum*; and an extremely strong Iron Goddess tea, favored by the Chiu Chow people, is perfect, they say, to counter the effects of foods that may be fatty or otherwise heavy.

However, it is not unusual for either a strong rice wine, or a millet-based liquor, or whiskey, or even brandy to be on the table with a Cantonese meal. In fact brandy, particularly Cognac, is a favorite among the Cantonese, and no formal meal or banquet is without it. A dish such as a hot pot, which is usually served in the colder winter months, is almost always accompanied by either whiskey or brandy, the theory being that both the food and the drink will heat the body.

247

Beer is drunk mostly at lunchtime by the Cantonese, not so often as tea, but in significant amounts. They rarely drink beer at an evening meal. Westerners, however, have made beer the drink of choice with Chinese food. Cold beer, particularly the German-inspired pilsner-like beers of Tsing Tao and Shanghai, have found acceptance throughout the world as drinks to go with Chinese foods, but any fine beer—I prefer the Dutch and German beers— will go well indeed.

Wine selection can be tricky, but it can be an interesting exercise as well. I have done menus for wine and food societies and for winegrowers' organizations that matched wines with Chinese dishes, and the efforts have been successful. I have paired Chardonnays with poached fish, Rieslings with fried seafoods and fish soups, Cabernet Sauvignons with strong fried rice, even a Pinot Noir with Peking Duck. The problems inherent in pairing wines and Chinese foods is that the sweet, sour, tart, salty, steamed, fried, roasted, stewed, and blanched all may be included in a single meal.

I am amused by Chinese restaurants that set out long wine lists with their menus. The essence of a fine Chinese meal, certainly a fine Cantonese meal, is variety and differences in tastes. What I do to avoid having to construct a miniature *ad hoc* cellar each time I create a menu is to opt for a wine that I believe will go well with everything I am preparing. For example, each Christmas I invite a houseful of friends for a Chinese buffet dinner. My typical table will contain at least two types of *dim sum* dumplings, a noodle dish, perhaps a satay beef, a roast fresh ham, cold chicken, vegetables, rice, and a variety of pickles and salads.

With these I have served vintage French Champagne, and it has been hugely successful. With similar party meals I have served a fine Chablis from France, fruity Chardonnays from California, and lively Alsatian Gewürztraminer. It is this last wine that consistently seems to go best with a varied Chinese meal, and I would suggest it as an almost foolproof wine for a multicourse Cantonese meal. However, I do not discourage attempts to match Cantonese foods with other wines, both domestic and imported.

Following are some sample luncheons and dinners, menus I have created from the recipes in this book. They are, to my mind, perfect meals for four people. My choice of wines with them would be first a Gewürztraminer, then a Chablis.

First is a luncheon menu for a warm day, a spring or summer day. All of the recipes can be made in advance and served cool or at room temperature:

White Cut Chicken (page 161)
Noodles with Ginger and Scallions (page 91)
Fillet of Beef Roasted in Satay Sauce (page 194)
Jade Flower Broccoli (page 110)
Tapioca Melon Soup (page 243)

The next menu is a hearty one with strong tastes, the contrasts of the Cauliflower Salad, the chives, the hot pot with scallops, shrimp, oysters, clams, and fish. A most filling dinner:

Water Dumplings with Chives (page 88)
Cauliflower Salad (page 112)
Seafood Hot Pot (page 134)
Sliced fresh pineapple

This menu illustrates quite well the variety of the Cantonese kitchen, as well as different cooking techniques:

Duck and Melon Salad (page 175)
Drunken Shrimp (page 143)
Honey Roast Pork with Scallions (page 182)
Cucumber Salad (page 111)
Almond Rice in Lotus Leaves (page 62)

And this demonstrates the virtues of steaming:

Won Tun with Veal (page 82)
Chicken Steamed with Fresh Lemon (page 167)
Spinach and Bean Thread Soup (page 108)
Steamed Sea Bass (page 120)
Pickled Pears (page 117), sliced and mixed with sliced fresh Bosc pears, garnished with fresh strawberries

Here is a menu with the food of the Hakka, and the Chiu Chow, blended with the Cantonese:

Stuffed Eight-Jewel Mushrooms (page 239)
Poached Fish with Two Sauces (page 226)
Lettuce with Oyster Sauce (page 107)
Scallion Pancakes (page 90)
Sweet Red Bean Soup (page 245)

And a touch of the same:

Chiu Chow Lo Soi Duck (page 214)
Shark Fin Soup (page 136)
Red Around Two Flowers (page 105)
Singapore Noodles (page 98)
Fresh oranges

Again, *Ho ho sik.*

EILEEN YIN-FEI LO

Table of Metric Equivalents

Volume (small measures)

¹/₄ teaspoon	= 1 mL
¹/₂ teaspoon	= 2 mL
³/₄ teaspoon	= 3 mL
1 teaspoon	= 5 mL
¹/₂ tablespoon	= 7 mL
1 tablespoon	= 15 mL
2 tablespoons	= 25 mL
3 tablespoons	= 50 mL
4 tablespoons	= 60 mL
5 tablespoons	= 75 mL

Volume (large measures)

¹/₄ cup	= 50 mL
¹/₃ cup	= 75 mL
¹/₂ cup	= 125 mL
²/₃ cup	= 150 mL
³/₄ cup	= 175 mL
1 cup	= 250 mL
2 cups	= 500 mL
4 cups/1 quart	= 1 L

Temperature

170°F	= 80°C
200°F	= 100°C
250°F	= 120°C
275°F	= 140°C
300°F	= 150°C
325°F	= 160°C
350°F	= 180°C
375°F	= 190°C
400°F	= 200°C
425°F	= 220°C
450°F	= 230°C
475°F	= 240°C
500°F	= 250°C

Length

¹/₈ inch	= 3 mm
¹/₄ inch	= 6 mm
¹/₂ inch	= 1 cm
³/₄ inch	= 2 cm
1 inch	= 2.5 cm
1¹/₂ inches	= 4 cm
2 inches	= 5 cm
12 inches	= 30.5 cm

Weight

1 ounce	= 30 g
¹/₄ pound	= 125 g
¹/₂ pound	= 250 g
³/₄ pound	= 375 g
1 pound	= 500 g
2 pounds	= 1 kg

Index